CW01464053

Praise

'Perfectly balancing sweetness and steam.'

PUBLISHERS WEEKLY, on *Stuck in the Country with You*

'A fun rom-com with plenty of warmth and heart.'

BOOKLIST on *Stuck in the Country with You*

'City meets country with explosive results in this escapist second-chance romance.'

THE BOOKSELLER on *Stuck in the Country with You*

Zuri Day is an award-winning, internationally bestselling author of books that make you think and tingle while wanting to mix and mingle! When not writing (say what?), she loves travelling the globe; being a famous vegan chef (in her own mind); gardening; convincing her ragdoll cat, Namaste, that she, not he, is the boss; and having similar fun conversations with family and friends.

Also by Zuri Day

Stuck in the Country with You

Discover more at afterglowbooks.co.uk

ZURI DAY

Champagne

TASTE ON A

Bad Boy

BUDGET

afterglow BOOKS

All rights reserved including the right of reproduction in whole or in part in any form. This edition is published by arrangement with Harlequin Enterprises ULC.

This is a work of fiction. Names, characters, places, locations and incidents are purely fictional and bear no relationship to any real life individuals, living or dead, or to any actual places, business establishments, locations, events or incidents. Any resemblance is entirely coincidental.

Without limiting the exclusive rights of any author, contributor or the publisher of this publication, any unauthorised use of this publication to train generative artificial intelligence (AI) technologies is expressly prohibited. HarperCollins also exercise their rights under Article 4(3) of the Digital Single Market Directive 2019/790 and expressly reserve this publication from the text and data mining exception.

® and ™ are trademarks owned and used by the trademark owner and/or its licensee. Trademarks marked with ® are registered with the United Kingdom Patent Office and/or the Office for Harmonisation in the Internal Market and in other countries.

First Published in Great Britain 2025 by
Afterglow Books by Mills & Boon, an imprint of HarperCollins*Publishers* Ltd
1 London Bridge Street, London, SE1 9GF

www.harpercollins.co.uk

HarperCollins*Publishers*
Macken House, 39/40 Mayor Street Upper,
Dublin 1, D01 C9W8, Ireland

Champagne Taste on a Bad Boy Budget © 2025 Zuri Day

ISBN: 978-0-263-39764-2

1225

MIX
Paper | Supporting
responsible forestry
FSC™ C007454

This book contains FSC™ certified paper and other controlled sources to ensure responsible forest management.

For more information visit: www.harpercollins.co.uk/green

Printed and Bound in the UK using 100% Renewable Electricity
at CPI Group (UK) Ltd, Croydon, CR0 4YY

Society and law have made up your stories
Enhanced wrongs and diminished your glory
Yet against hard hearts and minds you continue to shine
From behind the wall you continue with victories.

One

Jamilah turned up the volume on the R and B streaming channel and bobbed her head to the upbeat music as she crossed the kitchen floor. She was more tired than a swimmer doing laps in molasses, but in this moment? Life felt good. After months of watching her restaurant business Side Chic'k sink like the Titanic, an unexpected email in the restaurant's mailbox had changed her whole mood.

She pulled on thick gloves, wrestled a large pot from the six-burner chef stove, and carried it to the sink. While draining the pot, she leaned into the steam wafting from the boiled potatoes, giving herself an impromptu facial. The sound of a revving motorcycle engine quickly followed by the tinkling of door chimes brought on another rush of happiness. Blair. The lifeline she'd just received in the email would allow her the chance to give this ride-or-die chef a nice bonus, maybe even squeeze in a raise. Lord knows, Blair deserved it. After being the bearer of bad tidings for much of the year, Jamilah couldn't wait to share some good news.

"Good morning, Blair!"

Blair's grunt of a response wasn't exactly *Good morning, back-atcha*, but for flying-high Jamilah it would do.

Had she not been on such an email-induced high, Jamilah

might have realized that her red-, blue-, and blond-dyed short 'fro and sleeve-tatted chef's expression suggested there was nothing good about the day. That Blair barely returned the greeting should have been clue number two.

"I've got great news!" Jamilah continued, unbothered. She crossed over to a commercial-size fridge and pulled out fixings for the popular potato salad they offered, still talking while completely oblivious to the look of pained sadness her happy words painted on the face behind her.

"I've got news, too."

Jamilah's excitement was so high and Blair's tepid response so low that only the room heard it.

"I put in a crazy bid for this catering opportunity that opened up last minute, a pre-Halloween company-anniversary party happening at the end of the month."

Blair sighed. Loudly.

"I know. Late notice. Last minute. Sorry! Didn't dare tell you before now because I knew we'd never get it. Tech company. Two to three hundred guests, with imaginably varied palates. I offered a varied-meat menu, but since our restaurant only serves chicken…"

She shrugged and began peeling boiled eggs as she heard Blair's knives being sharpened. "I could not believe that email, Blair. They basically accepted my whole menu, so along with our famous fowl flavors—well, locally anyway—I hope you're ready to dust off those beef and pork recipes."

A snort made Blair sound as indifferent as Jamilah was excited. "Where are we getting all this money?"

"Don't worry about that. Like I said, since I thought there was no chance of getting the gig anyway, I swung for the financial fences. Their budget is hefty—a hundred per guest."

"Wow." Blair secured a red bandanna around her naturally tight curls and walked into the pantry.

"I know, right?" At another time, Jamilah's excitement would have been contagious.

"We're serving the good stuff. Barbecue brisket sliders and Wagyu burgers, pulled pork tacos. Ribs, of course, since this is Kansas City and we have barbecue sauce in our veins."

She reached for another egg to peel while in her mind the newly created menu was already expanding.

"I'm thinking about adding smoked turkey legs as another poultry dish, a seafood offering like salmon or lobster, and a vegetarian entrée to cover all the bases. What do you think?"

At the lack of response, Jamilah's hands stilled on the rim of the food processor. "Blair?"

Jamilah had been talking to an empty room. She walked to the pantry. Blair stood with her back to the door, staring at spices.

"Blair, are you okay?" Jamilah asked as she crossed the small room. "Look, I know it's going to be a lot of work, but it's a lot of money, too. I'll be able to pay you what you're worth for a change, plus a really good bonus, *and* hire extra hands."

Jamilah also thought she might be able to quit waiting tables and increase the days they were open from the current two and a half back to the original five. Hire back the waitstaff she'd been forced to let go. Expand the kitchen team.

Okay, girl, chill out. You're getting way ahead of yourself.

Especially since her chef didn't appear as pumped as she was. "This catering job will be great for business. We'll be fine."

Jamilah said this with more confidence than she felt. They'd be fine because that's how it had to be. She hadn't sacrificed the last few years of her life to fail. Hadn't watched her social life go down the drain along with a relationship—even one that was technically already washed-up—to end up with nothing to show for the high price she'd paid. This catering job had to be successful. Keeping the doors to her restaurant open, a dream she'd had since the age of thirteen, could very well depend on it.

Blair turned around. "Jam, I gotta tell you something."

The angst in her voice produced a chill at Jamilah's neck that ran down the length of her spine. "Is Leon… Did some-body… What's wrong?"

"Leon's company is going AI. He's being replaced by a robot."

Jamilah laughed. The idea sounded ridiculous, even in this AI age.

Blair didn't laugh.

"Are you serious?"

"Unfortunately."

"On the job or in the bedroom, too?"

Blair smiled. Or was it a grimace? Jamilah couldn't tell. All she knew was that nothing she'd hear today could steal her joy. It had been too long since experiencing the feeling.

"Losing his income is definitely a bummer, but you know he hated that job." Jamilah walked over and linked arms with Blair. "You're not alone, friend. We'll be okay. Your bonus will be enough to cushion you guys for the short term, during which Leon can work on the gaming app that's going to make you guys rich. He can help with the catering job, too. If you remember, at one time, I was going to hire your husband."

"Yeah, before you realized he couldn't boil water."

"Speaking of boiling." She walked over to a wall of shelving filled with canned goods and picked up a restaurant-size can of green beans for a casserole. "Time to get cooking. We open in two hours, and you know how slow I prep."

Jamilah turned to leave the pantry. Blair didn't move.

She walked back to find a woman normally tough-as-nails close to tears. "Oh, Blair, I'm sorry. Forgive me for being insensitive. Leon losing his job really sucks. I know it was less than a year ago that you purchased a house. With that and other monthly living expenses, I can imagine how scared you are to lose the security of a two-person income."

"It's not just that." Finally, Blair met Jamilah's eyes. "This affects you, too."

"Maybe," Jamilah replied, working to keep her voice light. "But unless you're leaving Side Chic'k, we have time to figure it out."

Jamilah bopped out of the pantry to the music playing. When

Blair failed to follow a second time, she backtracked so quickly it resembled Michael doing the moonwalk.

"Blair. What is it? Talk to me."

"I hate doing this to you, Jam, but I am leaving. I got a new job. They need me right away."

Arms crossed, brow creased, Jamilah asked, "What's *right away*?"

Blair visibly swallowed before answering. "Sunday."

"Next-week Sunday, right? Not Sunday as in two days from now."

"It's Prime Rib, Jam. They need someone ASAP."

For a moment Jamilah thought she might be sick. Prime Rib was an award-winning, five-star restaurant where anyone would kill a cow with their bare hands to work there. She closed her eyes and tried to remember the steps to an exercise in deep breathing, one that was supposed to help eliminate stress. Or, in this instant, stop a heart attack.

"Prime Rib, huh? That's, uh, great."

Like having a tooth pulled was great. With a pair of pliers. Without a numbing aid.

"I can't be mad at you, Blair. Working in their kitchen is a coveted spot."

Jamilah returned to the kitchen, this time with a somber Blair behind her.

"I thought that maybe we could bring in Ed. Give him a crash course in what I do. Have him fill in until you find someone permanent."

"Ed as in my uncle-with-an-attitude? The one with anosmia, a stiff knee, and a bad back? You're killing me right now."

"I feel terrible about the timing, Jam." Heavy sigh. "I might have another solution. Word has it there's a new chef in town."

"Well, unless their name is Bobby Flay, Delicious Miss Brown, or Tiffany Derry my arse is still up the creek."

Two

Rashad White leaned against his godmother Anna's kitchen counter, carefully stirring a broth he'd been perfecting for an hour. The kitchen was his favorite space. Where he felt most comfortable. A personal sanctuary, one that had saved his life.

He dipped a teaspoon into the gently boiling liquid, blew away the steam, and then slurped. Closing his eyes, he let the broth sit on his tongue, looking for the perfect blend of sweet, spice, and sour. His parole officer preferred he look for a job. Unfortunately, being a convicted felon made that a hard ask. No matter. Rashad aimed higher. He never again wanted someone else to have control over any part of his life. He didn't want to work for a boss. He wanted to be his own.

Thinking about what had or hadn't happened that got him locked up for three years, and the person who hadn't felt he was worth waiting for, made him heat up like the broth he was boiling. Replaying some of his family's actions or lack thereof while locked up only fanned the flames. He shut down the nonproductive trips down memory lane and refocused on food.

After adjusting the spices and adding more ginger paste, he dipped the spoon he'd rinsed off back into the brew. He savored the hot liquid as it slid down his throat. Clicked his tongue against the roof of his mouth. Caught the heat that crept up at the back of the bite. Subtle. Unexpected. *Nice.* He nodded, remembering his mentor's instructions, *Taste with your heart as well as your taste buds.* Passion was often the difference between a good dish and a great one. No one would ever accuse Rashad of having a lackluster attitude about anything. He brought the heat wherever he went, from the basketball court to the recording studio to the kitchen to the bedroom. Words like *intense* and *dramatic* were often used to describe him. Rashad Jamir White was a passionate man.

When Anna had first approached him about catering her bestie's fiftieth birthday party, Rashad had hesitated. Not only was she one of his favorite people on the planet but she'd believed in him when he hadn't believed in himself. Anna had been instrumental in his much-needed relocation and supported him once he arrived. She'd helped him with the interviews and paperwork that allowed him to leave the state of California and complete his parole in Missouri. That in itself was no easy feat. There'd been so much red tape that at times he'd felt like Anna was Moses trying to part the Red Sea and lead Rashad to a promised land of biblical proportions.

For the menu, Monique, Anna's best friend, had requested Chinese. Almost immediately the fear of failure crept in. Strangers rejecting his food was one thing. The person who'd been convinced to hire him by his godmother was quite another. Rashad was a chef in his own mind, true enough, who'd regularly prepared meals for a large, hungry crowd. He couldn't hang prestigious certificates or a framed culinary degree on the wall, but he knew one thing: he could cook. Everyone told him his food was the best. Eventually confidence, not cockiness, helped him accept this as fact.

But this situation was different. The success or failure of an entire dinner would rest on his shoulders. There'd be no mentor to hide behind. After almost two months in this new world called the Midwest, he'd find out if one of his passions, cooking, could sustain him. Keep him out of trouble. Cats had nine lives. In the system, men like Rashad didn't get that many. While California had relaxed the so-called tough on crime three strikes law that saw thousands of young men with minor felonies locked up for life, Rashad didn't want to take any chances. For him, the third time wasn't the charm but potentially the end of being a free man. For a very long time. When he heard the sound of those steel doors clink shut behind him, Rashad vowed to never go back. Ever. He'd breathe free air for the rest of his life. By any means necessary.

When he admitted his initial trepidation about catering the party to Anna, she wasn't having it.

"As you can see," she'd said, placing a meaty fist on an ample hip and running her other hand over her belly, "I've eaten a good meal or two in my day. You make champagne-level food on a tap-water budget. I'd put your plate next to anybody's anywhere."

Anna's words felt good, but Rashad wasn't a fool. He knew there were chefs who could cook rings around him. Her pep talk worked enough for Rashad to remember his reasons for taking the catering job: his empty pockets and the need to find work. Having gainful employment was a condition of his parole. Nichole, his California parole officer, and Thomas Turner, her Missouri counterpart who handled periodic, in-person visits, were pushing him to find a steady job soon. Maybe one of Anna's friends knew somebody who was looking to hire a man with exceptional skills honed through experiences most would deem unsuitable for a résumé.

Satisfied with the taste of his unique concoction, he reached for a package of ramen, a staple where he'd been housed before relocating to Kansas City. He tossed aside the square foil pouch of prepackaged spices and slid the dry square of noodles into the broth. A Kendrick Lamar song blasted from a phone on the opposite counter before his ringtone interrupted. Rashad smiled, tapped the speaker and answered as he placed it beside him, and continued stirring the soup.

"What up, cuz?"

"I'm a squirrel in your world, bro. Whatchu doin'?"

"Cookin'," Rashad replied without hesitation. He openly shared his culinary passion with most people, but not every-body. In certain circles, there was still the ignorant notion that men didn't belong in the kitchen. His cousin Juke and most of his friends appreciated his skills. His culinary chops had offered him protection behind bars. However, if some of the crew he once ran around with knew of his love for the kitchen and pro-ficiency with herbs, spices, and cooking utensils, they might revoke his cool card and his street cred would be shot.

"You get a job?" Juke asked.

"Yeah. Sorta." Rashad told Juke about the catering gig for the fiftieth birthday party he'd landed courtesy of Anna. "The guest of honor's favorite food is Chinese. That's not my usual wheelhouse, so I'm trying out a few things."

"You've got this, cousin. Everything you make tastes good."

Juke was a straight shooter, his compliment high praise. "But don't let that take you off your other goal."

"What's that?"

"You forgot already? The music, man."

"Music is who I am, Juke. That'll always be there."

"It better. You're too good, Ra God. Don't ever abandon your pen."

Rashad continued cooking with Juke's words swirling in his mind like noodles in boiling broth. His parole officer Nichole wanted him to make a living. Rashad wanted to make a life. As he cleaned up the kitchen with Kendrick rapping in the background, he pondered on whether or not he could have it all, feed his passions for both food and music. Rashad didn't know, but he knew one thing for sure. It was time to find out.

Three

Jamilah wasn't in a partying mood. In fact, if anyone asked what was the absolutely last thing on earth she wanted to do right now, her answer would involve socializing. She hadn't recovered from losing Blair as her ride-or-die chef and the main reason her restaurant was still open. Thanks to her mother, Jamilah already had abandonment issues. Blair quitting with no notice could have unraveled years of therapy. Yet here she sat, successfully holding it together in the parking lot of a small, private club in Grandview, Missouri, a suburb of Kansas City, while watching black, white and gold balloons dance in the wind to announce the nearby celebration.

She pulled down the visor and used an overhead light to check her makeup and ensure her don't-give-an-eff face had been properly hidden behind foundation and bronze. Wispy eyelashes covered worry, while shimmering cinnamon lipstick hid mounting stress. The makeup magic worked: pretty on the outside while inside feeling as ugly as a wart on a pig's snout. She blamed Blair, of course, even though, truth be told, there were other reasons for the psychological funk. Still, it was convenient to focus on her ex-cook. After dropping the nuclear bomb that had shifted Jamilah's world beneath her, Blair had

had the nerve to try to show her a bright side—a new cook in town looking for a job.

Fantastic was how Blair had described the man Jamilah would audition tonight without him knowing, the only reason she'd agreed to attend the party that Blair couldn't because she'd just started her new job and was working tonight. It was her mother-in-law's fiftieth birthday. Jamilah was there as a plus-one for Leon, Blair's husband and only son of Monique, the guest of honor.

Jamilah checked her watch. Fifteen minutes remained of the cocktail hour before dinner was served at eight. Perfect. She reached for the gift bag on the passenger seat and stepped out of her silver Lexus SUV. Showtime.

The fall temps had gone down along with the sun. It was unseasonably cold for October. Jamilah clutched her leather coat tighter, glad she'd passed on wearing the matching knee-highs with four-inch heels and selected the less flashy but more sensible two-inch suede ankle boots. A long, hip-hugging off-white sweater dress that suggested she might want to lay off dessert kept her in line with the host's white-only theme. She wasn't big, just curvy, a solid size ten. Her hair was swept up into a simple ponytail, highlighting the dangly diamonds she'd given herself four years ago as a twenty-fifth birthday present. They paired well with the diamond heart-shaped necklace from her father when she'd turned twenty-one. Next year she'd hit the big three-oh. Would there be a special someone in her life to buy her a new diamond or throw her a bash? Jamilah shook away the discomforting questions along with the depressing fact that there was no one in her life right now.

She followed the balloons up a flight of stairs and entered the building's small foyer. Nineties music and a din of chattering voices greeted her, as did the delicious aroma wafting from somewhere toward the back of the room. If the food tasted anything like it smelled, she was in for a good time.

Jamilah's mood lifted along with her attitude. Maybe tonight wouldn't be so bad after all. Working full-time as a restaurant server to pay the bills, juggling the Side Chic'k business part-time, and in between boyfriends, Jamilah needed some fun in her life. Nothing serious, mind you, wounds from her last breakup were still healing, but she'd welcome a nice distraction from her workaholic life.

Nodding at a few friendly faces, Jamilah took in a plain room with cream-colored walls decorated in black, white and gold. White cloth-covered tables and black folding chairs sporting white and gold bows continued the theme. Black strips of fabric across the tables further broke up the starkness. Gold candles flickered. White miniature lights glowed. Jamilah spotted a gift table and walked toward it. On the way she saw Leon with Anna, who'd previously visited Side Chic'k with the birthday girl, Monique.

"Hi, Jam," Leon greeted her.

"Hey, Leon." They shared a casual hug.

He looked awkward and a bit out of place in his khakis and plaid button-down shirt amid the more typical party attire. Still, Jamilah was grateful to see the easy smile on his boyishly handsome, freckled face. Leon wore his nerd membership proudly. And he should. He was smart, brilliant even. If he were as focused and driven as Blair, Jamilah believed he could someday be a wealthy man.

"You remember Anna," he said, motioning to the woman beside him.

"Of course," Jamilah replied, giving Anna a brief hug as well. "I'm Blair's friend, Jamilah. It's good to see you again."

"Likewise. You look nice. Love that dress."

"Thank you. Coming up with a look that's warm, cute, and comfortable ain't easy."

"Tell me about it. Trying to squeeze this size-eighteen ass into leather pants almost created internal combustion."

Jamilah held back a laugh with her hand.

A man Jamilah assumed was Anna's husband sidled up to her. "You're not fat, baby," he said with a squeeze. "You're thick."

"Yes, and so is a walrus." Anna gave him a talk-to-the-hand gesture. "In-tee-way…"

"I love your pants," Jamilah said. "You look very nice."

"You do look nice, Anna," Leon further affirmed.

"But not as good as the lady of the hour," Anna exclaimed. "Look at your mama, honey. She's doing the dang thang!"

A dinner bell tinkled. Jamilah followed Anna's gaze to a beautiful woman in the center of the room. She reminded Jamilah of Beyoncé's mom, Tina, looking regal and queenlike in a shimmering white mermaid-style gown, sparkly crystal-covered heels peeking from beneath the velvet fabric.

"Good evening, friends and family! For those just joining us, thank you so much for coming to help me celebrate this special milestone—the big five-oh!"

Claps and cheers mixed with the sound of party horns. The DJ added an exclamation point by blasting the music for a few beats before lowering the volume once again.

"Y'all have another five or ten minutes to get drunk, I mean, break my bank—oops, excuse me—choose a libation, before the open bar closes."

She paused as once again laughter and various reactions rang out around the room.

"After dinner and for the rest of the night there will still be a variety of beers and wines available. Hope you're hungry, because I've sampled dinner, and all of it is amazing. The cook is from California, and he's the real deal. Everybody here knows I'm addicted to the Cooking Channel and that Asian is my favorite cuisine. He stuck to that concept, at my request," she coyly added, giving a royal curtsy, "and created a wonderful menu. So sit back, relax, and enjoy!"

Jamilah followed Anna to a nearby table while Leon refreshed his and Anna's drinks and brought Jamilah her requested wine spritzer. She further relaxed into the evening's enjoyable vibe.

Mixing and mingling with a steady flow of patrons had been her favorite part of the restaurant's bustling days those first two years, until a popular chicken chain moved in nearby and sent her chick to the sidelines. Now she realized she missed that more than the money. She missed the restaurant constantly buzzing with guests. She missed her friends. Her ex, Walter, was involved in Kansas City's political scene, always getting invites to the latest events—concerts, the theater, grand openings, fundraising parties. His packed social calendar had been her social life. She missed that, too. Okay, and maybe him a little. She definitely missed having a man in her life.

"How's Blair?" Jamilah asked Leon, once he'd sat down.

"Exhausted."

"I bet. She texted when I called her and said she'd talk on her off day, whenever that is."

"Yeah, the hours are killer, but she really likes the chef. He's patient and doesn't mind sharing his secrets."

"Like Blair with me," Jamilah admitted. "I don't know how I'll ever replace her."

Anna eyed Jamilah as she sipped her drink. "That's why you're here, right? To try Rashad's food?"

"I told her," Leon said at Jamilah's mildly surprised expression. "Blair and I met him when he first came to town. Don't worry. She'll keep the secret. He's staying at her house."

"Oh, so you know Rashad?" Jamilah suddenly didn't care that her secret was out. The casual conversation was now a reconnaissance mission.

"A little bit," Anna answered slyly. "He's my godson."

"Really." Jamilah was all ears. "What can you tell me about him?"

"Nothing that he isn't more qualified to tell you about himself. Or convey through his food."

Jamilah picked up the unspoken message Anna had put down. She wasn't nearly as open to telling Rashad's business as Leon had been to share why Jamilah had RSVPed.

Before Jamilah could respond, the same big guy who'd spoken with Anna earlier, a good six-two or-three and around two fifty ambled over to the table and joined them.

"Baby, this is Jamilah. She owns that restaurant Side Chic'k that I told you about, the one where Blair worked. Jamilah, this is my husband, Charles."

"Nice to meet you, Charles."

He offered a bear paw-sized hand. "Likewise."

Jamilah watched as a small army of preteens dressed in all black approached the tables. They set down menu cards next to glasses of lemon water. She watched in surprise, trying not to let how impressed she was show all over her face.

After thanking the server for her lemon water, she picked up the menu card.

Wonton-O-Mo BBQ
Wingin' It
Kung Pow Platters
Fortune Cookie Custard Pie

"Cute," she said to no one in particular. "Rashad come up with this creative menu?"

"Sure did." Anna picked up her card, more than a little pride reflected on her face.

Jamilah fingered the card, two questions swirling in her mind. One, was his cooking as good as his creativity? And two, if it were, could he start this week?

Casual conversation continued until a TDH—tall, dark, and handsome—man materialized from the back of the room. He appeared slightly nervous, which Jamilah found endearing. She found herself leaning forward to catch every word getting ready to flow through a set of kissable lips.

"Um, good evening, everyone," he said, his deep, slightly raspy voice making Jamilah's lady parts tingle.

He unconsciously rubbed his hands together and took a breath. "My name is Rashad. I'm the chef. Okay, Monique already said that. Sorry, I'm kinda nervous. This is my first dinner party."

Jamilah decided nervous looked good on him. Even so, a list of ways to calm him down formed in her head, ways that involved her soft hands running over his hard chest, being wrapped in those chocolate-brown tatted muscular arms with their legs entwined. *Yum!*

"I'm here to help Monique celebrate her birthday and to help all of y'all enjoy it, too."

He winked at Monique. Jamilah decided that his eyes were as sexy as his lips. And that his obviously gym-ready body, strong and toned without being swole, gave no reason for the casual observer to be disappointed—from the tips of his shoulder-length locs to the soles of his Air Jordans.

"She says she's fifty, but until I see proof, I still think she's lying about her age."

"Flattery will get you everywhere, Rashad!" Monique sang out, having taken more than a few sips of her libation.

Her guests laughed while other women commented, creating a low buzz among the tables.

"Just speaking truth."

He flashed a set of perfectly white teeth that contrasted beautifully with his dark skin. Jamilah's fingers itched to run themselves along those chiseled cheeks and down the front of the plain black apron he wore over a stark white shirt.

What is he, about six feet, maybe one seventy-five?

Then directly behind that thought, what did his size matter? Um, *height* was the immediate and appropriate mental correction. The word *size* conjured up other fantastical body parts. His physicality had nothing to do with how well he cooked! She forced her attention back to the present, though wayward R-rated thoughts stayed on the back burner of her mind.

"I want to thank my godmother Anna for requesting me," Rashad was saying when her attention returned to where it should be. "And Monique for taking the chance on me to find out what I can do. Since y'all are all friends of hers, you know she's bougie."

More laughter.

"I like him," a woman at the next table said.

"He's cute," said another.

Jamilah told herself she didn't care that other women were eating him up with their eyes just like her. She lied to herself and decided he wasn't all that, too. There was no time in her life for fantasies that had no chance of going anywhere. If his food was as good as Anna said, and he became her chef, all of that chocolate and muscle would be strictly off-limits.

"To keep up the classy theme," Rashad continued, straightening his perfectly chiseled physique to stress the night's importance, "Monique wants each course announced. After taking a quick course at YouTube University, I'm ready!"

He laughed at his own joke. The room, every female under his spell, happily joined in. His smile wrapped itself around Jamilah, as warm and snuggly as her favorite cashmere blanket, and reminded her it had been almost a year since the breakup with Walter, and six months since the romp with an out-of-town and convenient friend with benefits that had left much to be desired.

"I've got a few courses I could teach him," murmured the same nearby woman who'd thought him cute.

"If he wants to be taught by an elder," Jamilah mumbled under her breath.

It wasn't like her to channel mean girl, and she was glad that it appeared no one heard her snide remark. She refocused her attention to why she was there, on business, to see if Rashad's skills could work for her.

When a middle-aged woman delivered a particularly scandalous comment, Anna turned and said, "that's my godson you're talking about," in a tone that silenced further conversation.

Not a piece of meat, Jamilah mentally added, even as she stilled her own spicy thoughts and refocused on the words coming out of Rashad's tantalizingly tasty-looking mouth.

"Tonight's theme is Asia Meets America. Um, for your first course I've prepared a wonton soup with mushrooms, shallots, and a secret ingredient, the barbecue in what I named the Wonton-O-Mo. I like cooking, but as you see, I like words, too. Enjoy."

Jamilah's eyes joined a few others' to follow Rashad's sure strides back through a set of double doors and undoubtedly appreciate the firm-looking ass that filled out his black jeans. When it came to whether or not she'd like his food, her confidence soared. Not only was Jamilah ready to taste his cooking. She wouldn't mind sampling the chef.

Four

The party was off to a loud and lively start when an organized group of young servers appeared with steaming bowls. A heavenly aroma wafted from the one set in front of Jamilah. She immediately detected a hint of citrus, a touch of ginger, smoked paprika and maybe…pork? The broth was clear with a light red tint, and the wontons looked airy and tender. She dipped her spoon into the broth. A chorus of flavors sang on her tongue. She took another spoonful, this time with one of the bite-sized wontons. The thinly cut shallot enhanced both the look and the taste of the dish.

Heavenly.

"Oh my God," Anna exclaimed, already scraping the bottom of her bowl. "That was even better than the sample he made last week."

Monique lightly touched her frosted lips with a napkin. "I was just thinking that exact same thing."

"That man can cook, no doubt about it." Charles picked up his bowl and drank the rest of the soup. "I didn't think I was going to like those soft noodles but wow. Delicious."

"Hey, son. Do you think Blair could make wontons this good?"

Leon smirked, the good vibes and comfortable atmosphere erasing his shyness. "Blair can cook anything better than anybody."

"Good answer," Charles said to Leon, raising his hand for a fist bump.

"The only correct one from her husband," Anna replied with a laugh, before turning to Jamilah. "Well, Ms. Restaurant Owner, what did you think of that first course?"

Jamilah was beyond impressed but hid her true feelings behind a bland smile. "I think I'm ready to experience the rest of his meal."

And what an experience it was. From winging it with the sticky spicy wing served on a bed of lemon and ginger-dressed red and green cabbage slaw to the main course, kung pao platters served in varying levels of spiciness with different meats, Rashad showed a level of cooking that surprised her. Jamilah didn't compare him with Blair. Their styles were different. But he could definitely hold his own with her in the kitchen and, Jamilah knew, handle the Side Chic'k menu.

Jamilah discreetly watched as he was stopped by another table of women who she assumed wanted to sing his culinary praises or maybe, given the murmurs around her, comment on his physical attributes. She noted his easy charm and personable tableside manner, an added benefit within a restaurant setting. Occasionally patrons at Side Chic'k asked questions Jamilah couldn't answer or specifically requested the chef. Blair was courteous during these exchanges, but Jamilah knew her comfort zone was less with customers and more when she cooked in the kitchen.

By the time Rashad served up a decadent chocolate custard pie with a fortune cookie crust, Jamilah had gone from wondering if he could handle the work in her restaurant to whether she could pay, even part-time, what this man's skills were worth.

She was mentally calculating a salary within her budget when Monique, who'd left the table earlier to dance, returned.

"This is a great party, Monique. The fun and the food. Blair told me that Rashad was an excellent cook," Jamilah told Anna. "She didn't lie."

"I tell him that every chance I get. He sometimes second-guesses himself because he hasn't been to culinary school. He wants to…"

Anna quieted, as though saying too much.

"I'd love to"—*give him whatever it is that he wants*—"speak with him about working at Side Chic'k."

Anna looked beyond Jamilah toward the double doors. "Here comes your chance."

Before announcing his last course, Rashad invited anyone interested in having him cater their event to let him know. Jamilah watched as several women rushed him as fans would a rock star, almost snatching the business cards from his hands.

"Let me go grab him from Monique's freaky friends," Anna said as she stood. "Or you'll be waiting all night to have that conversation."

To keep from staring as Rashad approached, Jamilah feigned deep interest in the game of Fortnite Leon was playing on his phone beside her. Still, she was uber aware of Rashad's presence, especially now as he stood right beside her.

"Rashad, I want to introduce you to Blair's good friend, Jamilah. She owns a restaurant called Side Chic'k, near downtown."

"Hello." His large fingers engulfed hers, rough with knife cuts and callouses.

His gaze was direct and friendly, his smile kind without being flirty. Still, a wave of attraction passed through her core as she returned the greeting.

Jamilah suddenly felt shy and girly and inwardly admonished her reaction. Who in the heck had taken over her body? She wasn't shy and hadn't considered herself girly since she was sixteen. No, she was all woman, a business owner seeking an employee to hire. In other words, she was a frickin' boss. It was time to act like one. She cleared her throat and added a slight tilt to her chin.

"The food tonight was"—*amazing, delicious, scrumptious, mouthwatering*—"very good."

The chef she could afford cooked average, even very good food. These more appropriate, more accurate words didn't fit her hiring budget.

"Thanks, I appreciate that. Your restaurant is named *Side Chic'k*?"

Again that sexy, almost irreverent grin that had Jamilah feeling a type of heat that didn't come from a stove.

"Yes, a play on the word chic meaning stylish, with an apostrophe between the *c* and *k*."

"Interesting word play," was Rashad's neutral response.

"It also defines our menu, a selection of sides built around chicken, the only meat offered. So *chic* and…*chick*."

"Creative. I like it."

Why did she feel like she'd just won the lottery? What this man thought about her business, well, it was no matter.

"I liked your creativity, too, especially the *wonton-o-mo*. That soup was delicious. What type of pork did you use?"

"Aw, come on, now." He leaned closer, his voice slipping into an effortless sexiness probably not intended. "We don't know each other well enough for me to be spilling chef secrets."

Well, baby, we can definitely correct that issue, she thought.

"I hear you're looking for a job," she said.

"Yes, and I hear you might be hiring." At Jamilah's questioning brow, Rashad continued. "Leon told me about his wife getting a new job at one of those upscale, five-star restaurants."

That Rashad already knew Blair and Leon, even casually, made her feel better about hiring a practical stranger and less upset that he already knew why she was there. Clearly, the judiciousness that made her father so good in law enforcement had not passed down to her.

"Yes, Blair is an amazing cook. I hate to lose her. So…are you interested?"

"It's definitely something I'd consider."

Jamilah forced herself not to squirm under his direct, intense gaze, even though the way he looked at her caused her Kegel muscles to contract and release.

"You probably don't have your phone on you."

"No, it's in the kitchen."

Instead of using a digital business card, she reached into her handbag and pulled out a paper one, glad to do something that felt professional, like she was in the driver's seat of this situation instead of trying to rein in an attraction careering all over the place.

"Does Monday at eleven work for you for an interview?"

"Sure." Rashad took the card and after a quick glance slid it into his jeans pocket. He looked out as the music changed and people began pairing up to shake a tail feather between a crowd of onlookers.

"Time to hit the dance floor," Anna said to Rashad and Jamilah as she tried to urge Charles out of his chair.

He shook his head. "Sorry, baby. My dogs are barking."

Jamilah laughed at the old-school way to say one's feet hurt. "It's all right, old man."

"Hmph." Charles's eyes twinkled as he looked at his wife. "We'll see if you're calling me that later on tonight."

Jamilah watched the intimate exchange, keenly aware of the potential hire, a strapping specimen of a young man, standing next to her and the antics he could undoubtedly perform later on.

Anna ignored her husband of more than two decades while a big smile broke out on her face. "Come on, y'all."

"Do your thing, goddess," Rashad said, giving Anna a quick hug. "I've got to finish up in the kitchen."

And then to Jamilah, "It was nice meeting you."

"Likewise. See you tomorrow."

"Looking forward to it."

With a slight bow, he turned and walked back into the house. Jamilah quickly devoured his retreating figure with her eyes, then felt self-conscious as she noticed other women doing the same.

Pull. Yourself. Together!

Jamilah joined the guests on the sidelines, cheering on those brave enough to stand the good-natured teasing while taking the spotlight down the middle aisle of another *Soul Train* line. Anna and Charles performed versions of eighties and nineties dances that brought down the house. After saying her good-byes and walking toward the car, though, Jamilah wasn't thinking about dance moves. She was thinking about food, more specifically the man who'd made her want to moan from the dishes he'd created, and wondering just what else those talented hands could do.

Five

Rashad finished writing a line in his rhyme book, placed Side Chic'k into the search engine, then tapped his phone's GPS system. He fired up the fifteen-year old Toyota 4-Runner that Charles had graciously said he could borrow indefinitely and sat while it idled to warm it up as he'd been instructed, blowing into his cold fingers to generate heat. One thing for sure, he'd never get used to the Midwest cold weather. Anna warned him this was just the beginning, that here in the heartland temps in the fifties were considered warm. When he learned the winter average hovered around thirty, sometimes lower, he'd gone out the next day and bought the heaviest coat available.

The car and Anna's husband were a godsend. Charles was a good dude, a role model who'd helped him navigate an unfamiliar city. Juke had given Rashad the name of a casual friend who'd relocated to KC years before, but aside from a quick meetup when he'd first arrived, Rashad had kept to himself. Trouble often followed this friend like a shadow. The last thing Rashad wanted was to get caught up in something shady. He wanted to turn the page on his old life and start a new chapter. Unfortunately that sometimes meant cutting off good people who had done nothing wrong to him personally, but whose energy he'd simply outgrown.

There were other reasons why Rashad was being careful about the company he kept. Removing people not headed in the same direction helped him stay focused. Life had given him another chance to get it right. To show the world who he really was. He didn't want to mess it up. He had some things to prove not only to himself but to others. Like the ex who'd betrayed him with the former friend she was now dating.

Since arriving in the middle of America, he'd spent most of his time with Charles, a solid man and Anna's second husband. Rashad respected how he'd provided for his family and Rashad's godmother with twenty-plus years at the post office and a musician side hustle good enough to secure weekend gigs. He'd even developed an unexpected friendship with Monique's son-in-law, Leon, whom he'd quickly nicknamed QNA, the Quiet Nerd Assassin, for his encyclopedic knowledge of hip-hop, expertise in programming and coding, and love for video games. When questioned about the nickname, Rashad explained to Leon that where he came from having one was almost a requirement. It meant that you'd graduated from acquaintance to friend.

Everyone who meant anything to Rashad had a nickname, as did almost everyone he knew back home. In LA circles he was the Ra God. Anna was Goddess. Charles was Pluck, for the way he handled the strings of his bass guitar. He thought of Jamilah, the slightly uptight but all right woman with the curvy figure and heart-shaped face and eyes that told him she was feeling a vibe between them even as she tried to keep it strictly professional. She reminded him of the women he'd met when hanging out in the valley with his engineer cousin. The ones who graduated college and attended church and joined groups with Greek names. The ones who acted all stuffy until the music turned up and the lights went down. The ones who, if seen later while out with their peers, would look through

him as though he were beneath them, as though they hadn't
sucked his blow pop days before.

He didn't quite get that feeling with Jamilah and felt her pos-
ture was more an act of defense than one of superiority. Something about that observation made him want to protect her, out
here ballin' with her own business and whatnot. This could be
a great opportunity, one where he could learn a lot. He'd keep
that in mind when they met later, and use the head above his
shoulders to check the one below his waist.

Rashad reached his destination and parked in front of a large
building that housed two spaces. He was immediately struck by
the location's proximity to Paseo, a major thoroughfare with
easy access and lots of traffic, great assets for a customer-driven
business. A popular chicken restaurant nearby also got his attention. It looked desperately out of place amid the area's rich
history, but had a line of cars at the drive-through. *Wonder how
her wings are holding up against that national chain?* He was about
to find out.

Rashad checked his reflection in the mirror, straightened the
signature black-and-white bandanna holding back his shoulder-
length locs and gave himself a quick pep talk.

"Nobody in this city cooks better than you. You've got this."

He walked to the door and turned the knob. The door was
locked. The business was closed. Their appointment was at
eleven. Not trusting a sometimes-flawed GPS navigation system, he'd left Anna's house early and arrived at Side Chic'k
with fifteen minutes to spare. He stood on the sidewalk and
took in his surroundings. The sun was bright, which made the
temperature feel closer to the fifty degrees registered on the
car's temperature gauge. Fifty was cold where he came from.
Sometimes he still marveled that he actually lived in Kansas
City, Missouri. It was where he needed to be, but he missed
California. No matter what, LA would always be home.

Looking around and not seeing another car nearby, Rashad decided to take a quick walk to stay warm and familiar-

ize himself with the area where he might be working. Just as he reached the corner, a silver Lexus SUV rounded it almost on two wheels, the driver honking as it sped by and pulled to the curb in front of the restaurant.

Jamilah. Last night he had returned to the kitchen, but not before taking a moment to check out the revelers on the dance floor. He hadn't seen her go down the line, but a vision of her laughing with Anna, the white dress she wore hugging all the right places, swam into view. His body immediately reacted. He moved to shift the hardening shaft in his jeans and pushed away the memory of how he'd low-key checked her out all last night. She was his type, physically, and he hadn't had sex since arriving in town. Before prison, being celibate was something Rashad never imagined. Discipline, however, was one good thing that had come from his time behind bars. His ex, Brigit, had taught him the other lesson that curbed most sexual promiscuity. After feeling what it was like to have his heart broken, he'd learned to have more care with those of the women he encountered.

Jamilah was fine, yes, and he was attracted. Still, he concluded that the only breast he needed to focus on right now was on a chicken connected to a paycheck. He exuded a casual confidence as he strolled back toward her car.

"Can you help me with these boxes?" she asked, opening the back door to her car without a direct look or greeting.

He almost replied with a knee-jerk answer about making demands without a proper salutation. But then he saw how well the ass sticking out toward him fit the corduroy slacks that covered it, and he swallowed the sarcasm.

He walked over and took the box she handed over. "Good morning to you, too."

"Good morning." Still in whirlwind mode, she hurriedly unlocked the door and headed back toward her car. "It's been a crazy morning. I just found out about a meeting I have to attend. We've got about thirty minutes, forty tops. I need to get the car unloaded. I usually pull around back," she continued, reaching for two recycled bags and heading into the building. "But I saw you on the corner and pulled up."

"What's all this?"

"Produce from a nearby urban garden, mostly organic."

"Isn't that expensive?"

"It can be."

Rashad detected a bit of snap in her answer. She did say the morning was hectic with the unexpected thrown in. Maybe that was it.

"Business must be good. Are you open five or six days a week?"

"Set that top box in the pantry," she all but commanded, ignoring his question. "Bring the ones with the lettuce, tomatoes and onions on top into the kitchen."

Rashad had spent too many years being bossed around and disrespected, treated as invisible by those who felt a right to do so. Behind bars, he'd been forced to take it. Not so on the outside. That shit was over. If he was going to work at Side Chic'k, he needed to get that straight right now.

"You're pretty bossy," he said, following her into the kitchen instead of out to the car. "Is that how you run your kitchen? More importantly, is that how you speak to your staff?"

Jamilah placed the bags of frozen items she carried onto the stainless steel counter. "Is my being direct a problem?"

He took a breath, the way he'd seen yoga instructors instruct on YouTube tutorials. Doing so was supposed to center you, help control your emotions. Rashad knew he could be a hothead, a trait that had gotten him into more trouble than he cared to remember. If he was going to get past the first stop on his journey to success, he'd best tame that beast right now.

"I don't mind direct conversation. In fact, I prefer straight talk. But being spoken *at* instead of to, like I'm a child? Not so much. Look, I know this is your restaurant and I'm here for a job interview. I've heard about kitchens where the chefs act crazy, like that dude from England who berates the cooks, slams shit around, gets in their faces. That's not the type of kitchen I want to work in. So if that's the kind of operation you're running, where being rude and disrespectful is considered part of the job, then we don't even need to do the interview, 'cause I'm not your guy."

He watched a myriad of emotions play across Jamilah's face before she stopped unpacking the bag of frozen items and placed her palms flat on the counter.

"My apologies," she said, without looking up. "I shouldn't have snapped at you."

After a couple seconds, she lifted her head and eyed him directly, undoubtedly having no idea how mentally arousing it was to watch her regain the same control he'd also fought for moments earlier.

"I'm having a bad morning, Rashad, one that doesn't need to be taken out on you. I'll come back and finish this later. Alone, so if I explode no one else will catch the shrapnel."

Rashad softened. "That's probably a good idea, unless you've got some hella workers' comp."

"If you'll have a seat in the dining room, I'll put these in the freezer and be right out."

"Or I can grab those veggies from the car."

"Thanks."

Rashad's heart warmed as he walked away. There was something about Jamilah that rubbed him the right way. Maybe they weren't as different as Rashad had imagined. He liked a fiery woman, one who could hold their own against his alpha nature. In the kitchen, if misused as it had been just now, it could be a liability. But in the bedroom, between two lovers, it was an asset he immensely enjoyed.

Six

Jamilah flung bags of frozen goods into the freezer before momentarily sticking her own head inside. She needed to cool off. A walk-in freezer would be nice. It wasn't just her misplaced anger and frustration that needed to chill but the kundalini energy spiraling inside her, craving a man's touch. A manly man like Rashad.

He hadn't meant to push her buttons. Yet his simple question—a fair one—had lit a fuse made ripe for striking by the morning's phone call from her bank. Was buying organic expensive? It could be. Should she decrease her overall spending by making wiser food choices? Definitely. One look at her rising debt from high-interest and almost predatory credit cards would tell the whole story. The *You've been preapproved* enticers had come at a time when she'd had little money in her bank account and mounting business expenses. The financial slump happened quickly and was completely unexpected. With a variety of chicken preparations and sides with names like Creepin' Cauli-bites, the TLT, Taste Like Tuna chickpea sandwich, Two-Timing Tomato Bisque, and Swipe Right Caesar Salad, the restaurant's popularity happened fast, mostly by word of mouth.

When the slump brought on by the chicken chain happened,

she'd hoped it would be a short one. It wasn't. The money dwindled along with her customers, forcing her into a countdown. Six days open, then five, four, three, to now—from noon on Friday until six on Sunday. She was forced to take a full-time job to make ends meet. Fortunately Gusto, a trendy, upscale eatery in a swanky suburb, had great tippers. Her already shaky social life became nonexistent. The chances to date? A pipe dream. Pun intended.

Rashad's question hit another soft spot. The one about being second-guessed. Even though he had no restaurant experience, Walter had questioned almost every choice she'd made, from naming the place Side Chic'k to the menu she created. Her father often joined Walter in these queries. She'd push back by telling them to stay in their lanes. It hurt to feel as though she'd been tag-teamed, even more so when after the breakup her father and Walter remained friendly.

Jamilah forced her thoughts from the past to the present. She and Walter were no longer together. Her father had slowly come around to trusting her choices. Frozen food stored, expensive organic vegetables on the counter, and control restored, Jamilah walked into the dining room. Rashad stood with his back to her looking out the window. His broad shoulders, tight butt, and long strong-looking legs were the stuff that dreams were made of.

"Why'd you decide on this location?" he asked, turning around as he heard her sandals on the laminate flooring.

"Opportunity. Let's sit by the window."

He joined her at the table.

"Did you bring a résumé?"

Rashad shook his head. "I know I should have, but—"

"Yes, you should have. But it's okay," she hurriedly continued to cover the fact that she'd snapped again. "This was short notice. Plus, I experienced an unofficial tasting of sorts at Monique's party."

He nodded.

"You're a good cook."

"I think I'm a great one, but...whatever."

Clearly, this man hadn't gone on many interviews. Patience was a virtue, and sometimes humility, too. She opened her mouth to share this POV but closed it just as quickly. She needed him more than he needed her.

"You're from California, correct?"

"LA, born and raised."

"How'd you get into cooking?"

"Necessity."

Jamilah felt a whole lifetime story existed behind that one-word answer but for now chose not to push for details.

"Obviously, you like it," she said, instead. "Would I be familiar with any of the places you worked?"

"I doubt it."

"Where did you train?"

"Home was the first place. Both my great-grandmother and grandmother are great cooks. I guess what you would call my professional training was under a guy named Francisco Cortez."

"How long did you work at his restaurant?"

Rashad shifted uncomfortably in his seat. "Um, three years."

"What kind of spot is it?" Jamilah reached for her phone. "I'll look it up. What's the name?"

"California State Prison."

Jamilah's thumb froze, hovering over the phone screen.

"Interesting name for a restaurant."

"Perfect for a jail."

She tried and failed to lighten the moment with laughter. It came out more like a burp. "You are kidding, right?"

"Straight talk, Jamilah. I was recently released from prison and am now on parole." He delivered the news in the same vein as someone saying *I attended Harvard and graduated last month.*

"Oh...wow."

Jamilah stood, walked to the door, and worked to change her expression from what-in-the-whole-hell to simply why-

were-you-in-there. Even more, she wondered how quickly the
conversation she'd had yesterday with her father would come
back to bite her.

She returned to the table and sat. "Please excuse my reaction. Your answer completely threw me. I...had no idea you'd
committed a...that you were a..."

"Criminal? It's not a label I claim, but I don't run from it
either. There are worse crimes out there being done by people
society respects. That's a whole other story. As for my situation,
engaging in illegal activities is what I've done, not who I am."

As Jamilah listened, she mentally ran through a list of options. Who could she call? Who could cook? Who was available
with zero notice? Who would work for what she could pay?

"I never thought to ask if you...had a record."

"One in three brothahs in this country are in the system.
But then, I suspect you know that, being a melanated sister
yourself and all."

"Mela-who?"

"Black," Rashad explained. "One who possesses a large
amount of melanin."

"Duly noted," Jamilah dryly replied. "I can't say I'm familiar with that statistic, and I'm around plenty of Black people,
or *melanated* as you call it, men included."

"And none of them have ever been pulled over for DWB?"
Jamilah scrunched her brows.

"Driving While Black."

Jamilah opened her mouth to refute his claim, then remembered an incident when she was in college. And another that
Walter had told her about before he got booted and suited and
joined the city council. She remembered stories shared by famous people who were pulled over and then apologized to after
being recognized.

Why? For driving a nice car. For being in certain neighborhoods. For shopping in stores considered above their pay grades.
Jamilah never allowed much reflection on these types of inci-

dents. Growing up with a father in law enforcement perhaps shielded her from such profiling and other forms of harassment. That, and his rigid stance in both following and upholding the law. She saw men in blue as the good guys and felt that if someone got arrested, let alone charged and convicted, they probably deserved it.

"Your food is some of the best I've tasted," Jamilah said. "But I…"

"Don't want to hire a felon?"

"As far as I know, I've never hired anyone with a criminal background." Nor would her dad have allowed it.

Rashad shrugged. "It's cool. Not the first time I've been turned down, won't be the last. That five-letter f-word keeps brothahs like me locked to our past like a pair of handcuffs. It allows something that happened when we're seventeen, eighteen, to affect us for the rest of our lives."

"Is that when it happened? When you were eighteen?"

"Aw, hell no. I was a badass long before that."

His bold, honest answer made Jamilah laugh out loud. *Straight talk* he'd called it, said without wavering and looking her dead in the eye. Something about his fearlessness was appealing. It showed a strength and resilience she wasn't sure she possessed.

"May I ask why you went to prison? It's really none of my—"

"There's no part of my past I'm ashamed of, and I don't live with regrets." Rashad leaned against the back of the chair, comfortable and easy.

"Growing up, police were always patrolling the Jungle, stirring up shit."

"The Jungle?"

"Yeah, the neighborhood my family moved to after…when I was ten years old. Had my first encounter at just eleven. I asked why they stopped me, what they wanted, and found my face smashed into the hood of a cruiser. Needless to say, that wasn't the way for them to win friends and influence people, not me anyway. That's where the antagonism began and my hatred started for anybody wearing a badge and carrying a gun."

"My dad's in law enforcement."

Jamilah was a daddy's girl from the womb and would check anyone who came for her father. It was her turn to look Rashad dead in his eye.

One second passed. Two. More.

"Your dad's a cop," Rashad finally repeated. "Good thing I'm only trying to be your cook and not your man."

Jamilah smiled, even as his comment hit a raw nerve. She had imagined that by now she and Walter would have been married, or at least engaged. Instead, a few months ago, she'd learned of his recent engagement to a popular attorney in *The Call* newspaper. While she knew ending their relationship had been the right thing to do, she missed being partnered up, missed the good times that she'd shared with her ex. Of course this wasn't a fact she'd ever acknowledge, at least not without a gun to her head.

"To answer your question, some friends and I were hanging out in my neighborhood, running a pharmaceutical operation." At Jamilah's confused expression he added, "Selling weed."

"Ah," she held out the word in understanding. "I see."

"Nah, you don't, but I won't go into that right now. Anyway, there was a gun in the car, a part of doing business and keeping from getting jumped or robbed. A situation went down, and the next thing we know we're surrounded by cops, getting searched and, of course, arrested. I was charged with possession with intent to distribute, and illegal possession of a firearm, even though the weapon wasn't mine. We later found out it legally belonged to my friend's father, who also owned the car. That information didn't matter. I was guilty by default. Got five years. Was out in thirteen months due to prison overcrowding. Three years ago, I was riding with friends. Got pulled over again for..."

"Driving while Black?"

"And male, four deep in the car. In LA more than two bro-thahs walking can be considered a gang. Of course the officers told another story, one about our ride fitting the description of a car reported stolen. That's one of their go-to excuses. Again it was later proven that car registration, insurance, everything was legit, but because I'd been caught in the company of other felons who just happened to be my cousins, my parole was revoked."

"Why didn't you just say who owned the car?"

Rashad's laugh contained no humor. "That's not how it works in the streets. There's more to the story, but being that your daddy is one of them, I'm sure you don't want to hear it. Bottom line is that I did the bid. And here I am."

"I'm sorry that happened. It doesn't seem fair."

"Life is fairer for some than others. But I'm not here to play victim. I just want to cook."

Jamilah straightened up and tried to shut down the sound of her law-enforcement father's accusatory, judgmental voice going off in her head. She closed out him dictating the steps to be taken to know the background of who was around her. She wasn't crazy about hiring a felon, but being between a rock and a hard place or, more specifically, a fried chicken leg and a catering gig, left her little choice. And something about Ra-shad's sincerity while sharing made her trust him.

"Everyone deserves the chance at a better life. I'll hire you on a trial basis. A ninety-day pro…"

Rashad laughed, this time low and easy. He shifted his body, crossed one ankle over the other. "Don't be nervous about put-ting me on probation, Jamilah. It won't be the first time."

She wasn't nervous about her position, which she felt was warranted given the circumstances, but about how her nipples hardened at the sound of his laughter and how good he looked simply slumped against a chair with those long strong legs on full display.

"It's standard. I'd do it for anyone."

Not exactly anyone. She hadn't done it for Blair but justified this discrepancy with the fact that her former chef had arrived with a stellar résumé and reference letters.

"Tell me more about your experience in California, the type of food you generally cooked and how many you served."

The interview flowed smoothly after that, with Jamilah learning more than she ever thought she'd know about prison chow. Given his vast experience with large crowds, she was confident he could easily handle the kitchen and also manage next week's catering event. He filled out an application, she gave him a tour, and they agreed he'd start that Friday. All the while, her feminine flower was very much aware of his masculine might. The attraction was incredible, but that's all it could be. They could be coworkers, cooking collaborators. But that was where Jamilah drew the line. The two of them were from different worlds. They could never be FWBs.

"Thanks for believing in me," he said sincerely, pulling Jamilah out of her thoughts.

"What got you the job is your belief in yourself."

Jamilah had been so caught off guard by and then caught up in Rashad's revelation, she almost ran late for her appointment at the bank. Her mind should have been focused on the loan she'd applied for and whether or not she got it. Instead it was filled with thoughts of a self-proclaimed badass who looked like a god, had the swagger of a hip-hop star, and could cook like a world-class chef.

Seven

Friday morning, Rashad emerged from the basement and was greeted by Anna's cheerful grin in the kitchen. She wore comfy-looking striped wide-leg pants and an oversize sweater. A large purse and even larger tote sat on the island separating the kitchen and dining room.

"Hey, handsome!"

"Grand rising, Goddess."

"Let me check you out," she cooed, giving him the once-over. "You look especially sharp today, Rashad. Locs freshly twisted. Wearing that tight pullover to show off those manly muscles, I see."

He laughed. "I ain't trying to show off nothing."

"Um-huh. And I see all that *nothing* you ain't showing off." She gave his arm a playful squeeze before walking over to grab a mug of coffee. "I'm messing with you, godson, but hey. Jamilah's a pretty girl. You're a nice-looking young man. Who knows the types of dishes that might get cooked up in that kitchen."

"Trust me, only those that can get plated. Jamilah is way too bougie for a brothah like me."

Anna waved off the comment, then picked up her purse

and tote. "Don't let her reaction to your background fool you. Women love a bad boy."

"How do you know?"

"Katrina," she replied.

"My mama?"

"She was a church girl before meeting your daddy." Sidling up to him she whispered, "After that party we snuck out of the house to attend...that all changed."

A teasing look accompanied the laughter that followed Anna out the door and continued in the garage. Rashad laughed, too, but sobered once his aunt had gone. He imagined that whatever had changed when Katrina married his father paled in comparison to how all of their lives changed once Corey White died. It's said that death either brings families together or pulls them apart. He and his mother had never been close, but after the murder, Katrina had shut down even more emotionally, withdrew into a world of reality shows, casinos, and the occasional male friend Katrina tried to hide from her children. Older sister Zara, a quiet, studious introvert, moved to Oakland to live with their dad's sister and was now a nurse. Born three years apart with opposing temperaments, they'd never been close either. She lived life on the straight and narrow. That had never been Rashad's style.

Eventually Katrina had worked through her grief. She returned to religion and, like her sister-in-law and daughter in Oakland, became very involved in church. She tried to persuade Rashad to join them. He declined. Not that he didn't believe in a power greater than himself. But it was too late to try to turn him into a holy roller. By then Rashad had found another cult: the streets. For all its bad rap, it was a school that taught him a valuable set of life skills that not only served him in prison but would give him an advantage for the rest of his life. Ironically, prison was the vehicle that drove the three of them closer. Even with his pushback against her constant proselytizing, Katrina's visits and Zara's letters became a source of light in that confined, dark space.

His family, food, and books protected his sanity. Authors like Frances Cress Welsing, Steve Cokely, Anthony Browder, and Dr. Yosef Ben-Jochannan. His absolute favorite, though, was *Hip Hop Decoded* by a former rapper and a conscience leader, Duane Bowser, also known as The Black Dot. If hip-hop was a religion, then *Hip Hop Decoded* was the official bible. Hands down.

Rashad made a quick omelet, ate, and left the house. On the drive to Side Chic'k he called Zara and got her voice mail, leaving him alone with the music and his thoughts. Anna's words continued to reverberate. Rashad allowed a moment to think about his dad: that the man was not there and why it was too painful to revisit most of the time. But Anna's comment took him back to those early years when his dad, mom, and Zara constituted the perfect family. His dad was a good man, always out hustling. But when he was home there was always music, rap mostly, but R and B, too, even a little jazz or blues if the mood was right. His father, a blue-collar mechanic who loved laughter, was a jokester who fashioned himself the next Bernie Mac. Loved comedies, too, and would let Rashad stay up late to watch them with him, even on school nights.

A half hour before his ten thirty start time, Rashad pulled around to the back of the row of buildings where he'd been told to park. His phone pinged. He pulled it out see a message from Anna.

Every trip to one's destination begins with the first step. Proud of you for taking this one. Much love and Happy Cooking!

"You're right," Rashad said to himself while nodding as if she could see him.

He reached for the door handle. His phone pinged again.

Thanks for letting me know about your new job!

He shook his head, his mother's message sending him on a short guilt trip. "I'm in trouble," he mumbled before texting her back.

I thought you were in Oakland?

My phone works here, too. Zara says congrats. We'll call you later.

Thankfully, the smiley emoji meant his mother wasn't truly offended, that they were still on speaking terms. He sent a quick thumbs-up before getting out of the car and walking toward the narrow concrete pathway between buildings. Last night, Charles had given him a quick history lesson of the area where he'd be working. Only a few blocks separated Side Chic'k from the famous Eighteenth and Vine intersection with attractions such as the Negro Leagues Baseball Museum and the GEM Theater. The Mutual Musicians Foundation, a National Historic Landmark, stood out on a block that was otherwise in a state of neglect. Rashad liked to be familiar with his surroundings, and for this music connoisseur the history sounded interesting. But a tour of the area would have to wait.

Rashad reached the sidewalk and noted that the space connected to Side Chic'k was empty. He pressed his hand against glass streaked with dirt and peeked inside. Except for an errant chair and piles of wood, the place was bare and covered in trash and dust. It obviously hadn't been occupied in a while. It looked roughly twice the size of Jamilah's restaurant. Rashad wondered what had existed there before and why she hadn't chosen the corner spot instead of the smaller space next door. Several more questions followed in succession. How much it would cost to buy or rent? Was there a kitchen and, if so, what shape was it in? Finally, how much would it cost to renovate, and who was the owner?

For a few precious seconds, Rashad allowed himself to fantasize. Images exploded inside his brain, warmth inside his chest. Reality quickly crashed the party. His bank account was nonexistent, as were the chances of this felon to secure a bank loan or get any other type of help for that matter. After reading about The Nacho Grill, a successful food truck owned by a friend in Detroit, he'd thought about taking that route. But even twenty-five thousand, the average cost of a basic food truck, was out of his reach.

Rashad checked his watch and hurried back to where Jamilah said she parked during business hours. He saw her Lexus as soon as he hit the alley. She must have entered from the other end of the block. He went to his car, pulled out the notebook that was always with him—he never knew when he'd be hit with a great rap or lyric—and walked to the door. It was unlocked. Was that safe? He walked in, noting a bathroom, what looked like a small storage area on one side and the pantry he'd entered the other day on the other side of the short hallway. Straight ahead was the dining room with its minimal design. He appreciated the simple aesthetics of steel, wood, and glass and liked how communal tables mixed seamlessly with tables for two or four but felt the space lacked personality. It needed color. Vibrancy. Energy. A dash of soul.

A movement caught the corner of his eye. Jamilah crossed the kitchen to the stove and poured salt into a huge pot of water just beginning to boil.

He stopped at the counter, allowed himself a slow sweep of the tantalizing backside view Jamilah presented, respectfully of course, and then placed his notebook on a shelf below it and cleared his throat. He reminded himself that the breasts he'd be stroking belonged to a bird.

"Good morning."

Jamilah looked over her shoulder. "Hi, Rashad."

"You always keep that back door unlocked?"

"Most of the time."

"You never worry about getting robbed?"

"This small business? I don't think most thieves would even bother. Police patrol the area regularly, too."

She nodded toward a large, well-used notebook he hadn't noticed. "I brought out Blair's bible so you can take a look and get up to speed on her recipes."

Rashad bristled, a raised brow contrasting his lowered voice. "Her recipes?"

Jamilah reached for a bottle of oil and poured some into the pot, then added macaroni. "Yes."

He pointedly ignored the notebook as he crossed the room, sort of like one would avoid poison ivy. "Thanks, but I think I know how to fry chicken."

"I'm sure you do, but not the way our customers are used to tasting it. I don't want them to be able to take a bite and notice we have a different chef."

"Why not?"

He watched Jamilah take a breath before giving him her full attention. "Because," she began as if she were speaking to a toddler, "Side Chic'k chicken has a specific taste, one that Blair developed. I don't want to change it. Hopefully, that's not a problem."

"Not at all."

It was totally a problem. One that grew bigger with each turn of the grease-stained notebook page. He and Blair had totally different cooking styles. She used a wet brine; he preferred dry. Her spices were minimal; he was the spice king. Most of her recipes were standard, predictable; Rashad prided his food on being anything but that.

"Listen, Jamilah, I…"

Every trip to one's destination begins with the first step. Proud of you for taking this one.

Anna's words put Rashad's ego in check. The empty space

next door and the possibilities it evoked further calmed him down. He wasn't trying to work here forever. Just long enough to take the next step toward the man he wanted to show the world he could be.

"Yes, Rashad. Did you have a question?"

Jamilah's tone suggested she was braced for a fight. Until seconds ago, Rashad was ready to give her one.

"I just wanted to thank you again for giving me this opportunity."

Jamilah's relief was evident in the way her face lit up. She had a smile that could separate a man from his money and lips that could make him work his ass off to get more.

"You're welcome, Rashad. Later, we can maybe talk about a catering job I have coming up soon. It's going to be a lot of work, but there will be extra money involved."

"I'm down for that."

"Good. The first thing for you to do is get the baked chicken in the oven. There's some brining in the fridge. Spices are there," she said and nodded toward a grouping of bottles and jars, "and in the pantry. In general, that was Blair's work area, so feel free to set it up any way you want."

"Cool." He walked to the fridge and pulled out the chicken, and after taking a look first at the menu and then at Blair's notebook, he began cutting up the birds.

"It looks like the breasts are the only baked option?" he asked.

"Those and the thighs that are used in the chicken salad."

"Got it."

Jamilah walked over to an MP3 player. "Mind listening to a little jazz?"

Rashad offered a lazy smile, thinking those smooth notes were a fitting genre for the way her body moved. No doubt those hips were made for holding, that waist one to wrap his arms around.

"Not at all."

Soon, the sounds of a Wes Montgomery classic filled the air.
"Rashad?"
"Yeah."
"I'm glad you're here."
Rashad turned back to his work, bobbed his head to the music, and tried to keep his expanding chest from filling the room.

Eight

Jamilah wasn't lying. Well, not exactly. She was relieved to find Blair's replacement so quickly and not lose the catering contract. She probably would have hired the Joker if he could crisp up a wing. But that wasn't all. She'd risked everything to leave corporate America and venture into the sharkish waters of the culinary world, a dream she'd held since the Food Network and Bravo TV replaced her mother's presence and she spent afternoons imagining herself the next Top Chef. Initially, everyone she cared about had been against her owning a restaurant—namely her ex and her conservative, take-no-chances dad. James had quickly come around, even helped her secure a start-up loan. At the end of the day, he just wanted his daughter to be successful doing what she loved.

Walter wasn't as easy to convert. Having a restaurant owner wife wasn't what he'd envisioned for his political career. His current fiancée, Olivia, an attorney, was much more aligned with the prestigious, influential lifestyle he desired. He'd tried to be supportive but in actuality was more a complainer and critic, questioning her decisions, causing her to second-guess what she knew for sure. Jamilah had spent her life trying to prove herself to others. Absent mom. Exacting dad. Judgmental ex. This time around there was only one person whose standards she wanted to satisfy: herself. For that reason, she couldn't fail.

On the way to the bank, she'd reached out to her cousin, Ed, and another man who occasionally helped out when needed. Neither was available. After the bank appointment, where her short-term loan application was denied, Jamilah went to work and spent the entire eight-hour shift grappling with the conflicting emotions that thoughts about hiring Rashad produced.

Rashad was the exact type of man her father had warned her to steer clear of, to not even entertain as an acquaintance, much less an employee. Until now, Jamilah had listened and obeyed. From the time he became a single father when she was ten, the words of James Carver Jr. were law. His beliefs were her beliefs. His point of view her own. She'd dated men who would meet his approval, like those in law enforcement. When the relationship with Walter didn't work out, she didn't know who was more heartbroken—her or James. Walter was a councilman now, engaged to Olivia, the perfect politician's wife. Jamilah had ended the relationship because while she loved Walter, she hadn't been in love with him. He felt like more of an obligation than a choice. On most days that decision still felt like the right one.

And now, here she was working side by side with a convicted criminal, a felon. She didn't even want to think about the inevitable father–daughter conversation about her newest employee. She hoped he'd be too busy to check out Rashad on his own.

She reached her restaurant and as always felt a tinge of pride as she gave a quick walk-through before settling into the kitchen. The subtle tans and grays accenting stark white walls were a clean backdrop to the sepia-tinted and black-and-white photos of vegetables hung throughout the space. Stainless steel light fixtures, exposed brick and laminate flooring seamlessly mixed a modern look with the building's eighty-year-old history. Authentic-looking floor plants added a touch of nature while not requiring the green thumb that Jamilah didn't possess.

"Who came up with the name Side Chic'k?" Rashad asked Jamilah, successfully distracting her inner angst.

"I did. Why?"

"No particular reason."

"Yes there is, or you wouldn't have asked."

Rashad picked up a large tray and headed toward the oven. "Most women don't want to be considered the side chick."

"I thought about that, but the name perfectly describes my business, different types of chicken with a variety of sides. I couldn't resist the double entendre, and the way I spell it makes it unique."

"So she's a chic side chick."

"You got it."

"I'd say that's false advertising."

"Why?" Jamilah was fully prepared to defend her restaurant's name like Mayweather defended his title.

Rashad turned and with a look that would linger long into her nighttime said, "Because I can't see you ever playing second fiddle in anybody's band."

Inside Jamilah preened like a peacock, realizing this was how it felt to be seen. To cover up the emotional moment, she grabbed a large block of cheese from the fridge, cut it into smaller chunks and began feeding them into a shredder.

"Why are you using that type of cheese?"

"What kind would you use?"

"Something you didn't have to cut or shred. Already in a creamy consistency that can be poured over the pasta."

"From a can?"

Rashad's eyes slid in her direction, accompanied by a smile that once again made her heart skip. This situation bordered on dangerous. He really was a nice-looking man. Suit and tie, close-cropped, and clean-shaven were more her type, but his locs were well-coiffed and highlighted a prominent nose and strong jawline, especially when pulled back and tied, as they were now.

"You have a problem with canned goods?"

"No. The box you carried into the pantry was full of them, so obviously they're okay sometimes."

His questions shouldn't have gotten under her skin. Chefs tended to be opinionated, with their own way of wanting to do things. Fortunately for Jamilah, she and Blair were on the same page, for the most part. For her and Rashad? If this convo were any indication, not at all.

A point further proven as she watched him carefully drop wings into the fryer. "Doesn't sound like that oil is hot enough."

"Don't worry." When Jamilah's skeptical expression remained, he added, "This is the first fry."

Jamilah walked over to the bible on the counter, the one opened to Blair's fried chicken recipe.

"That's not how wings are done here."

"Okay."

After a minute or so, he removed the wings from the fryer, then walked over and scanned the pages of Blair's book.

"Any questions?"

"None."

Said in such a way that instead of questions, he probably had comments that she didn't want to hear. She switched back to a safer topic, one that would familiarize Rashad a bit more with his workplace.

"FYI, the *chic* in Side Chic'k, is wordplay for the restaurant's decor."

Rashad looked around. "So I heard."

"Where?"

"You told me at Monique's party." A pause and then, "You think this decor is chic?"

She looked out at the blond wood she felt gave the room a quiet sophistication, the muted tan, black, gray, and white color scheme, the pictures on the wall and the stainless steel that tied it all together.

"What do you think?"

"I think…" he shrugged again "…to each his own."

So much for safe topics. Would she and this guy ever agree on anything? Once again, Jamilah worked to tamp down her frustration. What did she care about his random opinion? Rashad's background was cooking, not interior design. Good taste was subjective. The last person she needed to listen to for advice on style was a man who'd spent the last three years surrounded by concrete.

For the next several moments, the sounds of prepping and cooking filled the air, punctuated by a question here or comment there as Rashad settled into the routine. Jamilah finished shredding the blocks of cheese and assembled their second-most popular side dish. From the corner of her eye, she watched Rashad's knife skills as he cut up the remaining chicken pieces and began to fry them, before separating the drumsticks and thighs. She finished the mac 'n' cheese and potato salad, then focused on the remaining offerings for today's menu—candied yams, green bean casserole, a steamed broccoli/carrot/cauliflower combo and a standard garden salad.

When she returned to the kitchen from filling the warmers, Rashad was waiting.

"Taste."

"I know what fried chicken tastes like."

"Not the way I fry it."

"Yours?" Jamilah looked at her watch. Thirty minutes until the doors opened, ten before her lone server arrived. She didn't have time to argue with Rashad.

"You didn't follow Blair's recipe?" she quipped. "The one right here?"

She picked up Blair's kitchen bible, her anger rising as she flipped the pages. "*Heat oil to three hundred and fifty-five degrees. Drop each piece of chicken individually into the fryer, ensuring that pieces don't stick together and that oil keeps circulating as the pieces cook.* These instructions are simple. Why didn't you follow them as I asked?"

"I did as you requested, then finished frying the wings I'd started earlier."

His calm demeanor made her behavior seem slightly unhinged, though Jamilah felt being chagrinned was her right. He placed the wing on a saucer and returned his attention to the frying baskets.

"People love two things about chicken—tender, juicy, properly spiced meat and crispy skin."

He stirred the legs cooking in the first basket before dropping a batch of wings into the second.

"When you do a quick cook at a lower temperature, then fry the meat a second time in higher heat, it gives the skin that crispy texture that chicken lovers enjoy."

"You're right, and that's exactly what they get with Blair's recipe." Before he could interrupt, she held up her hands. "Look, I'm not questioning your cooking skills. I know you can cook. That's why you got hired."

He returned to the wing, brought it back over. "Jamilah, just taste it."

Jamilah raised a brow.

"My apologies. This is your business. But as a cook who knows chicken, I couldn't resist. I wanted you to have the comparison."

With her eyes on his smug face, she took a tentative bite. The skin was so crispy it literally crackled and popped when she bit into it, while inside it was succulent, flavorful, and fall-off-the-bone tender. It took everything in her not to close her eyes and emit an orgasmic whimper. If this man could do this to the wing of a chicken, she could only imagine the magic those gifted hands could perform on her legs, breasts, and thighs.

She chewed until her libido was under control, licked her fingers, and in a voice as casual as mentioning the weather, said, "That was all right."

Rashad burst out laughing. "Girl, you're tripping. You know that's the best wing you've ever tasted in your life."

Jamilah watched his confident stroll to the serving tray filled with the appendages that helped birds fly. He exuded authority and confidence, as though he owned the place. Jamilah wondered if some of that confidence could rub off on her. Then she imagined other ways the two of them could rub together and quickly looked away before that train of thought could leave the station.

"For the record," Rashad said, unaware of Jamilah's racy thoughts and temporary discomfort, "what I did is called the twice-fry method. But don't worry. I only made a few like that so you could taste them. The rest are the average kind that you get by following that book."

"Average? Blair would cut you for that comment."

"I've met her, and I agree she'd try."

They laughed.

"I can blend those cooked to perfection in with the rest, or put some sauce on them so they won't be so—" he snapped his fingers "—crispy, juicy, tasty, delicious. Or I keep them to the side so you can enjoy them later on, while deciding how to tell Blair that the new cook has a better recipe. Matter of fact, don't worry about that either. Next time I visit Leon, I'll tell her myself."

"Set them aside so what we serve is uniform." *And so later on I can gobble them up.*

Jamilah changed the subject. "You hang out with Leon? That's an unlikely friendship."

"I don't know many people here and, honestly, probably don't want to know too many." He walked over and dipped a spoon in a large stainless steel prep bowl. "He's quiet and geeky as hell, but he's a video gamer and a hip-hop head. What's not to like? Besides this bland-ass potato salad," he half murmured, half mumbled under his breath.

"What was that?"

"Nothing."

Their young, brunette and bubbly server Shasta arrived.

Jamilah made introductions. She and Rashad enjoyed an effortless working rhythm while disagreeing about everything—from gas versus electric to cooking totally from scratch versus adopting boxed and canned conveniences and everything in between, especially food. If asked, they'd probably disagree on whether grass was green and the sky was blue. Even so, the two worked together in a natural flow and were ready on time for the Friday lunch crowd.

Just after unlocking the door and flipping the Open sign, Jamilah tasted another of Rashad's "twice fry" wings and admitted the truth. It was amazing.

"I didn't have to tell you it was delicious," she said after admitting as much. "You already knew."

Rashad smiled, a simple act Jamilah felt should come with a Danger sign.

"Helps to hear it, though."

"In time, maybe after your ninety-day probation, we can do a few pop-ups and test out the new recipes. But not now. There's too much riding on what happens this month."

"Heard."

There was the occasional hiccup here and there, but overall, the first night of service with the new chef went well. A few customers noticed the change and asked about Blair but were quick to add that the food tasted great. Cleanup was smooth, accompanied by the even smoother sounds of singer and guitarist George Benson, one of her dad's favorites. During service, the stove wasn't the only hot spot in the kitchen. The new cook had Jamilah feeling the heat. She believed Rashad felt the energy, too. An accidental touch here. A lingering look there. Jamilah covered this attraction with denial, Rashad with professionalism. One thing was for sure, she finally admitted: A hot pot like this could only simmer so long before it boiled all the way over.

After the bulk of the work was done and everyone else had

left, she said, "I've got the rest of it, Rashad, so you can leave. Tomorrow's a long, hopefully busy day, so be ready."

Rashad walked over to where Jamilah stood. "Are you sure it's safe to be here by yourself?"

Was it just her or had his voice gone low and sexy? It had to be her imagination. Damn, she needed someone to scratch her sexual itch. Like him. Like now. She cleared her throat to force the thought away.

"I'll be fine. You did good."

He put a hand on her shoulder and squeezed. "Thanks. I appreciate that."

She broke contact while squeezing her cootchie muscles together. "Okay, see you tomorrow."

Rashad left. Shasta and the busboy, Caylen, too. The streaming station changed from George Benson to Norman Brown, a guitarist from Kansas City. He played a Janet Jackson cover.

"That's the way love goes," Jamilah sang as she danced around the room. Running the place without Blair had gone better than she could have imagined. Rashad fit right in with Shasta, Caylen, and the guests. There was only one problem: her father. He wouldn't be happy she'd hired someone with Rashad's background and would be disappointed that she had defied him. If the stars aligned and the gods were kind, he'd forget about her hiring someone new. She sure as heck wouldn't bring it up.

A few minutes later, her cell phone rang. *Dad.* She hesitated only briefly before answering the call, ready to take the conversation anywhere except near the man who'd just left her kitchen.

"Hey, Daddy! How's it going? Are you still at work?"

"Just finishing up some paperwork at the station. How'd your interview go?"

"Interview?" Jamilah parroted the word as though she *spoka no English*.

"Yeah, the one with Rashad White. I hope you haven't hired him already. That young man is six feet of bad news."

Nine

Jamilah's worst fear was confirmed. James had done a background check and if it was as thorough as some he'd conducted on her other friends, he probably now knew more about Rashad than Rashad did.

"Jamilah?"

"Yes, Dad?"

"Rashad White, did you interview him?"

"Yes, I did."

"And?"

"He's a talented and experienced cook. Everyone who attended Blair's mother-in-law's party raved about his food, and I concur."

"Don't tell me you hired that fool without a background—wait, hold on a minute."

Jamilah felt her heartbeat quicken as she did a final sweep of the kitchen before placing dirty towels and other items in the stackable washer and turning it on. She reached the door, looked out into the darkness and set the alarm before walking outside. The night air was cool, but she didn't think that was why goose bumps suddenly appeared on her arm. It had been the message her father delivered and what he might want her to do as a result of what he'd learned. She got into her car, turned the heat on full blast, and was hit with a jolt of cold air from the cold engine.

"Dammit!"

"Jamilah?"

"Sorry, Daddy. Just turned on the heat, and the air is freezing."

That's because you didn't let the car run for a few minutes, like I taught you when you were about sixteen and told you about a million times since then."

"You're right."

Jamilah turned off the fan, blew hot breath on her fingers to heat them up, and reminded herself to dig out an extra pair of gloves to put in the console. At the same time, she felt a tinge of anger at her father's tone, something that lately happened more and more. At first she blamed it on the stress of a sagging business, but tonight it felt more like a righteous indignation at being treated like a child. Growing up, her father's voice had been the voice of God. What he said was law. In nearly thirty years she'd rarely defied him, even when he acted as though her opinion didn't matter.

I'm not a baby anymore, she thought and immediately felt guilty. Her father had been there, always. Hadn't abandoned her like her mother had, which created a loyalty that Jamilah couldn't see might be a bit unhealthy. All she saw—felt, rather—was security. For any child growing up in a single-parent family, security and love were really all they wanted.

"I'm in the middle of an investigation and have to go right now. But we need to finish this conversation. In the meantime, find another chef."

"But Daddy—"

"No *but*s. He's not the one. I don't have time to go into it right now, and I'm disappointed that I even have to. Do you want to know why?"

Not really.

"Because me having to tell you what you should already know means you didn't follow rule number one on new hires."

"A background check," they said together.

"I didn't have to, Dad. He already told me—"

"I'm sure he told you a lot of things." Jamilah heard the squawk of her father's radio. "Look, I've got to go. Handle your business. Find somebody else to work with you. I'll call back when I can."

"Okay. Bye."

Jamilah breathed a sigh of relief as she ended the call and headed out of the parking lot. Just as she reached the end of the alley with a choice to go left or right, her phone dinged with a call she wasn't expecting.

"Blair!"

"Where are you?"

"In my car. And hello to you, too."

"No, I mean where, as in location."

"Just leaving work. I—"

"Never mind what you're about to say. There's a ticket waiting for you at the Uptown."

"For who?"

"Godfrey."

"The comedian?" One of her faves. Politically incorrect as hell and hilarious in the process.

"How many Godfreys do you know? I'm on break and only have ten minutes. Just wanted to catch you before you went home and took off your face."

"You know I don't work in makeup. I look like crap, jeans, an old Side Chic'k T-shirt, and a bomber jacket. Plus, my hair's not done."

"Who cares? One of Leon's friends got two tickets, and his date canceled. Leon is in St. Louis, and Simon is gay so you don't have to impress him. Anyway, you're a natural beauty."

"So I'll be sitting with a stranger?"

"About fifteen hundred, in fact. Now, go. Have a good time.

The late show is probably just getting underway. Thank me later."

Blair clicked off before Jamilah could respond. Didn't take long to decide what she'd do. Godfrey was hilarious, and after the day—week—months she'd had, she could use a good laugh. She headed up Broadway, parked on a residential side street, raced into the venue and laughed so hard she almost peed her pants. Leon's friend Simon, a Triple G—as in, *geeky gay guy*— was the perfect companion—dry British humor, irreverent, and awkwardly cool. She'd forgotten how much fun it was to be entertained, to be social in a way that had nothing to do with food. She told Simon as much as they stood in the lobby.

"Thank you, Simon. That was a good time that was sorely needed."

"Don't thank me," Simon replied, in a voice that reminded her of James Cordon. "Thank the unnamed online asshole who stood me up."

Jamilah eyed an imaginary body beside Simon and dutifully said, "Thanks, asshole."

He cracked up. She threw back her head in laughter. When she lowered it, her eyes met a pair staring at her discreetly from across the room.

Walter.

Jamilah hadn't seen her ex in person for over a month. Last time was much like this. Public place. From a distance. Each time it became easier. Even knowing it was the right thing to do, ending their relationship had been a rough ride. For many reasons. Her intuition had told her it was over long before she told him. Because of his cavalier attitude at her heartfelt admissions, and cold shoulder for months thereafter, she almost felt like the one who'd been dumped.

That was then, this was now, Jamilah reminded herself. No hard feelings. She smiled and gave a discreet wave. He waved back. His fiancée turned around and looked at her. Olivia. Jamilah knew her name because of the large spread on their engagement in the society pages. Jamilah forced herself not to be self-conscious about sweaty work attire and hair hidden beneath a greasy bandanna until two hours ago as she took in Olivia's casual, tailored elegance and well-coifed do. Watched as the woman who wore her attorney energy like a designer jacket placed a possessive hand on Walter's arm when she spoke to him. Turned her body away from Jamilah. Spoke into his ear. They both laughed. His arm slid around her waist as another couple approached them. The scene might have been funny had what Jamilah felt was a show of insecurity not hit close to home. Jamilah's clinginess toward the end of their relationship came from the fear of not measuring up in a thousand ways to people who shouldn't matter when it came to who shared her bedroom. Highlighted a lifetime of being a people pleaser, lest they abandon her like her mother had. It had taken all these months to rediscover herself. She was still healing. She'd had help from a variety of sources, including a dear friend in Cali who'd said after the breakup, "The only man you want to be with is the one who lets you be yourself."

Jamilah tried to shake off the across-the-room encounter, but the joy from Godfrey's comedy dissipated before she reached her car. In its place were thoughts of Walter and the possible conversations that had taken place with his lawyer girlfriend about her. An unwanted trip down memory lane rolled in her mind as smoothly as the wheels on her car returning her to her downtown loft. Memories that solidified a conclusion she'd come to before, that much of her life had been spent doing what others wanted, at the cost of her own desires. She'd chased the validation not shown by her mother from others, especially men. Bosses. Boyfriends. Schoolmates. Her dad. *Especially* her father. He was a hero she rarely crossed. Which is why his demand that she fire Rashad had her so conflicted. The only thought that made her feel even worse was of all that sexy swagger leaving her kitchen, of never seeing Rashad again.

Ten

A glint of silver and Rashad reached for the car handle. Jamilah was driving that Lexus like a bat out of hell. Couldn't blame her. Rashad liked speed. He also liked arriving at Side Chic'k early and wished he had a key. Being on probation and having unsupervised access to someone else's business was probably a huge ask, so he wouldn't. One day, though, he hoped she'd trust him enough to let him in the building without her. After that? Keys to a place of his own.

Rashad reached for his notebook and stepped out of the car. "Hey, Boss Lady."

Jamilah's expression teetered between a smile and a frown. "Excuse me?"

"I said, 'Hey, Boss Lady.'"

"Don't call me that," she replied with a slight shake of her head.

"This is your establishment, right?"

"Right."

"Aren't you the boss?"

"Definitely."

"And a lady, I presume." His voice dropped an octave, took on the quality of honey on a buttered biscuit.

She gave him a look over her shoulder before unlocking the door. Rashad wasn't buying the tough sistah act. She loved the compliment. He loved her perfume and their proximity while removing her hand from the knob.

Jamilah stepped back. "What are you doing?"

"I'm opening the door for you." He did so and stepped aside. "Ladies first."

"Thanks for that, but here in the workplace, that type of chivalry isn't necessary."

They entered the building, stopped at the coatrack, and after removing their outerwear proceeded down the hall.

"See, that's why a lot of y'all are still single. Too independent. Won't let a gentleman be a gentle man."

"You don't know my relationship status. Kindly mind your business." Jamilah's voice was stern, but Rashad peeped the flirt beneath it.

"Oh, so I'm wrong? You've got a man?"

"I've got a business to open and food to prep, that's what I've got."

"So the answer to my question is a strong negative." Rashad strolled to the counter and placed his notebook on the shelf beneath it.

"The answer to that question is *let's focus on work*."

"Point taken, Boss Lady," he continued in response to her scowl. "Aside from knowing how to handle a breast or a leg, I have no business in your business. Oops, I mean… Wait. That didn't come out right."

Jamilah looked at him, eyes narrowed. He adopted his most innocent face, lowered chin and doe eyes with shoulders hunched over. He watched Jamilah try to hold on to a frown that morphed into a smile and turned into a chuckle.

"You're a trip."

"Yep, and you just got a free ride."

An easy camaraderie swept into the room and quietly settled around their shoulders. She walked over to a rack and pulled down an apron. Rashad peeped the extra sway in her hips, a sure sign that she was picking up what he was putting down. He'd always been an ass man and her…asset was top-shelf. Yes, this was his workplace, and no, he wasn't trying to harass anybody. But at the end of the day he Tarzan, she Jane, and he couldn't help but wonder what it would be like for them to swing on a vine together.

He walked over and reached for the larger apron on the other side of the rack. Their fingers touched. Sensual electricity crackled. Both acted oblivious to the current that could have charged all the kitchen appliances.

Rashad bobbed his head to the rap playing out in his head.

Jamilah walked to the sink and washed her hands. "Somebody's in a good mood today."

Again, Rashad followed her and did the same. "I'm feeling optimistic. Yesterday was a good day, all things considered. I think me working here might work out."

"Glad to hear it."

"No more so than me or my parole officers."

Jamilah walked toward the fridge. "What does working here have to do with your parole?"

"Nothing directly. They'll just be happy to hear that I'm working."

Rashad checked himself for running his mouth. Barely five minutes around Jamilah and he'd gotten too comfortable and said too much. She'd stayed on his mind long after the business closed, so much so that seeing her today felt familiar, like they'd known each other for years instead of days. Still, he couldn't afford to let his guard down. Letting her know how important this job was to maintaining his freedom might give her the illusion of too much power. Sure, he could find another job like he'd found this one, but after job hunting for weeks, this felt like a good fit, where he'd be comfortable in his skin. All that time in prison with thousands of testosterone-driven, survival-of-the-fittest men locked down in cages made the simple act of feeling comfortable easier said than done.

Jamilah turned on the stereo to a local radio station. For the next several minutes the sounds of pop, rap, and R and B combined with the clanking of pots and pans, running water, and sharpening of knives.

Jamilah ran through the prep schedule. "Any questions?"

"Not yet. I was just here yesterday doing this exact same thing."

"Not everyone is such a fast learner or retains information the first time around. Plus, I want to make sure everything is done correctly. Our reputation is built on the taste of the plate. It's got to be right."

Rashad chuckled. "I like your style, Boss Lady."

"The name's Jamilah."

"My bad. Jamilah."

Rashad expertly cut up several chickens, then placed them in a brine. "What got you into cooking?" he asked, as he reached for a bowl filled with spices and herbs.

Jamilah smiled. "Food Network. Guess you could call me a latchkey kid. Daddy worked long hours and had strict rules about what I could and couldn't do. Hanging out with other kids or in other homes without him around was one of them. So after school until around seven, sometimes eight, I was on my own. While other kids were playing video games or outside socializing, I was studying Rachael Ray, Sunny Anderson, and Alex Guarnaschelli."

"Alex is a beast," Rashad replied with a nod.

"I love her passion. Her and Antonia Lofaso are my favorites to watch compete."

"You know Heavy D is Antonia's baby daddy."

Jamilah paused and looked over. "Wow, you really are a Food Network fan."

"I prefer *aficionado*."

"Ha! Okay."

"I know more about Heavy D than I do about Antonia. But she knows how to throw down in the kitchen."

"Is TV how you got into cooking?"

"No, my granny did that. But while locked up, I went to Food Network and Cooking Channel University. Even got the men in my unit hooked on the shows. They'd vote on what dishes I should try to make, then me and my mentor Francisco would come as close as we could, given the limits of our pantry."

"That's crazy," Jamilah said, eyes twinkling. "I'd do the same thing. Write down the recipes, then try and remake them. I liked Rachael's because hers were quick and fairly easy. I also loved watching the Neelys, but their recipes were above my twelve-, thirteen-year-old pay grade. But they had daughters about my age who'd occasionally join them in the kitchen. Seeing people who looked like me on TV, all professional and successful restaurant owners, made me believe that I could do that, too."

For a few moments the two worked in companionable silence.

Then Rashad paused in fixing food and said, "See that, Boss Lady? We're not so different after all."

He would have run a half marathon for the smile she gave before she replied, "Wonders never cease."

Eleven

At closing, Jamilah heard an Ice Cube verse in her head. She agreed with him. Today was a good day. Rashad had cooked the chicken to perfection, so much so that a table of women asked to compliment the chef. Jamilah figured at least one would rather commingle than simply compliment, but she followed the law she'd laid down with Rashad and told herself it was none of her business.

Over the next few days, she and her new hire continued to vibe. The other staff welcomed him with open arms. He fit right in. It wasn't all smooth sailing for Jamilah, though. There was still the issue with her dad, who was thankfully engrossed in a suddenly hot cold case. He'd texted and asked about Rashad's replacement. So far, she hadn't responded so she wouldn't have to lie.

What she *had* done was talk to Rashad and her meager staff about the late October cater. She'd hoped Blair could be of more assistance, but Prime Rib had her locked down. Jamilah had even looked into hiring a catering chef, but what they charged ate up more of her profits than she could afford. Rashad's food tasted great, and he'd cooked for large groups; however, Jamilah wasn't totally convinced that his experience was enough for this event. The next few months of Side Chic'k staying open hinged on the catering gig's success. She wouldn't get a second chance to make a first impression.

After closing Saturday night, she decided to be honest with Rashad and voice her concerns.

"There's no doubt you can cook," she said, after sharing with Rashad the proposed party menu. "I'm concerned about your being able to handle the menu, especially the high-end meats."

Rashad removed his bandanna and shook out his locs. Jamilah wondered if he knew how sexy that move was and how it had shifted her thinking to a whole other kind of beef.

"If I can make cheap meat taste amazing, don't you think I can do the same with a more expensive cut?"

"So far I've tasted Asian cuisine and fried chicken, so honestly, I don't know."

The next day Rashad arrived carrying a plastic grocery bag.

"What's that?" Jamilah asked, after he'd placed his ever-present notebook under the counter.

"Besides cooking, hip-hop is my other passion. I write rhymes." He walked to the fridge, placed the grocery bag inside, and pulled out a pan of chicken that had brined all night.

"Your loving hip-hop doesn't surprise me, and I noticed you always carry that notebook. But I was talking about the bag you just placed in the fridge."

"A little something for later," he replied nonchalantly. "Wanna cook a dish for you after we close, if you don't mind."

"I might mind. What is it?"

"Little surprise for you. Don't worry. All I need is a skillet, a few condiments, and what's in that bag."

Business was slow. The day dreary. The temps were unusually cold for October in the Show Me State. When there was an hour left to closing and no customers in the past thirty minutes, Jamilah released Shasta, told Caylen to start clearing the dining room, and asked Rashad to begin closing down, too. She returned to the cash register and began tallying up the day's meager receipts. Soon, a heavenly scent of beef and something else—pork, maybe—wafted from the kitchen. Her mouth watered, reminding her she hadn't eaten since breakfast. She looked out at the empty dining room, walked over to lock the front door, flipped over the Closed sign, and headed to the kitchen.

"Wait. Stop!" Rashad commanded.

"What are you making?"

"It's a secret. You can't come in here right now."

She gave the room an investigative sniff. "A hamburger?"

"Can't fool you, huh?"

"Seriously, Rashad?"

"Go handle your business, Boss Lady, then have a seat. Thought you might enjoy something besides chicken for a change."

Crossing her arms, she leaned against the doorjamb. "I don't exactly appreciate you making my chicken establishment smell like a burger joint."

The lopsided grin he gave her dissolved her anger faster than dry yeast in hot water. "I think after being served, you'll forgive me."

Five minutes later, Rashad entered the dining room and set a plate on the table.

"Jamilah...for you."

She walked over and sat down, examined the simple sandwich as though it held the nuclear codes.

"Not much to it," she said, lifting the top bun. "Mustard and pickles. That's it?"

He shrugged, sat down. "That's it."

She picked up the sandwich. "Pork and beef?"

"Jamilah. Eat."

Loving an alpha man like she did, how could Jamilah do anything other than take a bite? She did and was shocked. What looked like a simple sandwich wasn't simple at all. There were layers of flavor, hidden, unexpected. She took another bite, barely stopping herself from mewling like someone had stroked her G-spot.

"What's in here?"

"You like it?"

Jamilah felt that the way she licked her lips just then made it obvious, but she answered anyway.

"It's delicious. I mean, really *really* good. I'm tasting things I can't see, like a bacon jam, um, even a sour cream–like tang, and something smoky. I'm not even gonna lie, Rashad. This is the best burger I've ever eaten."

"Good. Let's talk about the catering job."

While closing up, Jamilah reiterated the menu she'd planned. Rashad made suggestions. Without even realizing she'd made a decision, Jamilah began tweaking what they'd offer. Rashad's burger had done the convincing. She'd roll the dinner dice with him.

That burger, and their conversation, rolled away the clouds from a super slow Saturday. Once again she felt hopeful, optimistic. Pulling off this catering event might lead to more offers, which would help sustain them until business picked up. Her mood light, she hurried Rashad out, telling him that she wanted to take a quick inventory before leaving. They said good-bye. She turned the music to a Quiet Storm station and was humming a Sade classic when her phone rang.

Her father.

His text she'd ignored.

She'd completely forgotten about it and steeled herself for what he'd say.

She tapped the Speaker button and walked to the pantry. "Hi, Daddy."

"Hey, Jamilah. I texted earlier."

"I saw that. Was gonna call you after work."

"I just want to confirm that you got rid of the felon. That we no longer have a criminal in the kitchen."

"Actually, Dad, no, I didn't fire him."

"What do you mean you didn't fire him?"

"Rashad still works here."

Silence as Jamilah imagined him processing her defiance.

"I know he has a record, but before you go off, let me explain."

"There's no explanation for willingly being around someone with a rap sheet."

Her father's words that painted Rashad as dishonorable made Jamilah want to defend her cook's honor.

"Rashad was upfront with me about his criminal history. I know he used to sell marijuana and was recently released from prison. His background isn't squeaky clean. But I like him, Dad. He seems like a good guy."

"What do you mean you like him?"

Meaning that she'd let him place his hot dog between her buns. Hypothetically, of course.

"He's not a bad person. In fact he comes off as a good person who did a bad thing."

"*A* bad thing? The word *a* implies a singular incident. That's not Rashad. His running with the wrong crowd goes back to include time spent in juvie."

He read off a list of infractions, including the theft and gun charges that Rashad had previously shared with her.

"Dad, everything isn't what it seems. Those charges, well, what's on paper doesn't tell the whole story."

"Are you defending this guy?"

"I'm saying sometimes the law declares you guilty by association."

"You dare to lecture me about the law?"

She heard him take a deep breath, his raised voice becoming calm once again. "In this world, baby girl, you are who you hang around. You don't know how it works in the streets. I kept you shielded from it.

"I know I wasn't always available when you needed me. That I worked too many days and too many hours. But I thought I taught you better than to hire a criminal and, even worse, to keep him working for you after knowing the facts."

"He doesn't come off as a criminal."

"Of course not. People like him are some of the most charismatic individuals walking the earth. How do you think they're able to operate successfully? Maybe I shouldn't have worked so hard to keep you sheltered, but, baby, trust me. In my twenty-plus years on the force, I've met men like this Rashad character coming and going. You do not want to get involved with the likes of him, in any capacity."

"He's a great cook," Jamilah countered. "Doesn't everyone deserve a second chance?"

"Absolutely. Just not there, with you."

The thoughts from the other night returned. About Jamilah, the people pleaser, doing what others wanted rather than standing up for herself. She stood a bit straighter, squared her shoulders, as if a straightened spine would provide the backbone needed to stand up to her dad.

"I respect your opinion, Daddy, but I don't agree. Rashad is a good guy and a great cook. And I… I need someone with his level of experience." She told him about the catering gig. "Cooking that amount of food isn't a job that just anyone can handle."

"But it's no problem for a man just out of prison? He's still on parole, Jamilah. Hasn't even been out three months."

"I appreciate your concern, but I've made my decision. Rashad is helping out with my next catering gig and is Side Chic'k's new chef."

Every second of silence that ticked by increased Jamilah's nervousness and probably ticked up her blood pressure, too. Her angst was warranted.

"I think you've forgotten a few things," he said, with a deceptive cool, calm collectedness that had shook more than one confession out of a guilty man.

"Like who helped with the start-up money to open your business. Who cosigned the loans. Whose name is on the lease. I don't want to play hardball, but I will."

There it was. The trump card. Jamilah's bravado backbone

slackened. She was so frustrated and angry she could all out boohoo. But she wouldn't. Couldn't. She had a business to run.

Returning to the kitchen to make a list, she asked him, "Are you threatening to shut down my business?"

"I'm helping you face facts. What are they?"

By rote, Jamilah regurgitated what her father had told her.

"Rashad's a criminal, a felon."

"One still on parole."

"Yes, and birds of a feather flock together. We are who we hang around."

"Which is why you can't have any wannabe thug working at your place of business. Have you talked to Ed?"

"Yes, I've talked to him."

"Good. Maybe he can help you out until you get someone else. Meanwhile, Rashad White needs to be fired. ASAP."

Jamilah's stomach dropped, the one full of the best burger she'd ever had.

"Is he still there, by any chance?" James continued.

"No. He left right before you called."

"You do see my point of view on this, don't you? Hiring a felon was a mistake."

"I can admit that now is not the time to take chances, especially when I'm trying to increase our profits and return to a full-time schedule."

"That's right, Jamilah. Public perception is everything."

"Agreed."

"Do you need me to be there when he's terminated?"

"No."

"Are you sure?"

"Yes," Jamilah said, on emotional autopilot, agreeing with her dad from muscle memory. "When delivering the bad news, I'll make sure we meet in a public place that's well-attended and safe. Don't worry. I'll figure it out."

"Let me help you do that," Rashad said, stepping out of the hallway and into the kitchen.

Jamilah jumped. Her hand flew to her throat. "Rashad."

"You don't have to fire me. I quit."

"Jamilah! Is that him? Is he back there?" James's voice boomed throughout the small space.

"Only long enough to get what's mine." His voice was deceptively quiet, but Rashad was close enough to Jamilah's cell phone for James to hear.

"Man, if you so much as lay a hand on my ___"

"Whoever this is, fuck your judgmental ass and whatever you think you know about me. You don't know shit."

With that he walked over to a shelf beneath the counter and picked up the notebook that Jamilah hadn't noticed still being there. Without another word or look in her direction, he walked out the door.

"Rashad, I'm sorry!"

"Is he gone?" James asked.

"Yes."

"Are you sure?"

Jamilah picked up the phone, walked down the hall and to the back door. The space next to her Lexus was empty, much like her heart felt right now.

"He's gone, Dad."

"Disrespectful sonofabitch, he'd better be glad I'm across town."

"I don't think he would have said that if he knew my dad was speaking."

"Men like him will say anything. Do anything. He quit not a moment too soon."

Just like that the irresistible felon-turned-fantastic cook Rashad White was out of her restaurant and presumably her life, the move her father wanted, that both of them agreed was for the best. Was it really? Jamilah asked herself. And if so, why did she feel like crap?

Twelve

Outside, Rashad rushed to his car, a string of curse words leading the charge even as he worked to calm down. He jumped inside, fired it up and sped off without waiting for the car to warm up. His fingers coiled into fists. He wanted to punch something. Somebody. In prison, what that person said on the phone could get you hurt. Rashad wasn't one to start a fight, but he was known for finishing them. With freedom stripped away and basic human rights taken, a man's respect was all he had left. At first Rashad had physically fought for what wasn't given when verbally demanded. Later, he earned it one plate at a time.

Rashad's trauma and stress had begun with the murder of his father. One of his coping mechanisms was turning off his emotions. Shutting down. That's what he did now. Eased his foot off the gas and concentrated on his breathing, allowing his natural heart rate to return. Stopped at a red light, he turned off the overheard conversation. Ignored the now familiar pain of betrayal from yet another woman he'd trusted. These moves to self-protect came naturally. Later, Rashad would learn that they were textbook for those who'd experienced emotionally or physically traumatic experiences. They all lived with a type of PTSD.

It was his PO Nichole who shared with him what she'd

learned while taking a few psych classes at UCLA. That children who grew up in violent or abusive situations or experienced them developed skills to shield their minds from the weight of whatever tragedy had happened. To block out egregious memories. Compartmentalize pain. Those in war zones, for instance—Syria, or Iraq, or Palestine, or the Congo, or disenfranchised neighborhoods in Chicago, or Philadelphia, or Memphis, or Compton. All involved suffered a form of what many soldiers in combat experienced, an illness more often than not left untreated, unrecognized, unacknowledged, undiagnosed.

Suddenly out of work and already out of options, Rashad drove home and parked with a mind on nothing and everything at once. The empty space next to Side Chic'k. His friends back home. His ex, Brigit, the other betrayer. His mom in Oakland with Zara and her steady, stable job as a nurse. Anna and Charles. Three years in purgatory, suspended animation of the mind, body, and soul. He tapped the phone flashlight and pulled out his notebook. His pencil struck a beat on the steering wheel, foot keeping time like a drum. No words came.

He walked into the basement that was his home. The dark was comforting, familiar. He lit a candle, his only light source, and pulled out his well-worn rhyme book. But still, the lyric bucket was empty. Pride, ego, and trustworthiness weren't the only aspects that had taken a mental beating. His creativity had also been traumatized.

Hours later, still restless and unable to sleep, Rashad reached for his phone and went online. The apology Jamilah shouted at his back as he walked out the door had pulled the scab off a heart wound he thought had healed. Created a tension that screamed for release. His right hand didn't offer the kind that he needed. Dating sites that offered casual meetups could do the trick. This work thing with Jamilah had been tenuous at best, but something that could have helped him get where he wanted to go. Now getting his own was of utmost priority. He'd do what he had to do until that happened, maybe even work at the competition down the street. But getting his own setup was now priority number one.

Rashad clicked on a dating app and began scrolling through pic after pretty pic. Whoever he chose wouldn't be disappointed. He knew he was a good lover. More than one woman had begged him to keep playing long after the song ended or had tracked him down for an encore. When he'd finally found the woman who felt like the right soprano to his bass, he got locked up and endured the dissonant chord of betrayal when she left him for a good friend. One of the best things about relocating to Kansas City was the distance it created between not only that sad situation but also him and the females who still wanted to play in his band.

Ten minutes later, he'd found a Band-Aid for his pain and anger. He fired up the car once again and drove toward the distraction.

The next morning, Rashad stood in a hotel bathroom. He toweled off from a hurriedly taken shower while dispassionately eyeing the bad BBL walking by in slow motion. The move to get his attention, get his soldier up again, wasn't working. The woman he'd swiped right to hook up with last night was pretty enough, blond hair from a bottle and lips that benefited from injections. Rashad wasn't judging, but when it came to asses he preferred those made by God, like Jamilah's—*damn, why did I think of her?*—to those from Brazil.

Jamilah. What a letdown. He should have known better than to believe her words about being happy to work with him while doling out second chances. At the least, she was a user, and at most, a woman insecure enough to be easily persuaded. Looking out for herself, what she could get, with no thought of a man's feelings, or that a thug like him, as the voice on Jamilah's phone had called him, might even possess a work-ing, beating heart.

He didn't have time for either.

Time to get out of the temporary pleasure portal and back

into the real world. He crossed the room, slid into his jeans, pulled on the wrinkled T-shirt by the bed and stuffed his boxers into his pocket.

The woman pulled on the black mini she'd arrived in and stepped into heels that were more appropriate under last night's moon than the midday sunshine. She slinked over to him. "Rashad," she purred, "you're in a much bigger hurry this morning than you were last night."

"Um, yeah, baby," he replied, using the catchall term that came in handy when forgetting someone's name. "I've got things to do."

"Work, huh? You're a chef, right?"

"I'm a lot of things," Rashad said, quickly deflecting the question and the cause for why he'd gone online in the first place. "Right now, I'm going to make like Casper and become a ghost."

A quick kiss and a wink softened the verbal blow. He laced up his sneakers and, after declining a sexcapade replay later tonight, prepared to beat a hasty exit. He walked to the door.

"Rashad!"

He paused, hand on the knob. "Yeah?"

His distraction sidled up beside him. "I need to ask a favor. I'm in a situation and could use a little help."

"What kind of help?"

"A little financial assistance."

Rashad had never paid to play, but he knew what it was like to need money.

"How much?"

"Like…five hundred, maybe?"

Rashad laughed. This was starting to feel less like a real problem and more like a game being played.

"Last night was good, baby, but not *that* good."

"Well, how much can you give me?" she pouted.

"Are you a ho or something?"

She reached up to slap him. He caught her wrist.

"How dare you!"

"It was a fair question," he said, gently yet firmly bringing her arm back down to her side. "Women who ask for money in exchange for sex are usually defined by that label."

"I'm not a prostitute. I just need some money."

"I'm sorry," Rashad answered, as he opened the door. "But I can't help you."

Rashad left regretting he'd swiped right last night. A man had needs. Rashad's sex drive was high. But that wasn't what made him bed a stranger. That culprit was Jamilah and the conversation he'd overheard. Not that he'd admit that fact, even to himself. He'd had a lifetime perfecting the art of hiding his emotions behind a scarred, iron-clad heart and a closed, don't-give-a-damn look. So what if she and whoever she was talking to had judged him? What else was new?

In the wee hours of the morning, after continuously replaying what happened the night before in his head, Rashad had vowed one thing. He was done allowing other people to define who he was. He had skills and confidence and was looking for a job when he got the one at Side Chic'k. No matter what, Rashad knew he'd be all right. As long as he believed in himself, realizing dreams was just a matter of time.

Rashad wasn't ready for a free afternoon. Not wanting to be alone with his thoughts or go home and stew at Anna's, he called Leon.

"Hey, man. What game are you playing?"

"Who says I'm playing anything?"

Rashad laughed. "The sound you just muted."

"Don't you have somewhere to be?"

"No."

"No? What, did your shift get shifted already?" Leon laughed at his own play on words.

"You could say that." Rashad paused for effect, turning on the freeway that would take him across town to where Blair and Leon lived. "I quit."

"You what?"

"You heard me. I'm done there. Side Chic'k is now Side Shit to me. I don't work there no more."

On the other side of the call, silence.

"Leon? You there?"

Leon cleared his throat. "Quit playing."

"I'm serious, man. Real talk."

"Where are you?"

"On my way to your house," Rashad replied, exiting the freeway.

"Cool. Come on through."

While driving over, Rashad got four calls. He ignored them all. Anna was just being mama bear, ready to play the role of the caring godmother while trying to get all up in his business. His parole officer Nichole was just doing her job. No doubt she'd received his text about getting a job. He wasn't ready to reveal that he no longer had one. Hopefully he'd get hired somewhere else before their next conversation. The last calls? Jamilah. Twice. Nothing else for them to talk about. She'd said more than enough last night.

He reached Leon and Blair's house and pulled into the driveway. It was an older home in a transitioning neighborhood, the status quo surrounded by new possibilities. There were cracks in the concrete. A silver state-of-the-art security system stood in stark contrast to fading siding with peeling paint. Still, there was something welcoming about the yard in need of mowing and beds of errant flowers on either side of the door. That friends his age paid a mortgage and not rent was impressive. They were adulting nicely and basically on a chef's salary. Making their way in the world. Just the thought strengthened Rashad's resolve.

The door opened before he could knock. It was Blair, not Leon, who let him in.

"Dude! What's going on? Jamilah's been blowing up my phone. Leon says you quit. What the hell?"

"Good afternoon to you too, Blair." Rashad continued to the back where Leon had transformed what might have been a den into a game room/man cave, with Blair yapping at his heels.

"Seriously, Rashad. What could have happened that was so bad you quit? You literally just started working!"

"What up, Leon?"

Leon nodded, his eyes glued to the TV screen. "Nothing to it."

Blair continued, relentlessly. "I'm the one who hyped you up like damn near the Second Coming. For that alone I deserve an explanation."

Blair huffed and puffed, her eyes going from Leon to Rashad, then back to her husband.

Leon got the memo and paused the game.

Rashad plopped on the couch. Blair sat in a chair.

"Yesterday after my shift was over, I accidentally left my book in the kitchen."

"Why would you have a notebook in the kitchen?" she asked. "Creating your own bible?"

"Creating rhymes," Leon interjected. "When he doesn't cook, he raps."

"Not really. More of a spoken-word artist."

"Don't rappers speak words?"

Glares from both Rashad and Blair now.

Leon shrank. "Sorry."

"Anyway," Rashad continued with a sigh, "I went back for it and overheard a conversation. About me. Jamilah was on the phone with someone calling me a thug and telling her I should be immediately replaced. Your girl agreed. Not a good look."

"Hmm." Blair considered Rashad's words. "That doesn't sound like Jamilah. She's not two-faced like that. What exactly did she say, or even more important, what did you hear?"

"Her agreeing with this jerk acting like he knew my whole life."

"Probably her father," Leon said. "He works in law enforcement."

Her father? Damn.

Given the words they'd exchanged, Rashad hoped it wasn't her dad. In hindsight, however, Leon was probably right. The man definitely sounded overly protective, as though he was ready to kick Rashad's ass on sight. Or try. Rashad wasn't a lightweight. He knew how to throw paws.

"Well, if it was her father, I cussed him out."

Blair brought a hand to her forehead. "Oh boy."

"He was saying all kinds of foul shit about me. I had every right to defend myself. But still, if I'd known it was her pops, I would have expressed my thoughts differently."

Rashad had the decency to feel bad. His grandmother, who helped raise him, would definitely not cosign his behavior. She was one of those God-fearing, church-going sisters who'd give you a dollar if she had two and at the same time take that Bible she loved to quote from and use it to pop you upside the head. Granny didn't play.

"She told me her dad was a police officer or detective, whatever. I walked in on him running down my criminal history, pointing out every mistake I'd made from the time I was fourteen."

"How'd he know?"

"Background check," Blair and Rashad said at once.

"That's standard in hiring these days," Blair pointed out. "Probably did one on me. They weren't singling you out."

"Doing a background check wasn't the problem. I told her myself that I'd been to jail and that it wasn't the first time. The problem was her talking about me behind my back. Listening to and making assumptions about my character when asking me directly would have been a much better move."

"I'm sorry that happened, dog," Leon said, sincerity and compassion pressed between each consonant and vowel. "That's really effed up."

It was the perfect answer from a friend to a man who was hurting, especially one of the rare ones who Rashad had trusted with his background. Kids weren't born bad. Urban teens didn't just wake up with violence in them. There were hidden agendas, plans made in high places, that created the worlds with crime as one of their few options. Rashad appreciated Leon agreeing that he'd been wronged.

A phone rang from another room.

"That's probably Jamilah again," Blair said, rising. "Or my boss. Either way I've got to go. But do me a favor, Rashad? Please talk to Jamilah. Give her a chance to tell her side."

"I already heard her side!"

"What you heard sounds horrible. I'd be mad, too. Jamilah's naïve, but she means well. I'm not excusing her actions or ignoring your feelings. I just know how excited she was to have you come work for her and how desperately she needs you right now. There's a huge job coming up and I can't think of anyone better than you to help her pull it off."

"Oh, so this isn't about her righting a wrong, it's about me saving her ass?"

The phone stopped ringing.

Blair walked over and placed a hand on Rashad's shoulder. "No, Rashad. It's about both of you taking a breath and giving each other grace. She's stressed the hell out. You're sensitive about this and understandably so. Just… I think the two of you together could be really successful, could help each other get what both of you want. You've messed up, and people gave you second chances. I'm just asking you to think about returning that favor."

When he got home and talked to Anna, her position was much like what Blair said. His friend Juke had his back, used words not spoken in polite company to encourage Rashad to do his own thing.

"T-Bone's been asking around about you, man. He's looking for you."

"He's not going to find me. Hanging out with so-called felons is what got me three years."

"No, this jacked-up system did that."

Rashad nodded even though Juke couldn't see his agreement. "Anyway, Tee is on the straight and narrow. Flipped a bunch of stacks and is now flipping houses. Some in Vegas, where he lives, and somewhere in Mississippi where his folk are from. All one hundred percent legit."

This was news to Rashad. He hadn't spoken to any of the Andersons since doing the bid for his boy Drew by not snitching to police that night about who possessed the weapon found in the car they pulled over.

"They owe you, man, and who knows? Maybe he can help you get your own biz."

Rashad took in all of what everyone said. Later that night, he sat alone in the quiet of his room, dark except for a small desk lamp and his imagination. Again, he resorted to his best friend, the pen, to work out the feelings roiling in his stomach, smoldering between each heartbeat. Pressing pen to paper, he took a deep breath. This time, the words flowed.

All society everywhere wants to be judge and jury
Causing inner fury. Their critique can't cure me
Rest assured it's a blurred line, a fake deed
Society's sobriety from unkind minds who lured me
Who grew up in the vicinity of classmates for enemies
Gunshots for lullabies. Dead daddies. No last goodbye. Like Corey White. Rashad closed his eyes and searched for the elusive memory of his father's touch. He couldn't feel it.

NO space to cry. Powers that be who lie.
NO place to hide. Wide open genocide.

Again, Rashad paused as the faces of friends he'd lost swam into view. Rather than tamp down the roiling emotions, he allowed himself the rare moment to feel them and pressed the pain through his pen.

NO answers why. No better by and by.

NO recognition for tries. NO chance reaching for skies.
Only judgments and juries sending men to purgatory
NO grit all glories the pen behind their own stories
Behind the wall the unmitigated gall
To shine in concrete creative laboratories

Rashad smiled at this line. That some of the world's most creative geniuses languished in prison was a fact!

Honorable roots grown through street soldier boots
Yet the truth that soothes makes the pathway smooth
Is this. Found guilty from a not-guilty plea
The twist. No losing dignity no spilling tea
Ten toes down for loyalty. A conscience free.

At the end of the day, Rashad could look in the mirror and be proud of maintaining his integrity, his character, of representing honor among those who mattered most.

YES. To mental sovereignty. YES. A bittersweet victory.
YES. A heart passed test. No stress. Say less.
YES. That energy best for me.

Rashad filled ten pages with emotions, song snippets, rhymes, raps, verses, or whatever these feelings ended up being, then cut out the light and lay back, fully clothed. He stared at the ceiling, looking for the thing that was searching for him.

His phone dinged. He lifted it up, read the name. Jamilah.

Sorry for what happened. Please call.

He tossed the phone, stripped naked, and strolled into the shower. Once finished, he returned to bed and slid between the covers.

Replayed everyone's advice. Listened to his own.

Didn't call her back.

Thirteen

Jamilah paced the length of her open-concept, downtown loft, unaware of the bright sun shining through the panoramic windows that had sealed the deal for her home choice selection and helped justify the rent that hadn't seemed so high when the restaurant flourished.

"I know it's a lot to ask, Ed, especially after saving me today, and with your condition. But my back is against the wall. If I'm going to pull off this catering event, then everything to make that happen—shopping, major prep, and some of the cooking—has to start next week."

"I wish I could help you. But with this pain, I don't think so. What about Blair?"

"First person I called. I've left several messages, but haven't heard back."

Jamilah didn't take it personally. She knew how brutal kitchens could be when trying to establish one's place there.

"I could ask Russell," Ed offered. "Good cook, but he drinks. War messed him up. So I don't know if I'd trust him to be reliable."

"What about some of the women who cook for the functions at the VFW?"

"Major grocery store chains provide those meals. The women don't cook, they heat up. Hold on, Jamilah. Got a call coming in."

Jamilah sat on one of her counter bar stools, scrolling through her Contacts list for the umpteenth time. She tried hard to not feel dejected, to convince herself that what happened last night, while awkward and not how she wanted to end Rashad's employment, was probably for the best. Her father had made a career in law enforcement. Had spent decades around criminals. Perhaps he could see what she couldn't. Jamilah knew that he loved her. Had never lied to her. Had never steered her wrong.

Yet.

Restless, unresolved energy pulled Jamilah from the stool. She walked to the window. Instead of the burst of autumn's colors, she saw Rashad's face. Angry. Dejected. And something else, something that looked like hurt but went deeper. Glancing back at the room behind her, the sun jumped off a familiar brass frame. She walked over to the wall that held a grouping of pictures and picked up one sitting on the table, amid another collection of memories. This one a favorite, a picture of Jamilah and her father when she'd just turned thirteen.

He'd allowed her to get her ears pierced and her hair braided, long plaits that fell in curls down her back. His lady friend at the time had taken Jamilah shopping and helped her pick out a dress. The age-appropriate maxi with pastel colors cinched at the waist and fell to the floor in soft pleats. They'd gone to dinner. Not a place for kids but a real dinner, a steak house for grown-ups. He'd opened the doors for her, pulled out her chair. Told her that these acts were how a princess should get treated. Jamilah had indeed felt like royalty that night.

She picked up another picture, this one at around age eighteen. A name came to mind: Matthew Lindsay. Her first love she hadn't thought about in years. Artistic, sensitive, and introverted, with a slight build and bright smile, Jamilah had been smitten from the start. They'd bonded over a love for wonderfully weird art house movies and Bruno Mars. Daddy didn't like him. Not manly enough. She accompanied him to his senior dance, but the relationship fizzled under the heat of parental displeasure. On the opposite side were the men she'd dated for longer periods, ones who met with her father's approval. Had she liked them more because they met her dad's standard? Had she endured an unhealthy relationship with Walter because their being together pleased James? The questions hung in the air like Midwest humidity, the answers hovered like a rain cloud.

Again, an image of Rashad's expression from that night sprang up unbidden. The feeling of being betrayed etched on his face made her heart ache all over again. She labeled the feeling compassion and embarrassment when in actuality attraction and shame were closer to truth.

There were other feelings, too, ones Jamilah could not yet explore. Ones that would surely lead to her father's displeasure. She wasn't ready to brave that storm.

"That was Russell. He might be able to help with the catering."

"Thank God. And thank you, uncle."

"Anything for family," Ed replied. "I can help out at the restaurant. As long as I have a stool to sit on, I should be okay to help you prep and fry up chicken. I'll talk to Russell and make a few phone calls but can't make any promises. Keep doing what you can to get others to help you, especially with the catering job."

Jamilah continued down the list, leaving messages or reaching out to people who weren't available. Finally, with zero remaining options, she phoned Rita, a good enough worker but messy friend who loved to gossip, speculate, and lie. They'd met as freshmen at a local college and became friends while doing a class project together. At first, Jamilah liked Rita's funny, effervescent personality. It wasn't until the venom Rita shot at other friends became aimed at her that Jamilah understood the meaning of a forked tongue and lessened their interactions. Rita left college, got married and, after her husband joined the navy, moved to California.

Jamilah learned they'd returned to the city by running into Rita at a grocery store. Her husband had been honorably discharged. Rita needed a job and had kitchen experience. Jamilah hired her right away. It didn't take long before the kitchen that had previously been drama free deteriorated into a bickering beehive of he said, she said, with Rita at the center of it all. Just when Jamilah felt she had no choice but to fire her, fate intervened. Rita got pregnant with her second child. Jamilah attended the baby shower and knew they'd welcomed another girl but hadn't tried to stay in touch. As far as she knew, Rita might be a stay-at-home mom with no need for extra cash.

Nothing beat a failure but a try.

"Jamilah?" Incredulity was wrapped around the greeting. "I was just talking about you!"

Again?

"All good, I hope." Jamilah sounded unconvinced even to herself.

"Of course! Remember Everett? That server who also wanted to learn how to cook? I ran into him the other day. He said you were still open but only on weekends. What happened? Money problems? You were doing so well."

"You've never driven past Fly the Coop, the one near Eighteenth on Paseo?"

"Ooh, girl, I eat there all the time. I didn't even think about how their business might affect you. No wonder you're barely hanging on."

Jamilah desperately wanted to end the call. Defying her father and rehiring Rashad would probably be easier than this.

"We're doing fine," she lied, proud of how easily the words slid off her tongue. "I wanted to expand my brand and have started a selective catering business for high-end clients."

Jamilah was okay with Rita repeating this, which she certainly would, to any mutual acquaintances and maybe strangers, too. The creative storytelling sounded good to Jamilah's own ears.

"Tell me more."

"I have an event coming up at the end of the month, one the client booked at the last minute."

"A Halloween party? I love those."

"Company anniversary, but because of how close it is to Halloween, costumes wouldn't surprise me. My usual crew isn't available. I'm calling to see if you might be interested in helping out. With pay, of course."

The conversation had probably removed years from her life, but once it was over, Jamilah had a potential crew of six, her employees Shasta and Caylen, Rita and Everett, five counting Ed, six if Russell was riding the wagon. There was only one critical piece missing: a real chef.

With a final swipe of her thumb she scanned the remaining names in her Contacts. Her thumb tapped the screen when reaching the *W*s, hovered over a name that shouldn't even still be in her phone. Her ex, Walter Overton. Walter was a Kansas City native who knew everybody. The councilman position he held at City Hall probably gave him access to a variety of lists and groups throughout Kansas City, information that could help Jamilah save this job. She was just about to peel off the little dignity that remained after speaking with Rita and call him when her ringtone chimed.

She couldn't jab the phone icon fast enough and hoped she'd been saved by the bell.

Fourteen

"Blair! Oh my God, finally!"

"Hi."

"Sorry for all the calls back-to-back," Jamilah said, assuming that as the reason for Blair's lackluster greeting. She knew through texts that her former chef was still in hell's kitchen, pulling seventy-, sometimes eighty-hour shifts a week.

"Hope I didn't disturb your sleep, but, girl... I've got a huge emergency. You're not going to believe what happened."

"I already know."

"Know what?"

"Hold on."

Jamilah listened to what sounded like Blair moving around, confirmed when she heard a door shut.

"Rashad's here."

"At your house?"

"No, at the White House, Jam."

"What's he doing there?"

"I imagine trying to stanch the flow of blood from the dagger thrown in his back."

"Whoa! You can't mean by me?"

"A hit dog will holler. How could you talk about him like that, especially about his past, a very touchy subject?"

"I didn't intend for him to hear me."

"Clearly, which for him was even worse."

This was not the phone call Jamilah expected. She felt confused, experiencing remorse and righteous indignation at the same time. Already feeling lower than a whale's belly at the bottom of the ocean, she went on the defensive.

"He's not the only one feeling badly. Daddy did a background check, Blair."

"And told you he'd been to prison, which you already knew."

Jamilah looked at her phone as if the inanimate object had spoken.

"I messed up, Blair. I hired him too quickly."

"You messed up by firing him, Jam. And talking about someone behind their back doesn't sound like you at all."

Jamilah imagined Blair getting dressed for work, her voice at different levels as she walked around the room.

"I thought he'd left."

"That would have made it right, then, if he hadn't heard you?"

"Why are you on his side?" Jamilah said, fighting back. "Along with being a decent cook"—*amazing, stellar, but why be technical?*—"he's a felon. There's no telling what would have happened had I kept him on."

"Oh, really? Well, I have a few ideas. His high-level cooking skills and charming personality would have done wonders for your restaurant. His presence alone would have likely pulled in more female customers. Word of mouth about his cooking would have done the rest.

"Rashad isn't just a good cook, Jam. He's a good man. Smart. Driven. Full of ideas."

"And just out of prison."

"That wasn't a secret. He told you during the interview."

"Sounds like he told you his side of everything."

"This isn't about sides. It's about right and wrong. And you feeling a type of way because Rashad has a past, one that he's trying hard to put behind him. It's not fair."

"I know. You're right. And I already get how crazy this question is going to sound, but—"

"No," Blair interrupted. "I can't help you with your event. Unfortunately, the only other person I know who is qualified enough to recommend on such short notice is a brothah just out of prison and still on parole. I don't know what else to say. Hold on."

Jamilah heard Blair tell the guys good-bye. The more her ex-chef said, the less sure Jamilah felt about the high horse she rode on.

"I'm not as bad as the person you're painting," she continued when the convo resumed. "I was pressured to do what I did."

"Just how long are you going to let your father run your life?"

That was a good question. It joined the others Jamilah had shoved in a mental carry-on that would someday have to be unpacked. Meanwhile, she needed to get out of the house and out of her head. Time for some retail therapy that she couldn't afford.

"Thanks for listening to me rant, Blair, and being honest about how you feel. Let's talk later, okay? I need to get some fresh air."

"What you need to do is check your ego, call Rashad, and do whatever it takes to get him back in your kitchen."

"I've tried that. Sent texts last night and this morning. He doesn't want to talk to me."

"I hope you two can work it out. Rashad cooks better than most of the trained chefs I've worked with, and I've worked with some of the best."

"He's very talented. I can't lie about that. But even if he agreed to come back, if Daddy found out he'd have a fit."

"Okay, cool, but can your daddy cook? Can he break down those chickens, barbecue beans, fix mac 'n' cheese?"

"Ed worked the shift yesterday."

"As head chef?"

"You don't have to say what I'm already thinking. As backup, he'll have your bible."

"Jam, no disrespect to the veteran, but the way he cooks you're going to need the one commissioned by King James. If you want to save your restaurant and have a chance in hell of pulling off that catering gig, you need Rashad. This situation is less about how your father might feel later and more about what you need right now."

"I've tried reaching out to him, Blair. What else can I do?"

"Whatever it takes to save yourself from bankruptcy or worse. You need to check your ego and make Rashad your hero."

"Cute." Jamilah smiled, remembering Rashad's strong presence in her kitchen. "I don't know what I'd say to him."

"How about the truth? That you were wrong to judge him. That you effed up. Tell him about your dad's influence, and why you acted like a judgmental bit—"

"Hey!"

"Person."

Jamilah smiled again, and this time her heart joined in with a tiny shred of hope on its wings.

"Tell him you'll double his salary, take him off probation, give him full run of the kitchen, heck, give him a little, you know...kitty-kitty."

"Blair! No, you did not just say that!"

Blair laughed. "Hey, sometimes a girl's gotta do what a girl's gotta do. Besides, it's been a while since I've heard you mention a man. You've probably got cobwebs."

"You know what, you may be right," Jamilah said, laughing, too. "Last night I woke up to something scratching my leg. Now that you mention it, might have been a spider."

They howled.

"Rashad is very good-looking. There could be harder sacrifices, pun intended."

"You're disgusting."

"I love you, too. Look, Jam, I just pulled up. Time to clock in. Now pull that Spike Lee classic out of your bag, and do the right thing. Text and let me know what happens."

Jamilah left the house and headed for a strip mall. Rashad stayed on her mind. By the time she reached her favorite discount retailer, she had an idea. Her father was emphatic about Rashad not working at the restaurant he'd helped get started. But the catering event was hers alone. She sat in her car and pulled up Rashad's number. Then, on second thought, she put the car back in Drive and headed to Blair's house. Damn her and all that talk about sex. Just the thought of seeing that "hard sacrifice" made Jamilah's cat purr.

She saw Rashad's SUV before she reached Blair's house. Once in their driveway, Jamilah hopped out of the car and marched to the porch like who she was: a woman on a mission with a dream to save. She knocked on the door like law enforcement. Her daddy would have been proud. After a couple of minutes—okay, seconds—she reached for her phone to call Leon. No way was she leaving this house as long as Rashad was inside.

Leon opened the door. "Dang, girl, you're knocking at the door like you're running from trouble."

Straight into it, more likely.

"Blair's already left for work."

"I'm here to speak with Rashad."

Leon's response was a slightly raised brow. He stepped onto the porch and shut the door behind him.

"I'm not sure that's such a good idea."

"It's probably a really bad idea. But one I'm determined to see through, so would you kindly go back in there and let him know that the last woman on earth he wants to see right now will take up residence on this porch until he comes outside?"

Leon peered at her with an unreadable expression, then shook his head. "Women."

As Jamilah waited for the outcome of her request, her bold veneer began to slip. What the heck had she been thinking to come barging over here like she had a right to conversation? She had no idea how Rashad would react. How he'd behave when he was angry.

You can't have any wannabe thug working at your place of business.

Did Jamilah want smoke with a—

"Yeah."

Jamilah whipped around. Deep in thought, she hadn't heard the screen door open.

"Rashad, hi."

He verbalized nothing, but his body language spoke clearly. *Get to the point.*

"I came over to apologize for what you heard the other night…and what you didn't."

His face was a mask.

"Your words were clear. No interpretation or translation needed."

"True, but context might help."

"Was that your pops on the phone?"

"Yes, that was my father."

"He was out of line. But I didn't mean to be disrespectful."

"I'm very sorry, Rashad, about this whole situation. I feel horrible that you overheard our conversation."

"But not what was said."

"I'm especially sorry for that." A gust of wind came up out of nowhere. Jamilah looked at the sky. It looked like rain. "Is there any way we can go somewhere and talk?"

"Why?"

Rashad wasn't going to make this easy. And why should he? She'd put him in the hot seat until she was comfortable enough to offer the grand privilege of sweating over a fryer. He didn't owe her leniency. Turnabout was fair play.

Fifteen

Rashad didn't agree to a meetup right away. Allowed a few days to pass before he texted with the message that he'd see her on Friday, that he'd come down to Side Chic'k after closing and hear her out. During that time, he clicked onto the dating site he'd used a couple days ago. His phone had been blowing up with notifications. Ninety percent were from Dee-Lite, his latest swipe-right choice.

Probably still after money. Or his body. Damn.

A slight chill passed through him as he remembered other women who wanted more from him than he could give. He'd dodged his share of drama-laced bullets, one of the reasons he'd welcomed relocating from LA. The last thing he needed was a repeat of those situations now. He quickly blocked her profile, changed his to private, and breathed a sigh of relief.

Once done, he'd gone back in Leon's house and vented about Jamilah again. Leon had intervened, a voice of reason.

"She was dead wrong to talk about you. No one is disputing that," he'd said, the moment serious enough for him to put down his console. "But I've known Jamilah almost as long as I've known Blair, and I can tell you there isn't an intentionally cruel bone in her body. I know her father, James, too. He's military, obstinate, sees the world in black-and-white. But he's not all bad either. She gave you a chance. Don't you think you should give her one?"

Still not sure he'd meet with her even after Leon's sound advice, Rashad had gone home, gotten online, and scrolled ads seeking a cook. There were plenty of them. He had choices. One place wanted someone who specialized in Cajun and Creole cooking. Another was upscale, perhaps above his pay grade. He was also almost certain they'd do a background check. Rashad wasn't sure he could handle past mistakes preventing present opportunities again. A bunch of eateries needed prep and line cooks, dishwashers, and servers. There was an assisted-living facility wanting someone to cook their breakfast and lunch meals. He'd taken a few screenshots, then heard Anna and went upstairs for a second opinion.

"I can't stand people like that," she admitted after Rashad shared what he'd overheard and learning he'd quit because of it. "I'm surprised, though. She doesn't come off as that type of person. And I know for a fact she's attracted to you. It wasn't just your food that had her ringing your phone."

"Even if she were interested, her dad would shut it down, and she'd let him. I can't deal with a woman like that. Not sure I'd even want to work with one."

"Don't focus on her. Focus on you and your goals. It's only one conversation, Rashad. What do you have to lose?"

"I want my own place but need help to get it started. There's an empty space next to Side Chic'k that would be perfect. Maybe you and Charles could come on as investors or silent partners."

"Rashad, you know we'd do anything to help you. But our money is so quiet right now we can't find it."

Friday night, as he pulled into a parking space behind Side Chic'k, the back door opened. An older man with a bald head, big gut, and stained apron stepped outside. He leaned heavily on a cane and then on the wall. While lighting a cigarette and taking a long drag, he eyed Rashad with mild interest, like someone used to scoping out his surroundings. Rashad didn't want to come off looking suspicious. He gave the older man a head nod before stepping out of the car.

"Closed yet?" he asked.

"No, but customers enter around front."

"I'm here to speak with Jamilah."

"Oh, you're the brothah who quit on her."

"Yeah," Rashad said, reaching for the door handle, wondering yet again if coming here had been the right thing to do. "I'm that brothah."

He eased down the familiar hallway, his mind going back to the words he'd heard that night as he neared the kitchen. This time the only sound was water running, people laughing, and dishes being stacked in the dishwasher.

Before entering the kitchen, he glanced out at the dining room and identified the source of laughter. Jamilah stood at a table socializing with two couples clearly having a good time. He took in the easy interaction, and her. She wore a pair of black jeans that emphasized the curves he'd first admired, with a white baby doll T-shirt boasting the restaurant's name across the chest. Her hair was pulled back in a messy ponytail, emphasizing high cheekbones and nicely shaped lips. She really was a pretty woman, definitely the kind of attractive he liked. What went on inside that beautiful head? Not so much.

She must have felt his eyes on her. She turned. The humor drained from her eyes and was replaced by something he couldn't quite identify. She said something to the foursome, put a slip on the table and walked toward him.

"Hello, Rashad."

"Sup."

He wished his body could stay as neutral as his expression. It had only been a few days, but seeing Jamilah was like water to a thirsty man.

"Thanks for agreeing to meet me. I was hoping you wouldn't change your mind."

"My word is bond."

Jamilah looked around the nearly empty dining room. "Can we sit on the stools over by the window? It's more private."

Without waiting for an answer, she led the way. Rashad tried and failed to not watch the sexy swaying ass, further deflating the anger he'd built up against her and weakening his resolve to maintain the second impression she gave him, the one that completely obliterated the first.

"Have you eaten? Do you want anything, something to drink?"

"No, I'm good."

He watched Jamilah twist a ring she wore on the middle finger of her right hand and then adjust a grouping of bangles on her arm. She was nervous, Rashad knew, but when she began speaking, she looked at him directly.

"Rashad, I'm sorry. For everything. What you overheard my dad say, my reaction to what he said, everything."

"You've said that already, so I'll ask again. Are you sorry because you didn't mean what you said or only sorry because I overheard it?"

Jamilah put her chin in the palm of her hand, looked out on a quiet street, empty except for the cars of the two couples still inside. She dropped her head, then looked up. Her vulnerability was like kryptonite. He forced his attention back to why he was here, which shored up his resolve.

"The truth?"

"They say that is what will set you free."

"Both. You didn't hear the whole conversation. My father—"

"He's a cop, right?" Rashad's tone was sharper than intended.

"A detective."

"Well, now it all makes sense."

"He's always been a detective, Rashad, when it comes to me. It was wrong for him to judge you, but it wasn't personal."

"That's a damn lie." His voice was low and calm. His eyes, fire.

Ed walked up. "We're done in the kitchen. The last customers just left. Do you need me to stick around?"

His question was to Jamilah, while his eyes never left Rashad's face.

Rashad stared back.

"No, Ed. I'm fine. Did you meet Rashad?"

"Yeah, we met," Rashad said, still eyeing Ed while sending a telepathic message.

I don't want any trouble here. Don't start none, won't be none.

Ed caught the vibe that Rashad threw out. "All right, then," he said with a curt nod to Rashad before turning to his niece. "I'll see you in the morning?"

"Please, and thank you." Jamilah brought her hands together as if in prayer.

They both waited until Ed was gone. Rashad continued as if there had been no interruption.

"What you said was about me as a person. About the crimes I committed as a person, involving other people. You and your old man's judgmental opinions affect my life as a *person*. So don't give me that spiritual, hocus-pocus, *Four Agreements* bullshit about not taking it personally."

Jamilah's eyes widened in surprise.

"Oh, you're surprised I'm familiar with a spiritual guru? A lot of what I know would surprise you. I'm very well read, with a diverse palate. When you do time, you *have* time, know what I'm saying? If you're smart, you take advantage of the opportunity and work the system rather than letting the system work you.

"Now, do I get what the author meant, that opinions are formed from an individual's experience and perspective, and at the end of the day have nothing to do with who I really am? Of course. But to say it ain't personal is just po-TAY-to, po-TAH-to, to-MAY-to, to-MAH-to, you feel me? If it involves a person, it's personal. That's *another* perspective, from Guru Rashad."

"I don't necessarily agree, but I get your point." Jamilah eyed him intently, flickers of warmth, and something else, shining in her eyes. Rashad didn't look away. The heat intensified.

"Did you do all of what's on your record, what my dad pulled up of your criminal history?"

"No," Rashad stated emphatically. "About ninety percent, though."

He smiled. She didn't.

"Why?" Spoken barely above a whisper.

"Different reasons for different situations. Consequences of a very long, meandering story. You probably don't have that type of interest, and I don't have that kind of time."

"I am interested. I want to know and have time to listen."

"Okay."

"Excuse me for a moment."

Rashad watched Jamilah disappear into the kitchen. Her seemingly genuine interest moved something deep within him. The easy way they'd worked together and how she'd begun to see him as a peer, not an ex-offender, was the sexiest encounter he'd had since being released.

She returned with two glasses, a couple bottles of sparkling water, and a bottle of wine.

"Wine or water?"

"Water."

She set a bottle of water in front of him and slid over a glass before unscrewing the cap on the wine bottle and pouring herself a liberal portion. She sat down and held up her glass.

"To a better understanding?"

"Hold up, Michelle Obama, we're not quite at kumbaya."

"Fair enough." Jamilah sat back, took a small sip of wine, set down her glass, and waited.

"I lost my dad at ten years old. Murder. Rocked my world.

There was a lot of speculation, but we never got a clear reason why."

Rashad drank the water in his glass and refilled it. "After my father was killed, I didn't care about living either. I lost all boundaries. I had no fear. It was grief, but I didn't have a therapist to help me process that anger. The streets are enticing. And the money is good."

"Did you sell drugs?"

"I moved around a little marijuana. A lot of us did. In neighborhoods like mine, it's one of the few economies being offered. People have to eat. It's all good, though. No losses, only lessons. My past is the stepping-stone into the gift of my present and the door to my future."

"Spoken like a true guru." Finally, she smiled.

"Say less."

Rashad rested against the back of the chair, temporarily soaking up Jamilah, the one who crept into his thoughts at night, that made him want to step up as a man. But when he spoke, it was to the woman who'd betrayed him.

"What about you? Is growing up in a sheltered environment with a cop for a father what made you so quick to not only judge me but also easy to toss me out of your kitchen like trash?"

Sixteen

His question stopped her heartbeat. The calm, honest way he asked it snatched her breath. Just before he'd asked that question, Jamilah thought she'd seen a flicker of forgiveness in his eyes, fondness even. His expression changed, his tone low and direct. His eyes probed into her soul and demanded an honest answer. She searched for it, too. Her point of view morphed in the moment. New rules were being written in her head and heart.

"When Daddy called with your background report, I was quick to tell him I knew all about it. That you'd been honest from the jump about doing time and just getting out of prison. Being a career officer with a life spent around criminals, no doubt his opinion is jaded. Still, I defended you, Rashad. Told my dad he was wrong. That the report contained what you did, not who you were."

"And after that?"

Jamilah hesitated, took a deep breath. "My dad helped me get this place, helped me get a loan, cosigned the lease. He became very adamant about you not working here. Used the rhetoric I've heard since a child and, yes, was very convincing. When he gets like that, there's no changing his mind. So I changed mine. I'm sorry."

His hand rested on the table. She reached out and grabbed it, because if she didn't, she might float away on a sea of raging emotions.

He looked at their hands and back at her. Now along with strength and pride was something else. Something almost intangible. Vulnerability? No, Jamilah deduced. Never that.

"That I would ever make anyone feel the way you did—not valued, dispensable—is not acceptable at all. Will you forgive me?"

He stared for a beat, then looked away.

She reached out, now holding his hand with both of hers. Crazy how his energy worked like an anchor, settling her deeper into her truth. "Please?"

Something happened then. She felt it and was sure he did, too. A sensation, raw heat, that brushed over her skin like a summer kiss. An unnamable emotion seeped out of them both, intermingled, and poured itself over the moment. She wanted to kiss him. Ridiculous: this was the man who, at her dad's command, she'd been prepared to fire. But his eyes, lips, and more than anything his words pulled her in. She closed her eyes and imagined it, was just about to toss fate to the wind when…

"I forgive you."

She drew a breath. Squeezed his hand, then quickly released it in hopes that breaking contact would also break the seductive spell.

"Thank you." For several seconds, they simply looked at each other. Finally, Jamilah held up her glass.

"To new beginnings?"

He played with the stem of his glass but didn't pick it up. "We'll see."

"I'm an unapologetic daddy's girl," Jamilah said, setting down her glass without drinking to answer the question he'd asked. She thought of her dad and smiled. "You and I grew up in different worlds—mine, suburban, middle-class. I make no apologies for that, nor for my dad's attitude. Like you said, environment and experiences shape us. The father I've always known is a law-abiding, no-nonsense, straight-line kind of guy. A stint in the military and a career in law enforcement made him fairly rigid as well. He sees life in black-and-white. Not even one shade of gray. I'm not saying it's right. Just the way it is. And it's how I was taught. But we're not completely dissimilar. When I was ten, my mom…"

Jamilah hesitated. Very few people know what she was about to share. Not even Blair or Leon, whom she considered great friends. But since the system made sure anyone with money and an internet connection could reveal Rashad's history, she felt it only fair that she share her secrets, too.

She began again, with more resolve. "When I was ten, my mom left my dad."

Rashad's eyes widened ever so slightly. He nodded once, silent encouragement that boosted her courage.

"I won't get into the long version right now, but the short one is that she reunited with her first love, had an affair, and moved with him to another state to begin a new life. Like most kids, I thought her leaving was my fault. That somehow I wasn't good enough for her to stick around. Unlike you, however, Daddy recognized my depression and put me in therapy. I went for five years. My therapist is still on speed dial."

"I'm sorry that happened to you, Jam. Life ain't fair."

"It was horrible. Created all kinds of abandonment and insecurity issues. Made me cling even tighter to my father. He became a larger-than-life hero in what had become an unstable world."

"Where's your mom now?"

"Denver."

"Do y'all talk?"

Jamilah shrugged. "A little more now than before. After almost twenty years that included having a son with her new husband, they got divorced. She started reaching out, invited me to Denver for the holidays two years ago. Guess becoming a single mother caused her to imagine what it was like for Dad."

"Did you go?" Jamilah nodded. "How was it?"

"Awkward as hell. It's a little late for her to step into the mother role, but one day, who knows? Maybe we can be friends."

"I can see now how what your father says means so much. And why you don't want to disappoint him or go against his rules. And he helped start your business? That's a tough spot."

"I may be giving him too much power," Jamilah replied, a comment that came as a surprise to her own ears. "I shared a part of my life to let you know I can identify with the feeling of being discarded. That's why I would never..."

She hadn't cried from that memory for over a decade and couldn't afford the tears that now threatened. The last thing she wanted was to come off as a victim. To have Rashad feeling sorry for her was not the goal.

She held her jaw until the feeling subsided.

"My daddy loves me more than anyone on this earth. I trust him implicitly and rarely go against his advice. In the conversation you overheard, I agreed with him. Tonight, I've changed my mind. I was wrong to think the way I did about you. For judging you. For making a decision to terminate you based on your past alone. My life has been good but not perfect. Nothing like what you've been through, but enough to know the kind of pain that can overshadow right thinking."

Rashad nodded slowly, with upturned lips that could pass for a smile. He felt that stirring again, an emotional pull toward Jamilah that had nothing to do with Side Chic'k. He tried to dismiss it, reminded himself that women weren't to be trusted. Thought about the casual hookup he'd just had to block. Conjured up a mental picture of the ex who'd betrayed him. Instead of resolve, he felt even more conflicted. Jamilah was nothing like other women he'd known.

"Thank you for sharing your story with me, Jamilah. It's not always easy opening up those doors and walking back into yesterday."

"No, but I feel better that you know the truth, including the part of the conversation that you didn't hear. My dad chose not to hear that part either. I know you're a good guy. Guests at the party, customers at work, everyone likes you."

He raised a brow. "Everyone?"

Again, that feeling. The one that made her want to take Blair's suggestion and offer up body parts for his pleasure.

And then her father. *You* like him like him? Jamilah had sometimes chosen selective hearing as well.

"Everyone, me included. I meant what I said about being glad to have you in my kitchen. Working with you was easy, a smooth operation."

"But I'm not welcome back there because of your dad."

"You quit, remember?"

"And if I hadn't?"

Jamilah stood and paced the length of the room. She returned to the table, drank the rest of her wine. "Ed did okay today, so I think he can handle this weekend. Next weekend, the job is yours if you want it. Meanwhile I have another offer, the catering gig. I'd like to bring you on as head chef."

"Damn, girl!" Rashad became animated. "You're really desperate, huh?"

"Depressingly so, and out of options. You said you forgave me. Will you come back?"

"What about your law-abiding, law-enforcement father? He already don't like me. Your defying him won't help."

"You handle the kitchen. I'll handle Daddy."

"Standing ten toes down. That's what's up, Boss Lady. There's only one thing. It's regarding that probation."

Jamilah waved away the comment. "Don't worry about it. I don't need ninety days to know you're the man for this job."

"I appreciate that, but I'm not talking about me. I'm talking about you."

"Me?" She spoke with such incredulity that Rashad laughed out loud.

"Yeah. I'll do the catering gig. Depending on how that goes,

I'll come back to work here. But there's no guarantee I'll stick around. Any problem with your father or lip from you, and I'm out."

Said with such bluntness that Jamilah's mouth opened and closed several times, like a fish out of water sucking air.

Rashad laughed again. "I'm mostly kidding about that last part, but I do need to see what the action behind those words looks like, see if you can really step back and let me run things."

Jamilah shifted uncomfortably. "What exactly does my stepping back look like to you?"

"Not me taking over, but us working together. You trusting my skills for the catering event. With as many as you're expecting us to feed, I need to work the way I work. I'm going to need to know there's one person in charge, and that's me. And back here, not throwing Blair's bible at me, literally. If everything works out...you know...we'll see."

Jamilah didn't hesitate. With the clock ticking like a time bomb, how could she? Her relief wasn't just about the catering gig either. It was about not having Rashad walk out of her life completely so soon after arriving, of looking forward to their banter and working side by side. Of maybe one day even letting him pet her kitty.

She laughed.

"What's funny?"

"Something Blair said earlier."

"About me?"

"Yes."

"What'd she say?"

"To check my ego and try to get you back."

"Sit down and be humble, huh?"

"Pretty much." For the third time that night she held up her wine glass. "To my probation," she said with clarity.

Rashad held up his glass as well. "Cheers."

Seventeen

Jamilah survived the weekend with Ed. Because of the upcoming catering job, she'd taken the week off from her second gig, and posted a Closed This Saturday/Back Sunday! on the restaurant website. Later today, she'd meet with Rashad to make the shopping list and a plan for where to purchase what for the biggest bang and best quality product. Right now she was at her favorite off-price retail chain, getting the shopping therapy missed the other day. With every item examined, she thought of Rashad and whether or not he'd like it. Silly, she knew, but since their truce, he'd all but become a permanent fixture in her head. Conversations with her father were strained. Yes, Ed worked last weekend. No, Rashad hadn't shown up. Yes, she'd spoken with him. No, Rashad didn't seem to hold hard feelings against her.

Not mentioned was her provocative fantasy of him holding something else, like a particular appendage, hard against her.

The time would quickly come when she'd have to tell her father the truth. Too many law-enforcement guys that he knew were her customers. Rashad was too magnetic a secret to hide. If things went as planned, she hoped to use the catering event as leverage. How could he argue with success? Three hundred techies from a thriving company couldn't be wrong.

Jamilah found herself in the lingerie department and had just picked up a two-piece lacy PJ set, wondering who besides her was going to see it, when her cell phone dinged.

"Hmm, three-one-zero..." She almost didn't answer, then remembered why California could be calling.

"Cheyenne?"

"Oh thank God. You still have my number. I was afraid you wouldn't recognize it and send me to voicemail."

"I almost did," Jamilah admitted to this college friend from back in the day. "It's been forever."

"My apologies for being so out of touch. I've been busy."

"I know. *Love on the Air* is one of my favorite podcasts. You and Donte are relationship goals."

"Aw, thanks, sis. But don't believe everything you hear on a podcast."

"Cheyenne, please don't tell me what we see is all for show."

"The relationship comes with ups and downs, but Donte and I are definitely a couple. In fact, make sure your passport is up to date. Next year, you might need it."

"Ooh, a destination wedding?"

Jamilah rehung the nonsensical nightwear choice and moved on to the housewares aisle. Kitchen knickknacks were like chicken soup, good for the soul.

"Could be, and a romantic getaway for you and Walter."

It wasn't lost on Jamilah that these words came just as she stood in front of a selection of oils and vinegars, reminding her of just how much she and her ex had not truly mixed.

"Jamilah? There is still a you-and-Walter, right?"

"No, we broke up."

"Oh, sis, I'm sorry to hear that. What happened?"

Jamilah resisted the urge to deliver a Credo Mutwa tome the size of his seven-hundred—page *Indaba, My Children* and shared a novella instead.

"I was in the relationship for all the wrong reasons," she finished. "In the end, it's for the best."

"You are courageous for shunning appearances and following your heart. Just promise me one thing?"

"What's that?"

"There's someone perfect for you out there. Don't give up on love."

After agreeing to talk more and see each other soon, the call ended. Jamilah reshelved a stainless steel salad spinner and a musical teapot and, following her friend's advice, returned to the lingerie aisle for the lacy booty short set and a silky see-through mini. She wasn't completely cured as she left her therapy session, but the dose of shopping and convo with Cheyenne sure felt good.

The food shopping expeditions with Rashad felt even better. Having him back was a gift from God. He was knowledgeable and sensible and made choices that cut corners and saved money without sacrificing quality. Two days before the catering gig, the bulk of the cooking got underway. Jamilah, Rashad, Ed, and Russell, thankfully sober, arrived at the restaurant before daybreak. Everett, Rita, and a friend of hers named Shelby, who Jamilah vaguely remembered meeting one time before, arrived around nine. Jamilah was immediately reminded why she'd curtailed her friendship. Rita was loud and brash, although productive and organized. Her friend seemed more interested in flirting than food prep, a fact that Jamilah tried without success to ignore.

"You write, too?" she heard Shelby ask Rashad after shamelessly following him back to the pantry. Jamilah quietly fell in step behind them and positioned herself within earshot, for informational purposes only, and held up a nearby wall on the pretext of checking her phone.

"A little bit," he replied, his tone distracted. "Do you see the tomato sauce over there? I think I remember seeing several large cans."

"I'll look."

Jamilah detected enough saccharine in the answer to produce two cavities. Did the girl plan to search in his boxers for the sauce? The blatant gall of it all! Only Jamilah's resolve to know more kept her planted where she was, her phone now in Airplane mode to prevent getting busted by a ringtone.

"Here they are!"

An eye roll followed Jamilah's silent tsk. *Girl, you found cans of tomato sauce, not a cure for cancer.*

She heard Rashad's footsteps across the concrete floor. "Thanks."

"What do you write?"

"Rhymes, mostly."

"Rhymes? Really? Like rap bars? I'd love to get together sometime. I write novels and am working on a storyline about a rapper."

That was enough. Next thing, the girl would be filming a movie and wanting Rashad for the bedroom scenes. Jamilah stepped into the pantry.

"Finding everything okay?"

Shelby jumped as though caught stealing.

Rashad had no reaction, almost as though he'd expected her. That thought was reinforced by the twinkle in his eye.

"Did we get that gallon of hot sauce from that big box store?"

"No, I have some here. Shelby, can you help Ed and Rita in the kitchen?"

"I don't cook," was followed by a petulant expression that bloomed on Shelby's face.

"In that case, then, we don't need you. Today is all about cooking. You can meet us at the venue to help with service. I'll text you the address."

Shelby smirked in Jamilah's direction before looking at Rashad, hopeful. "I'll see if Rita needs my help."

Did she just shoot shade to the woman signing her upcoming paycheck? Any other time Jamilah would have checked her. But she understood. Men like Rashad could make a woman do crazy things. He'd made her think crazy things, like how it would be to hold on to his locs while he pounded her. See? Crazy. Plus, Jamilah was already short on help. She was still hoping some of Ed's VFW friends could help them serve tomorrow.

Ignoring the slight, she waited until Shelby had left, then walked over to a metal cabinet, opened it, and pulled out two large bottles of hot sauce.

Rashad reached for them. "Thank you."

"You're welcome."

She prepared to leave. He stepped in front of her.

"Not for the hot sauce," he continued, his seductive eyes affecting her like a dimmer in the bedroom, the one you turned down just before panties got dropped. His gaze made her feel like she'd drank the hot sauce straight, no chaser. Her body threatened to catch fire.

He cocked his head toward the door Shelby just exited. "For rescuing me. I appreciate it."

She chuckled and worked not to sound all gushy like Shelby had just seconds before. "No problem."

He motioned for her to go out first. Walking through the narrow doorway, she brushed against the side of his body. The hardness didn't surprise her. It was the spicy scent with hints of patchouli or something equally earthy that made her want to bury her head in his chest.

Fortunately, or unfortunately, depending on Jamilah's changing thoughts, the next two days were too busy for her to inhale anything but the smell of food. By the time Saturday and the catering event arrived, Jamilah was almost too tired to think. Fortunately, she didn't have to. Rashad stepped up and into the leadership role as though he'd been born into it.

"All right, everybody, listen up. It's game time. I want everyone focused on the task at hand, while remembering to have a good time. People don't only like food because of how it tastes, but also because of how the person serving it makes them feel.

"Ed, because of the dishes we're dropping to order, it's going to get hectic. I'ma need you to stay cool and have my back. Heard?"

"Got it."

"Everett, I need you to be the floater."

"Heard."

"Servers, keep the trays full and makes sure the food is hot. Rita, you're in charge of knowing when to change them out. Shasta, I need you to make sure all of the napkins, eating utensils, condiments, and stuff like that are always ready for whoever needs them.

"Russell, no bottoms up until we pack up, feel me?"

"I got you, boss."

"I want *everybody* to remember to encourage *everybody* to scan the QR code for the website. There are a couple poster boards hanging and cards on the tables. We want the people eating here today to be at the restaurant tomorrow. We're all here because of Jamilah. We're all representing Side Chic'k. Let's not let her down."

Jamilah was impressed, and moved. Rashad truly belonged here. She wished her dad could see him in action.

There were a few challenges with set up, but once everything had been unloaded, set up, and Rashad had assigned stations, the process he'd organized began to flow. From the first crispy wing until the last pumpkin-spiced cookie served, Jamilah heard nothing but compliments. The crowd, many dressed in wacky Halloween garb, came back for seconds and thirds. One man whose brother owned a bar in Olathe tried to hire Rashad on the spot.

"Appreciate that, brothah," Rashad had glibly replied. "But I'm a side chick."

Everyone around cracked up.

Although exhausting, their job was a success. All evening she saw people aiming their phones at the QR codes. Several people promised to visit the restaurant. Everyone, especially the women, loved Rashad.

"Next Friday at Side Chic'k?" she asked once they'd packed up and were ready to leave the venue grounds.

He didn't immediately answer. The few seconds of hesitation felt like days. When he nodded and answered in the affirmative, Jamilah could have kissed him. Later that night, when remembering how good he'd looked in his bandanna, black jeans, and black T-shirt emblazoned with *Side Chic'k* across that patchouli-scented chest she wanted to explore, she almost wished she'd kissed him for real.

Eighteen

Rashad awoke to a new day. Not just on the calendar but within himself. He felt different. More self-assured. Like he mattered. Undoubtedly Jamilah had something to do with that. Not that he was ready to admit the obvious. He was still hiding behind heartbreak, still determined to never again be the trusting soul who'd laid bare his emotions and gotten played as a thank-you. Not only by the woman he loved but by the friend he thought was ride-or-die. A man he'd known since high school. No, sir. Not worth it. But still, Jamilah was an amazing woman. One that he doubted would be down for a casual hookup. Not that that would even work, since he was her employee. Yet if he ever decided to get serious and give away his heart again, it would be to a woman like Jamilah.

He'd come a long way, sure, but his path to redemption wasn't over. Until the fall of next year, he had weekly required phone calls and/or visits to the parole office, a constant reminder that he was still tied to the system. He still wasn't free. He was still working for someone else, someone who'd allowed another person to color her idea of him, to use his past as a way to taint his present reality. He couldn't yet see the financial path to owning his own business. Not legally. Rashad was done with the shady side of the highway but understood those who still drove down that road. His street mentor once taught him that if your enterprise didn't make big dollars, then it didn't make good sense. Society was quick to judge young men who became street-pharmaceuticals salespeople to take care of their families. Felt nothing about suggesting they exchange a minimum two to three thousand a week for fifteen dollars an hour. It took money to make money, and right now Rashad could barely pay attention, let alone a monthly lease. He didn't have a list of potential investors or silent partners. Or a winning lottery ticket. Or a daddy like James to cosign a loan.

No, he was nowhere near being able to stroll down Easy Street with the world in his back pocket. Rashad knew he'd do well to remember that the justice system wasn't the only probation he was under. Being a Black man in America came with a guilty label, automatically suspect, instantly doubted, whether the world wanted to admit that or not.

After a long, body-aligning stretch, he flopped over on his back, looked at the ceiling, and untangled his emotions.

Satisfaction. Accomplishment. Those words popped up. He kept them. They fit the vibe of what had happened the past few days. Plans were created and executed under his leadership.

Respect. Yeah, definitely that, too. Recognizing not only his talent as a cook but that he knew what he was doing. Both Ed and Jamilah had acquiesced to following his lead. His experience in feeding thousands three squares a day from limited funds and even fewer choices made cooking for three hundred a breeze. Toss in the comfortable budget and bountiful ingredients, and the job was a lay-up he could almost have made in his sleep.

Rashad sat up against the headboard and reached for his notebook, thought about the crew all looking to him for marching orders. It had felt good to be trusted, for his opinion to be valued, his instructions followed. And to have those instructions lead to success. He looked across the room, tried to pull up the last memory he'd had with these feelings. He flipped through months, and then years, to one particular visit with his father's brother, Uncle Melvin. After Rashad's father's death, Melvin had tried to step in and fill unfillable shoes. He'd tried to keep Rashad on the right path, teach the young tween how to be a young man. In his grief, Rashad had rebelled. But there was that one weekend he'd spent in San Bernadino at his uncle's house. An electrician by trade who could fix anything broken and build anything needed, they'd spent the weekend constructing a shed for his wife, Whitney. A *she-shed* he'd called it, which to Rashad sounded corny. What fool would be dumb enough to give a shed a gender?

The shed was a surprise for Whitney, who'd just received her master's degree a few months before. Melvin had kept all the components in the garage, but on the Saturday Rashad visited, while Whitney went to a hair appointment, installing micro braids which was sure to take six to eight hours, Melvin roused Rashad from bed and put him to work. He'd balked at the assignment, but as board by board and nail by nail the shed moved from a drawing on paper to a tangible structure, Rashad's attitude shifted, as did his respect for Melvin. When Whitney returned to find a shed complete with electricity, running water, skylights, and shelving for her books, she burst into tears.

"Couldn't have done it without Rashad," Melvin proudly stated.

Whitney had come over and given him the biggest hug. "Thank you."

Rashad had felt accomplished, satisfied, respected...the way he did now. Last night, Jamilah had given him a big thank-you hug, too. It had elicited a whole different kind of emotion. He flipped to a clean sheet of paper and began to write.

Started at a party this part that would rock my world
Where an urban man did a scan on a suburban girl
Played no fool. LA cool. Not my type anyway
Let's ride with the lie locked up inside

Mental games that players play
Then...

He looked toward the ceiling to contemplate the next line. His eye scanned the clock.

Gotdammit!

Rashad bounded out of bed and headed to the shower. While packing away the last of the supplies and standing by Ed's van sharing *Good jobs* and *Good byes*, and after agreeing that he'd see her on Friday, Jamilah had shown her faith in him by giving him the keys to the kingdom—to Side Chic'k.

"This was Blair's set," she'd said by way of explanation.

Four words, but a lot more meaning in their implication. Again, she trusted him. He was part of the team, part of the family, a member she thought would stay awhile. Rashad couldn't guarantee that the latter was true, but while there, he would make the kitchen his own. To do so he was going in early—to rearrange his station and break some of Blair's bible rules.

Instead of leaving through the basement walkout, Rashad headed upstairs for an energy drink. He was surprised to hear footsteps this early in the day.

"Goddess, is that you?"

He rounded the corner to see Charles at the stove. "Sup, Pluck!"

"Me, and too early," Charles grumbled.

"I see. What are you doing, getting ready to serve breakfast in bed?"

"I wish. Anna's gone already. A meeting with her women's group. Some type of fundraiser or something they're planning. One I'll get wrangled into most likely."

Rashad grabbed the drink and a banana from a nearby fruit basket. "If I can help, count me in, too."

An hour later, he was knee-deep in the kitchen transformation. Cooking utensils were on the counter. He hadn't touched the prep station, but basically everything else had been taken down to be rearranged. Planks of plywood balanced against the wall with a tool set and construction items beside them. Potatoes baked in the oven. Macaroni performed a low boil in two different pots. Blocks of cheese, a pot of rice, and a variety of root vegetables were in various stages of preparation. A hip-hop station streamed in the background. Rashad acted as though this was his spot, imagined the changes he'd make to fit the establishment he envisioned. A stage for sure, maybe a small dance floor. The tables set up in a way that encouraged customer socialization and conversation. His dishes would be award-winning. His the most popular space in town. If, that is, someone forgot he was a felon long enough to give him a loan, or at least a chance.

At one point, however, he'd looked around and had to fight off panic as questions like *What the heck are you doing?* and *Have you lost your mind?* swirled around in his head. Jamilah had agreed to give him the lead and do things his way, but had he overdone it? If so, oh-the-hell well. In for a penny, in for a pound.

Rashad had just measured the wall where a plank of wood would be hung to make equipment more easily accessible when he heard footsteps. He glanced at the wall clock.

Someone here already? Jamilah usually began prep ninety minutes early, a whole hour from now. He walked toward the sound with only the slightest caution. Unlike Jamilah, Rashad locked the back door.

Jamilah rounded the corner. Her jaw dropped. She gasped, then angrily plunked a filled recycle bag on the counter.

"Rashad!" she yelled. "What the heck is going on?"

Almost the exact swirling question he'd thought earlier had jumped from his mind into Jamilah's mouth. He steeled himself against the nerves that threatened to bust in his gut and presented an unflappable demeanor.

"Calm down, Boss Lady—"

"Don't call me that, and don't tell me to calm down. You've

destroyed my kitchen! And what the hell is all that on the stove!"

Jamilah marched over to the stuff boiling, baking, and simmering, then whipped around in battle stance—arms crossed, legs spread, frown chiseled.

"What are you doing?"

Rashad remained as cool as a cucumber waiting for mayo and dill. "I'm running my kitchen."

"*Running* or *ruining*? Because right now," she said as she flung an arm while doing a three-sixty turn, "I can't tell."

"I'm rearranging my section of the kitchen and prepping a few dishes. You got a problem with that? And before you answer, remember you gave me a key I didn't ask for, and…you're on probation."

If there was a face made when swallowing words, whole sentences even, Rashad witnessed it with Jamilah. She worked her jaw with a hand to her throat as though aiding digestion. After taking a moment to collect herself, her thoughts, and/or errant curse words strewn across brain waves, she responded.

"While this is your kitchen, this is *my* business. So yes, I have a problem with entering my establishment and seeing it in this state of disarray. I also have every right not only to be upset about it but to ask what the hell is going on." A beat and then, "Respectfully."

Rashad watched Jamilah work to control her anger, breathing slowly, chest heaving up and down. She probably didn't know how sexy all that strength and power looked wrapped in that Side Chic'k sweatshirt paired with tight-fitting corduroys tucked inside cute ankle boots. He liked a woman who could hold her own, who didn't back down from her truth. But she didn't have to know that.

He tossed down the dish towel he held and headed toward the doorway. "I'm out."

"Rashad!" Those six letters she yelled held ten pounds of panic.

He quickly turned around. "Just kidding."

Again, a slew of emotions played Ping-Pong on her face. "Ooh," she finally managed between gritted teeth. "I could douse you with that whole pot of macaroni right now!"

"Which would put me in even more hot water."

Rashad kept his straight face and watched Jamilah try to match it. Her eyes sparkled with the mischief he felt. That comeback was funny. She wanted to laugh so bad but was too mad and had too much pride to give in to the punch line. He knew because he would have reacted the same way.

He held her gaze. She didn't blink or laugh. He thought of the lines he'd scribbled earlier before jumping out of bed and heading this way. The rhyme, spoken word, rap, whatever it turned out to be, that was all about her.

"What are you doing?" she asked again.

"Creating the same type of system here that made the catering gig flow so smoothly."

For the next several minutes he relayed the vision in his head, how every item was placed for not only easy access but also for greater functionality in the limited space.

"I probably should have texted you," he finished.

"How about *definitely*?"

"You're right. I was just so excited, Jamilah. Turning a dream into reality, taking something from paper to product, turns me all the way on."

The way you do, he wanted to add but didn't, even as his eyes traveled the length of her body and back, and their chemistry sizzled like a Bunsen burner. He could tell she was feeling him, and not because he was a conceited jerk who felt he could pull any lady. For the record, he just about could. No, his opinion was based on years of studying a woman's body language, from the time he'd lost his virginity at too early an age. It was the way her eyes fluttered and her body shifted ever so slighted. The way she licked her lips before quickly turning away and gave him a view of a heavenly moon.

"What's all happening on the stove?"

"More great ideas."

"That's what I'm afraid of."

"You're going to love them. Hear me out."

"*Them*, as in plural?"

"So picture this." Rashad spread out his hands like a banner. "Surprise Side Sunday."

"Paint me that picture."

"Sure." He walks over and picks up a plank of wood and a hammer. "Do me a favor and grab those nails."

While reimagining the cooking area (and the prep area, once Jamilah caught the vision), Rashad shared the idea that had come to him while inventorying the pantry. A way to maximize food usage and minimize waste. Using one product for multiple dishes, such as macaroni and cheese and macaroni salad. Baking instead of boiling the potatoes for potato salad and potato boats.

"What would you charge for this plate of sides?"

"Five dollars. Surprise Sides for five. Add two chicken legs, double the price, and call it Surprise Sides Walking."

He explained other benefits. How this surprise option gave the restaurant a chance to use up produce before having to toss it, how the name could be branded and marketed to draw in those visiting nearby businesses and a younger crowd.

"You thought all of this up this morning?"

"Wait until you see what I've got for you by this afternoon."

He winked. She smiled, a coy, slight upturn of the lips as she looked away. Rashad's insides tightened. Certain body parts took notice, too. Rashad increased the distance between them to break the sensual connection infusing them both. He nailed hooks onto the wood, then began placing cookware and other items within easy reach. Once done, both he and Jamilah stood back and surveyed the newly appointed kitchen.

She looked at Rashad.

He stared back with a self-assured grin.

"I know you hate to say it, but go ahead and say it."

"This is wonderful, Rashad. The kitchen looks bigger. It's functional. Convenient. I'd love to have a setup like this in my closet!"

He nodded toward the counter. "There's extra wood left."

Before heading down the hall, Jamilah looked at him with an expression as close to admiration as she could probably allow herself and something else. Lust, maybe? No way she wasn't feeling the same for him as he was for her. If she was going to keep looking at him like that and making him feel the way he did now, working here wasn't going to be easy, and he needed to limit the time that they were alone.

He forced his thoughts from sex to the stove. *Focus on the macaroni, man. The macaroni!*

He appeared busy, but his whole body tensed as a certain perfume wafted back into the kitchen. Tension turned to tingling as Jamilah approached.

"Rashad?"

She gently touched his shoulder. He turned around.

"Thank you." Then, as if she couldn't help it, she reached up and gave him a quick hug.

The woman was playing with dynamite. The restraint Rashad practiced could have ignited a rocket with enough juice for a moon landing. He wanted to wrap his arms around her, erase the space between their bodies, and let their tongues get acquainted. Instead, he leaned down and lightly kissed her forehead.

"You're welcome."

Nineteen

The next day, Jamilah was happy to see Rashad's SUV when she pulled in behind Side Chic'k. He didn't look up as she parked beside him and turned off the engine. He wore a pair of headphones, head bobbing up and down as he wrote something in a notebook, perhaps the one he had come back for during the infamous conversation with her dad.

She studied him in silence, remembering his scent while their bodies were in close contact the day before, the strength of his hands as they squeezed her shoulders, the feel of his lips on her skin. Not even a minute near him and already her mind was cooking up a meal not meant for the kitchen. Jamilah hopped out of her car, walked over to his, and tapped the window. He didn't jump, which for Jamilah meant he was aware of her presence the entire time, yet too into whatever he was writing or hearing to acknowledge her. Or perhaps she was purposely being ignored.

If so…*ouch!*

Rashad closed the notebook and pulled off the headphones. Reaching for his signature black-and-white bandanna, he held onto the notebook and opened the car door.

"Good morning, Boss Lady."

"Good morning, Rashad. You do not have to call me that."

"I like calling you that. All of my friends have nicknames. That's mine for you."

Jamilah didn't miss that he'd called her a friend. Something about how he said it made her believe she could live up to the name.

They walked toward the back entrance. "Is that the famous notebook? The one you came back for that night?"

"Affirmative."

"Rhymes, right?"

"Mostly."

"Because when you're not cooking, you're rapping."

His eyes slid in her direction as he opened the door.

"You were listening to music when I drove up."

"Something like that."

Jamilah remembered the conversation he'd had with Rita's friend Shelby, that hip-hop was his other passion besides food. Made her want to sneak and take a look at his notebook. She'd never dare to make such an intrusion without permission. The words contained inside were probably more sacred to him than those in Scripture.

They reached the kitchen. He placed the book on the shelf beneath the counter, then tied on his bandanna, a sign that he was ready to work. Sensing his hesitancy to share more about music, Jamilah switched the conversation to cooking. Ed arrived a short time later. Before the catering event, she'd talked to Ed and made it clear about Rashad's leadership position in the kitchen. Ed said he'd only been looking out for her. Jamilah had responded that it was time she do that herself. Since then, to her relief, both men acted like they had some sense and weren't neighing stallions impressing a mare. Ed complimented Rashad's knife skills. Rashad remarked on Ed's tats, which set off an ongoing conversation about life as a veteran. Like Rashad's uncle Melvin, Ed too had been in the army. Prep was quick and efficient, much as it had been before Blair left. Proof yet again that she'd been right to meet with Rashad and ask—beg, bribe, grovel—him to give Side Chic'k a second chance. The only thing left was to convince her father to do the same thing.

Two hours later, work was in full swing, with the dining room more crowded than it had been in months. Whether from the QR Code on cards placed on the catering event's tables or those recently handed out at nearby businesses, Jamilah didn't know. But she was grateful.

"I don't come over this way much," a customer was saying when she walked up to the table. "I'd heard of Eighteenth and Vine but had no idea about all the things going on down here."

"All finished?" Jamilah politely interrupted, before removing empty plates from the table. "We're closing soon. Anything else I can get you? A to-go order, perhaps?"

A young man wearing a backward baseball cap and matching sweatshirt answered. "Everything was delicious. Those drumsticks were the best I've ever tasted."

"I'll be sure and tell the chef."

The woman next to him asked, "The same guy from our Halloween anniversary party? What's his name?"

"Rashad."

"He's cute."

Jamilah hid her mild annoyance behind a smile. "I'll also relay that message."

She placed their bill on the table and headed toward the kitchen but not before hearing, "I wish that chef was on the menu."

The comment was followed by laughter and groans.

The business closed for the night. The crew cleaned up. Finally it was just Rashad and Jamilah alone in the space. Words became few. The air became thick. Jamilah waged a silent war between what had always been expected of someone like her and what she wanted to experience right here, right now.

"Should I put these in the storage room?" Rashad asked,

pointing toward the extra boards from his rearrangement project that had been temporarily stacked in a corner.

"Actually, as I said earlier, I could use that shelving setup in my closet." Jamilah nodded her head toward the newly organized wall. "Like those."

"No problem. I'll put them in your car."

"Um, is there any way you could like…install them?"

A slightly raised brow was his only reaction. Jamilah got busy wiping off an already clean counter. "But if you can't, I understand."

"No, I can do it. If that's what you want."

What she wanted involved a whole other type of wood, but he didn't need to know that yet.

"I'd appreciate it. I can pay you."

"No need for that. Just let me know when you want me to come over."

"Would now be too inconvenient?"

"It wouldn't be inconvenient, but it might not be wise."

"Why not?"

"Why not?" he mimicked. "Come on now, Boss Lady. I'm a man. You're a woman. We're feeling each other. Don't even try to deny it. We started out rocky, but I think this past week showed both of us that when we work together, it leads to success. I like what you've achieved. I respect your hustle and your vision. I wouldn't want sex to get in the way of that."

"Who said anything about sex?"

He stared at her in a way that made her panties wet. She fought to not squirm. He held her eyes for a second. Then a second more. Then a slow move of said eyes down the length of her body. She swore she could feel his hands.

"Never mind." She started to brush past him.

He caught her arm. "I'll do it to you, I mean, *for* you. The shelves. But it's late. All the bangin' I'll be doing might wake the neighbors."

It was her turn for a raised brow.

"With hammer and nail, of course."

"Of course. But no worries. There's a foot of concrete between floors which gives all of us there complete and total privacy."

Jamilah locked up, then typed her address into his GPS. He followed her to the car. Placed the planks sideways and through a window of his larger SUV for the short commute to her downtown loft. On the way there, she second , third , and fourth-guessed the reasons behind her actions. She wasn't into casual sex. Had never experienced a one-night stand. Rashad wasn't the type of man she was normally attracted to, certainly not like anyone she'd ever dated.

Rashad entered a home that smelled like vanilla—all Wayfair and Etsy and Bed, Bath and Beyond—and took in the decidedly feminine decor.

"You surprise me, Boss Lady."

"I asked you not to call me that."

"Why? You look like a lady and act like a boss." He reached over and fingered a very real-looking bamboo plant on an end table. "Would you prefer Suburban?"

"How about Jamilah? Or Jam. That's Blair's nickname for me that others who've heard it have adopted."

"Nah, I'm not into doing what others do."

"Why does my decor surprise you?"

"It looks…soft. Dainty."

"You just said I look like a lady."

His eyes raked her with that sexy look that scrambled her insides, before walking over to the art she was told would add a pop to her subtle living room canvas of lavender, pale yellow and bright blond wood.

"I was expecting something bolder, more modern, like this." He turned. His voice deepened. "Like you."

He kept surprising her, this supposed walking stereotype her father warned her about. Ironically, the painting was a gift to herself from an artist on Etsy, an abstract picture of a chicken, a beautifully illustrated interpretation that captured her brand completely. When the painting arrived, she called Walter and asked him to help her hang it. He almost refused. That's how much he hated it. Said it was *too loud* and *gaudy.* That it ruined the calm, sophisticated aesthetic she'd achieved.

Rashad saw the picture as she did. Because he saw her. All of this passed through her mind in a matter of seconds, the amount of time it took for him to walk over to where he'd leaned the planks and pick them up.

"You should add something like that to the walls at Side Chic'k."

"Chickens?"

"Color." He looked toward the hall. "Where do you want the shelving?"

"In my bedroom." Jamilah closed her eyes against how that sounded.

"Naturally."

"Stop thinking everything is about you and sex." Although it was about him and sex. "I've been wanting shelving in my closet for a while. When I saw what you did in the kitchen—"

"I'm just messing with you, shorty. No need to explain."

Jamilah whipped around and all but stomped to her bedroom, her feelings a mix of frustration and eroticism. In her home, everything about Rashad turned her on.

She was uber aware of him as they entered her bedroom. His body seemed to fill up the room, all strong arms, tight butt, long legs, and effortless swagger. She tried to see everything through his eyes, while walking into a closet that suddenly seemed way too small.

"Dang, Jamilah. You've got a lot of clothes." He stepped to her.

"I know." Flummoxed, she reached for an armful of clothes, walked over and dumped them on the bed, then headed back for a second trip. "It's just this one wall where I—"

"Come here."

Rashad pulled Jamilah into his chest, wrapped his arms around her, and rocked them slow.

"Slow down, baby. I know what you're feeling. I'm feeling it, too."

The kiss at her temple was so light that Jamilah wondered if she'd imagined it. The hand that rubbed up and down her back, though, and the hard chest and strong back that her hands traveled down on a get-to-know were all very real.

Her heart raced. She felt his, too. Or was it just hers beating out of her chest and into his? That chest. Her girls. They fit together perfectly. All muscle and survival and dogged determination. He continued to rock them as he ran his hand over her hair and down the side of face. Kissed her forehead. Settled his chin on top of her head. Took a deep, satisfied breath. His embrace made her feel safe. Treasured. Wanted.

Ooh, how badly she wanted him, too. More than a hug. Or a kiss. She wanted all of him. She wanted to feel all of that unapologetic authenticity. Her nipples began to harden. Her yoni pulsed. Her breath increased as she lifted her lips in search of his, as though she were parched and he were a fountain. His lips lowered to hers.

The kiss was light, magical, filled with promises that Jamilah believed could actually be kept. His lips skimmed over hers, back and forth and back again, his tongue following their shape like lip liner before slowly sliding into her mouth, as though coming home. His deliberate patience had her whole body reacting. Jamilah wanted to devour him like a Happy Meal. When he finally increased the pressure and kissed her in earnest, she was ready to tear his clothes off and be taken on the floor.

The kiss was too short, yet it lasted forever. He pulled her closer, placed a hand on her ass. Pressed her stomach against his burgeoning dick, its size living up to the timber she'd envisioned. She pulled at his shirt, the button at the top of his jeans. Perhaps it was the time that had passed since her last benefits.

Maybe the enhanced bad-boy allure. All Jamilah knew was that she wanted him here, now, deep inside her.

She broke the kiss. "I've got condoms."

Wobbly legs took her from the closet to the nearby night-stand. Shutting down all thoughts, cautionary dribble and self-judgmental blah, blah, blah, she pulled a box of Trojans from the drawer and hoped the ultra thins that Benefits had used could cover that eggplant that had just tickled her navel. Tomorrow would be enough time for that other *R* word, *regret*. Now the only *R* she wanted was the one who could massage her breasts and spread her legs like he did the ones in the kitchen.

Shaky fingers pulled out a familiar square foil, then turned to face Rashad. She was surprised to find him directly behind her. He took the condom, read the front, and smiled before tossing it on the nightstand.

"I like that heat you're coming with, Jamilah. But there will be no fucking tonight."

His coarseness did little to douse the flame licking the flower between her dewy folds. She hoped she'd heard incorrectly.

"You don't want to have sex?"

"Baby, you have no idea. But I can't. Not like this."

"Like what?"

Jamilah wanted to ask him to explain it to her like English wasn't her first language, because for the life of her she couldn't imagine why a testosterone-driven man like the one standing in front of her was turning down pussy-on-a-platter.

"Like doing something in the heat of the moment that we might regret tomorrow."

He was thinking about the *R* word, too?

"You don't come across as the type of woman who has casual sex. At least, that's not how I see you. If we ever do anything, I want it to mean something. I don't want it to be like all of my other encounters with casuals I've shopped for online, where a cute face, big tits, or a nice ass got the click."

Jamilah plopped on the bed.

"What if casual sex is what I want?"

"How many times has that happened? That you had a one-night stand or a casual dally with a brothah you just met a few weeks prior?"

Never.

Rashad read the answer on her face. "Exactly."

He turned back toward the closet. "Now, grab that bag of supplies off the counter, and help me hang your shelves."

Jamilah obeyed his command like the good girl she was trying hard not to be. She didn't want to help hang shelves. She wanted to help herself to the appendage he had hanging.

Twenty

Rashad stood at the stove, one of his favorite places to be, stirring up a variation on a dish that had helped secure his reputation as a bona fide cook behind the wall. The ability to create restaurant-quality cuisine using only the prison commissary and a hot pot, the only cookware option when in his cell instead of the kitchen, had set him apart from the other inmates and was great for bartering. Cooking and the talented pen that made him a credible rapper had given him a level of respect and camaraderie among the men, regardless of race or gang affiliation. His cooking skills were also what made Francisco decide to mentor him, to set Rashad up so that on the outside he could always get a job.

He poured a bowl of whipped eggs with a touch of cream into a skillet of sautéing peppers and mushrooms. Thick, crispy pieces of slab bacon replaced the pig skins he would have used from the commissary. Ramen noodle seasoning packets, a staple of both prison cell cuisine and in Rashad's cooking, were added, along with cheese and ketchup, another secret weapon for those with limited funds or food. He placed a top on the concoction. Once the eggs were almost set and the cheese melted, he crumbled French fried onion rings over the top, another cell secret, and turned off the burner. Moments later he, Charles, and Anna sat enjoying his breakfast fare.

"I tell you what, man," Charles said, after following a large forkful of the omelet with an equally voracious bite of toast. "If you can cook like this using humble ingredients, I can't wait to see how you'd throw down with an unlimited budget."

"Delicious as always," Anna added.

"Pluck, I'd cook this way even with a lot of money. I like the creativity. Plus, not wasting food is one of the forty-two laws of Ma'at."

"Oh Lord, not the encyclopedia," Charles groaned, his way of teasing Rashad about all the knowledge he acquired from reading so many books.

"Speaking of the Lord," Anna segued, "the committee can use both of y'all's help. We've got an exciting fundraising idea for next year, probably around the Fourth of July."

Rashad stood, placed Charles's clean plate on top of his, and headed toward the kitchen. "What is it?"

"A *Soul Train* line."

"*Soul Train*," Charles grunted and reached for his juice. "How is that going to make money?"

"We're hoping through corporate sponsorships. We're going to break the world record." Anna gave the guys a brief rundown of their plans.

"What, you're gonna try to be Damita Jo and that guy who was the breakdancing brothah?"

"I think you're going back to the seventies," Anna quipped. "Before my time, old man."

"No, you didn't."

"Did too."

Rashad smiled at their back-and-forth while wondering if he could ever have a solid love like theirs. Jamilah crossed his mind for the hundredth time since the kiss. How her lips felt. How she smelled. What she'd offered him. Turning down that sex had been harder than doing the three-year bid.

He headed downstairs to grab his notebook before heading out. "Sounds like fun," he tossed over his shoulder. "Count me in."

On the way to Side Chic'k, Rashad's head bopped to the silent beat of his current rhyme in progress, one inspired by Jamilah and a certain eighties throwback he'd heard Charles and Anna dancing to last night. He woke up with the hook from that R and B classic by Babyface playing on loop inside his head. The sexy smooth groove and how the beat lay deep in the cut begged to be rapped over, for bars to be laid down on top. The lyrics invoked a double, even triple entendre—whipping up something delicious in the kitchen, being P-whipped by a woman's charm, and/or the overwhelming appeal of a fine female to get into a man's bedroom…and his heart.

With Charles and Anna's muffled conversation and overhead footsteps in the background, he'd fleshed out a second verse to add to the first.

In the kitchen whipped up getting gripped up for last call
Shorty walked into the room with a badaboom that made giants fall
Tried to play it off like a hungry man turning down a meal
Couldn't fake the funk gotta get a chunk of that whip appeal…
"No one does it like me…"

He rapped the lines aloud in the car, reaching the chorus of the Babyface classic as he pulled into a spot behind Side Chic'k. Minutes later, hair tucked, hands washed, he turned the streaming channel from his usual hip-hop go-to and continued the old-school vibe. After checking inventory and going over the kitchen notes he'd placed at the back of his notebook, his own bible of sorts, he began prep. Because of how the catering crowd had raved about his extra crispy chicken wings, Jamilah agreed to switch to his method. He mixed up his signature dry brine and began the manual rubbing and massaging that made his meat so tender. The actions were comforting, routine. He'd already made a roux for the green bean casserole and warmed up potatoes for salad when he heard the back-door lock release.

It had been years since his heart raced at the thought of see-ing a girl. His sprinted.

Jamilah came around the corner looking naturally fabu-lous. Her messy curls, black jeans, and blinged-out Side Chic'k sweatshirt were all warmth and sunshine against the cool, gray day. And completely above his pay grade.

"Hey, Rashad! Wasn't sure it was you in here."

"Who else would it be?"

"Somebody who likes something besides rap." She walked over and grabbed an apron off the hook. "Am I rubbing off on you?"

"I like all kinds of music. Just for the record, you can rub off on me anytime."

Later he'd question this act of madness, but he walked over and greeted her with a quick kiss. Like they were a couple. As though it was the most natural thing to do in the world.

She kissed him back but said, "We probably shouldn't do that here."

"What, are we on camera or something?"

"Security cameras are outside, not in here. Yet."

"You lock the door?"

At that exact second, Rashad's spidey senses kicked in. He reflexively stepped in front of Jamilah.

"Yo, who is it?"

Footsteps now, slow and deliberate. Since a felon possess-ing a gun was illegal, Rashad would have to depend on what the good Lord gave him. He'd been in his share of street fights and wasn't too worried about a brawl. An armed robber would prove different. His fists were no match for a bullet.

He felt Jamilah's hand squeeze his biceps as the footsteps drew closer.

"It's me, Jamilah," a familiar voice said.

Rashad's brow creased. Where had he heard that voice be-fore?

Jamilah gasped softly before giving him the answer.

"Daddy? What are you doing here?"

Detective James Carver stepped into the kitchen, hand resting on his weapon. "I was just about to ask a similar question. What is he doing here?"

Rashad's back straightened. His chin lifted. The stance of a warrior, one chief to another. He'd stared down too many officers to count. Felt different when they looked like you, but his motto was the same with James as it was with any other man.

Don't start none. Won't be none.

Twenty-One

Jamilah stood transfixed by her own worst-case scenario. This was not how she'd wanted her dad to meet Rashad. There was supposed to have been a conversation. An explanation over lunch or dinner. Perhaps softened with her dad's favorite bourbon or a glass of red wine. She was supposed to convince him with themes of forgiveness and compassion and second and third chances. Instead she watched as World War Three looked about to break out. Sheesh! Time to try and wave the white flag.

"Dad, this is—"

"Rashad White?"

"That's right," Rashad answered, even though James aimed the question at his daughter. He stepped toward him with his hand outstretched.

James eyed the hand, then Rashad, then Jamilah. Nothing else moved.

Rashad shrugged, stood straighter, and placed a sly hand on the small of Jamilah's back. His strength flowed from his hand to her. She stood straighter, too.

"What's he doing here, Jamilah?"

"I work here."

"Does it look like I'm talking to you?"

"You more comfortable talking *about* me? Like the other night with her on the phone?"

Jamilah watched in awe as Rashad took control of a conversation that with every other human being on the planet her father would own, then watched her dad try to regain it.

James offered a sneer. "Clearly, you haven't learned to respect your elders, or the law."

"Where I come from," Rashad replied with a casual lean against the counter, which somewhat shifted the air in the room, "respect isn't learned, it's earned. That's how my granny taught me. But even for those who haven't shown themselves worthy," he paused to let that particular choice of words sink in, "I've learned to not let my ego be so big that I can't apologize when that's the right thing to do. Even though you were wrong for stating facts without knowing truth, I'm sorry for cussing you out that night. I wouldn't have spoken that way if I'd known it was you."

Jamilah offered Rashad a grateful smile. He acknowledged it with a slight nod.

James fixed Rashad with an unreadable look, then said, "Jamilah, I need to speak with you."

"Did you hear Rashad, Daddy? He apologized for his rude behavior."

"Did you hear me? We need to talk. Now."

"We open in just over an hour."

"This won't take long." James turned and left the kitchen without waiting for a reply.

"I'll be right back," Jamilah told Rashad, then followed her father out of the kitchen.

They went into the pantry. Jamilah closed the door.

"I already know what you're thinking," she began, her hands up in a sign of surrender.

"You have no idea what's on my mind."

"I know you don't like him, Daddy, but—"

"This isn't about me *liking* somebody." James used air quotes on his emphasized word. "I know what type of character you're dealing with. He's already affecting your behavior."

"How so?"

"How? You lied to me. When is the last time that happened?"

Jamilah worked to keep her voice low and calm. The walls had ears, and if Rashad pressed his against the wall hard enough, he'd hear every word.

"I never lied to you."

"When I asked if he was still working here, what did you tell me?"

"That Ed was helping me, and a few others. For one weekend, that was true. I didn't have to fire Rashad. If you'll remember, he quit after hearing your tirade. But after a long conversation with Blair and a sit with my conscience, I did what was right. For the business. And for myself."

"You wouldn't have this business if not for me."

"I'd be nothing without you, Daddy." Tears sprang into her eyes. She didn't try to stop them. "You stayed when Mom left. Raised me, taught me everything I know, including how to think for myself, how to make sound choices, how to follow my gut.

"Daddy, I appreciate all your help in opening this restaurant. I also see how now you're using that assistance to try to control how I run it, the same way you've controlled other parts of my life."

"Listen, Jamilah—"

"Please, let me finish. I'm not blaming you for being overprotective. I know your actions come out of love. But I'm almost thirty years old. It's time for me to make my own rules. To live or die by my own choices. If you can't trust Rashad, I'm asking you to trust your daughter. Give me a chance to prove that I'm not an imbecile and can think for myself."

She watched as James processed what she'd said, felt him battle his emotions.

"I don't like this, Jamilah."

"I know."

"You're inviting trouble with him around."

"What he's done isn't who he is."

"I don't feel you're safe with him working here."

Jamilah had never felt safer. "I'm sorry you're upset. But since being hired, Rashad has only made the business better. He's an exceptional cook. Gets along well with the staff and customers. The tech company we catered for loved him. The reality of the man working here doesn't match what's shown on paper."

James's eyes narrowed. "Are you into this guy romantically?"

She wanted to say that who she was or wasn't into was none of her father's business. She wanted to ask him if he was into anyone romantically, and if so, whether she had a right to know the details. She wanted to tell him to mind his own business. She didn't want to lie.

"What Rashad and I have in common is keeping the doors open. I've given this place the last few years of my life. Gainful employment is a condition of his parole. Neither one of us can afford to see it fail."

"In the near thirty years you've been on this earth, I've never known you to defy me."

"I'm sorry, Daddy, but honestly… I did what I had to do."

He looked at her intently, his expression unreadable, then left without a word.

Jamilah slumped against the shelving holding dry ingredients and canned goods. She could have released a lifetime of tears, but one look at the clock and she shelved that emotion. Time was ticking. She had a business to operate.

After splashes of cold water in the restroom to try and reset, Jamilah squared her shoulders and walked into the kitchen.

Rashad looked over his shoulder. "You all right?"

"I'm fine." She reached for trays and began filling them with the day's sides.

"You sure?"

"I said yes." Jamilah hadn't meant to snap. Clearly, her father's words had affected her more than she cared to admit.

They worked silently side by side until the crew arrived and business began. Thankfully, it was another busy day. Jamilah noticed a couple people from the tech event and a few tables of first-time customers scattered among more familiar faces. On the outside, she was the hostess with the mostest, the server with a smile, the pleasant one with a constant conversation. Inside, she barely held it together. Jamilah knew the kitchen was much too small to accommodate the elephant taking up space.

Hours later, Jamilah bid farewell to the last customer and locked the door. She entered the kitchen where Rashad and Everett were having a friendly conversation about sports. When he saw her, however, Everett beat a hasty exit. One would have had to be clueless or dead to not have felt the tension that hung in the kitchen all afternoon.

"Your Surprise Sides idea was a hit," Jamilah said, hoping to steer the conversation in a positive direction…and keep it there. "And the Surprise Sides Walking, adding the two chicken legs? That was the most popular to-go order. We've never had this much walk-up traffic. They were flying out the door."

Rashad nodded but continued methodically cleaning his station.

His body language transmitted being troubled, upset. Not surprising. Her dad had run more than one man away with his commanding persona. She hoped Rashad would be different. If not, it was just as well to find out sooner than later. Before they became lovers. Life would go on.

Maybe.

"We sold out of the potato boats." Jamilah went into the back for storage containers, then retrieved a couple trays and began transferring leftover sides.

"Surprisingly, we sold more macaroni salad than macaroni and cheese. Until now that dish was one of our biggest sellers. You're really adding to this business, Ra—"

"You're really gonna do this? Act like the most important thing we have to discuss are chicken legs and side dishes?"

"No. I need to apologize. I'm sorry for snapping at you earlier. And about my dad…"

"It's not about your pops. It's hard to do, but I can't take what he says or does personally. You're his daughter, his little princess. He's being protective, as he should. Plus, he's law enforcement. So by design, he has to be an asshole."

"No, you didn't just call my dad—"

"I did. And if you were being truthful, you'd have to admit you've seen that side of him, too."

Jamilah reached for a cloth and began wiping the counter. "My conversation with Daddy was very upsetting."

"What'd he say?"

She paused midswipe. "Do you really want to know?"

"I asked, didn't I?"

"It's what I said that matters."

"What was that?"

Jamilah finished cleaning the counter, then tossed the throwaway towel. "That this is my business, and as long as I'm running it, you're the head chef."

"You didn't talk that smack to pops," Rashad said.

"I might be paraphrasing a little, but that's basically what I said."

"So he's cool with me working here."

"No, but I am."

Actually, Jamilah's heart was breaking. She'd never been this at odds with her dad before.

Rashad walked over, pulled her close, and kissed her gently on the lips.

And like a parent kissing a boo-boo, a bit of her pain eased away.

Back at home, the ten o'clock news went off, and Jamilah was still traumatized. She'd wallowed in sadness, allowed herself a good cry, then pulled on a pair of chenille PJs, popped some corn and fixed some tea. She'd plopped in front of her sixty-five-inch distraction, one she hoped would clear her mind of the other inches she imagined swung between the legs of her cook. She'd shut out what she believed was her dad's disappointment and prayed for sleep to come on the couch. The bed was just too big to occupy alone.

Another hour and her thoughts were less about her father and more about her cook. She couldn't stop thinking about how he made her feel. How a few words and a light kiss had worked better than ibuprofen. And if she felt that good with only a kiss, how much better to enjoy his whole body? Those crazy thoughts she shouldn't entertain returned. She attempted mental reasoning with thoughts like him being her employee, of not trying to be a booty call, of keeping their relationship professional, of wishing she was into vibrators.

She wasn't, and the thoughts were no deterrent for what she wanted. Jamilah decided to take her own advice, to live or die by her own choices, no matter how reasonable or insane. She made one now, threw off the comforter, and walked into the bedroom. She quickly touched up her ponytail, changed out of her oversize PJs, slid on a pair of boots and returned to the living room for her coat and purse. Before heading out she sent a text to Leon.

Jamilah reached her car. Got in and took a breath. A part of her wondered what the heck was she doing, but the part that kept replaying what happened earlier knew it was time to choose a different action to get a different result. Her world had been shaped by her father, the most influential man in her life. It was time to influence her own destiny.

Her phone pinged. Leon had texted back with Rashad's address. She backed out of the garage and headed to Anna's house. For once, Jamilah decided to not overthink but instead to follow her heart. To experience life on her own terms, not that of others. To live up to Rashad's nickname and be her own boss.

Twenty-Two

Rashad emerged from a hot shower. He exchanged the thick towel he'd dried off with for the warmth of soft cotton sheets, an old quilt and faux-fur comforter. All of that and the downstairs thermostat was still set to eighty. This California native wasn't a fan of the colder weather, with temps Anna assured him would drop further once winter arrived.

He positioned the pillows behind him, reached for his notebook and rested his head against the headboard. After leaving Side Chic'k, he'd driven around the Eighteenth and Vine area with no destination in mind, only the conversation that happened between him and Jamilah's dad, and the uncomfortable work environment that played out the rest of the day. He thought he'd found a spot to find his groove and perfect his craft. But the last problem he needed while still on parole, or ever, was an overly protective father who also just happened to be a detective, one who might have been responsible for the patrol car he'd seen near Side Chic'k when he circled the block.

Funny how earlier he for sure thought his pen would be on Jamilah. Instead other, more serious thoughts flowed from the ink.

Stereotyped. Profiled.

Misjudged. Lost juvenile.
Grown up. Changed mind.
Major shift not duly noted.
Lost rage. Turned page.
Still judged—got outvoted.
Family affairs. Cops. Bold stares.
I'm…

Rashad's phone beeped. *Probably Juke, he thought*, noting it was almost midnight. Most of his calls or texts this late were from California.

It wasn't the West Coast.

Hey, Rashad. You up? It's Jamilah

I'm up

Good. I'm outside

Even though far from the basement window, Rashad looked toward the street. His thumbs flew across the keys.

Outside where?

Anna's house

WTH?

I know it's late. Can I come in?

Rashad almost said no, but curiosity won. What did she have to say now that couldn't have been said at the restaurant?

Come around to the side and down the stairs to the basement entrance

He rolled out of bed and slid into a pair of sweats. Just as he pulled on a T-shirt, Jamilah tapped on the door.

He opened it.

She stood unmoving, as if suddenly unsure of the decision that brought her there.

"You coming in, or are you going to stay outside?"

Rashad observed her brief, nervous smile as she entered.

"What's up, Jamilah?"

Her expression changed as she took a step toward him. It went from being shy and uncertain to more serious and determined. Instead of an answer, she flung her purse on a nearby chair and hungrily kissed a stunned Rashad like she needed his breath to live.

"Hold up. Baby, wait—"

"I don't want to wait," she all but growled without removing her lips from his. "I want you. Now."

She stepped back, let her coat fall and revealed a black silk nighty embellished with roses that hit the top of her thighs.

"Jamilah, I think we should talk—"

As he said this, she removed her boots. Then down came one strap of the nighty, followed by the other. She stepped out of the lingerie and stood bare-ass naked, hands on hips, titties jiggling.

"Do I look like I came here for conversation?"

Rashad visibly swallowed as he took in the tempting feast before him.

"Got damn, Boss Lady."

She shimmied past him and climbed into the bed, intentionally swaying her natural bubble ass as she crawled toward the middle. Whatever rebuttal he was trying to formulate evaporated like smoke in the wind. He slid off the sweatpants he'd hurriedly donned to cover his nakedness. In hindsight he realized there'd been no need for that. A T-shirt quickly joined the pile of clothes on the floor. He crawled into bed and on top of Jamilah, determined to give her everything she'd come for.

For that to happen, he'd have to slow things down. He replaced her ravenous actions with a slow grazing of his lips against hers, his tongue gently poking, prodding, but not dipping deep. She moaned, placed her arms around his neck and tried to control the pace.

With an alpha man like Rashad, that was never going to happen.

His tongue slid from her mouth to her chin and down to her neck, where he kissed her gently, almost reverently, as his thumb lazily stroked her nipple into a hardened peak. Soon his lips were on a journey to get acquainted with said peak. He dipped his head and captured it with his teeth, swiped it with his tongue while his thumb gave attention to her other breast.

She hissed. "Rashad…"

"Relax, baby. This is gonna take a while."

He continued to assault her breasts, one after the other, as Jamilah squirmed impatiently. He blew against the wet nipples, watched the goose bumps pop up all over her chest. This was the kind of sex Rashad preferred. The type where two people weren't just fucking, not just having sex, but making love. Right or wrong, orthodox or not, that's what Rashad wanted to do with Jamilah—make the kind of slow, thoughtful love that would stamp him on her heart forever.

He felt her hands slide through his locs as he shifted and continued his trek down her body, mapping out her curves with his lips, tongue, and fingers, appreciating every inch of soft brown skin. The scent of her essence wafted into his nostrils and went straight to his dick, which thickened and elongated with anticipation.

But it wasn't time for that. Not yet.

He kissed the top of her mound, licked her folds ever so lightly. Just enough to let her know he had special plans for that particular part of her body. Then he went to his knees, spread her legs and kissed the sensitive insides near her throbbing heat, watched as her nub grew and quivered. At that moment, Rashad believed that if clits could talk, hers would be shouting *Here! I'm right here!*

The thought made Rashad smile, give it a kiss, then continue his journey to know the rest of her. He sought out and gave attention to the sensitive places. The tender, insides of her legs. Behind the knees. Her ankles. Toes.

When he sucked in her cute, manicured big toe, Jamilah gasped loudly, clutching fistfuls of sheet in both hands.

"We've got to be quiet, baby," Rashad warned. "Charles and Anna are on the third level, but the vents might pick up loud noises."

"Please, just…"

"Don't worry. I'm definitely going to do that."

Rashad decided she'd waited long enough to experience her first release. He slid back up between her legs and began to worship her pussy with his skilled tongue. He used his middle finger to toy with another entry. Almost immediately, Jamilah's legs began to shake. She began to thrash around on the bed. He held her in place, forcing her to endure every second of the sensual assault. He kissed and licked and nibbled until the mewling stopped and the shaking subsided, then covered her body and sealed this first act with a deep, French kiss. He ground himself against her, giving her a feel of the pleasure to come, then rolled off the bed, retrieved a Magnum, and rejoined her. The smile she gave him, one both tentative and thankful, her eyes piercing through to his soul even as tiny teardrops hovered at the corner of her eye.

"That was incredible," she whispered. "I've never—"

He swallowed the rest of her sentence in a kiss that turned back on her juices. He slid his masterful manhood up and down her wetness, getting harder with every moan, every gyration. She shifted and widened her legs to give him greater access. Nothing about the woman beneath him resembled the conservative, bougie sistah he'd met that first day. No, this woman was all fire, desire, and wild abandon. A boss in the bed.

He raised her to her knees and began a slow journey into the caverns of her heat. The friction was delicious, his patience incredible. He gyrated slowly, teasing in and out as her body adjusted, admiring the beautiful round ass being presented before him. He dipped into her star, eased in farther. Massaged her cheeks. Squeezed her hips. Again, he felt Jamilah's annoyance at his slow pace. She pushed back against him. This time, he allowed it. Wider. Deeper. Until he was fully inside her. Then the fun truly began.

After a few rounds of lovemaking, the pair fell asleep. Rashad woke up around four, went into the bathroom, and wet a warm cloth. He brought it back out and began a thoughtful ablution of Jamilah's sweet spot. She stirred, then awakened with a smile.

"What are you doing?"

"You were tight," he said, while continuing his ritual. "Might be a little sore tomorrow."

He left for a sec and returned with a rinsed, hot towel and placed it at the door to her paradise. After taking turns in the bathroom, they cuddled beneath the sheets.

"Yeah, it's been a while. Plus, you're rather…blessed…in that area."

He leaned over, kissed the top of her head. "You all right?"

He felt her nod.

"You were the aggressor tonight."

"I'm sorry—"

"Don't you dare apologize. I liked it. You knew what you wanted and went after it. That takes courage. Being self-assured looks amazing on your fine, naked ass."

He squeezed a cheek for emphasis. She kissed his shoulder in gratitude.

"Thanks for saying that. It means a lot. This is new territory for me. I'm still not sure how I feel about it."

"Do you regret coming over?"

"Not yet."

He chuckled. "The jury is still out, huh?"

"Following my heart isn't a common occurrence. There are so many reasons I can cite for why this shouldn't have happened. Standing on my own is the right thing to do, but I've never gone against my father. Defending you felt both correct and disloyal. It's a lot of stuff to unpack. Most other men I've dated have been the kind my father would have chosen."

"Do you think it right that he make those types of decisions for you?"

"Obviously not." Said with a playful nudge. "Unlike you, I wasn't the rebellious kid. The obedient lifestyle is the only one I've known."

"That being said, what if your father never comes around? What if he never accepts me? What will you do then?"

Jamilah turned away from him. "I don't know."

Her answer was barely audible, but Rashad heard it loud and clear.

Twenty-Three

Jamilah arrived home before the sun kissed the sky. A telltale throbbing persisted between her thighs, as though Rashad's energy was still present. As she walked from the garage to the lobby and into the elevator that would take her to her floor, she was uber aware of all the places Rashad had pleasured. Tender nipples. Kiss-stung lips. Sensitive spots all over, down to her big toe. For Jamilah, one thing was for sure. She was in trouble. Big trouble. And in the light of the sun-filled morning, the possible consequences of her actions came out of hiding.

Going against her father by employing Rashad was one thing. Sleeping with him took the situation to a whole other level. Rashad represented everything her dad had warned her about. She remembered one of his sayings growing up, one that gave a nod to his extensive album collection: *Don't date anyone with a record that is not made of wax.*

Using that analogy, not only did Rashad have a record, but several. He'd been incarcerated more than once and even now was on parole. Jamilah couldn't even put all of her uncertainty on her father. In the light of day, the weight of her spontaneity settled around her like Rashad's arms had last night.

Was she okay if what they had was only temporary? Could

they still work together if the sex went south? Suppose their dalliance turned serious? How would their future look? Rashad was a great guy, but facts were facts. Men with felonies couldn't vote. It was hard to get gainful employment. She'd needed her father to help get a loan. What chance did Rashad have with his record? Could he buy a house? Get a car? Pass the scrutiny of any bank-loan application? These were questions for which she didn't have answers. Ones her father had probably considered when he called Rashad *six feet of bad news*.

Jamilah stripped and stepped into a steamy, hot shower, grateful for the warmth of the water and the power of the showerhead that massaged her body. She soaped herself, thinking of Rashad as her hands glided over her skin. She could never tell anyone that she wasn't warned, that there hadn't been mental caution lights blinking from the time she'd donned the negligee to when she'd trekked across town. As she'd neared Anna's home, they'd become more pronounced. That's until she walked into his basement abode and into his arms. From then the goal became clear, as did purposeful intent. There was certainty when she shed her clothes and climbed into his bed, feeling his eyes pour over her like the water did now. All doubt fled when she kissed him. When he kissed her back with a deliberate tenderness that was the very opposite of her aggression. The foreplay? Goodness. She would never be able to see his tongue and not remember all the places on her body that it had touched. And when he'd entered her? That slow thrusting when it was no longer possible to detect where he ended and she began? Followed by the light flashes and thunder roars that were her multiple orgasms? Game over. As she lay cuddled in his arms, satiated to the point of wanting to purr like a kitten, Jamilah knew she'd jumped from the frying pan into the fire, ready to get burned over and over again.

With a few hours until her server shift at Gusto, Jamilah forced her thoughts away from Rashad and on to her business. She pulled out her tablet and pulled up the spreadsheets that mapped out the Side Chic'k budget. Thanks to the recent catering job, the generous tip given to her at the end of the evening, and growing profits from being open two and a half days, she could comfortably handle expenses for the next few months, more if repeat customer business continued and she managed inventory correctly.

An image of Rashad laughing with customers brought a smile to her face. She was sure his presence played a role in the increased female patronage. There was no denying the animal magnetism and charisma. In her life for less than a month, and she couldn't go more than fifteen minutes without thinking about him.

She studied payroll. Thankfully her work at Gusto paid her personal bills. She paid herself after everyone else, and only if there was enough without cutting into other responsibilities. It was nice having her former employee Everett back, but she could let him go if doing so would stretch the bank account. What would really be great during this holiday season was another catering job or three. She clicked on the Side Chic'k website, looking at the home page for ideas on how to better advertise their catering arm to be more attractive to potential clients. While finishing up a text to her web administrator, the phone rang. She took a fortifying breath, hoped for the best, then answered.

"Hey, Daddy."

"Jamilah. How are you?"

"I'm okay."

"Really? I'm not."

Several seconds ticked by. Jamilah remained quiet. What could she say? She had no control over her father's feelings, and sat ready to stand her ground even as she felt it shift beneath her.

"I'm in the middle of a delicate investigation that I can't focus fully on for worrying about you."

"Don't worry. I'm fine."

Deliciously so, fully satiated.

"Why can't you just find another cook?"

"Why can't you just stay out of my business?"

"What did you just say?"

Jamilah took another breath. Maybe having this conversation over the phone wasn't the best idea. Then again, maybe the physical distance was exactly what was needed for Jamilah to put on her big-girl panties and not run from this tough yet much-needed exchange.

"I apologize for my tone, but not for what I said. I know you love me, Daddy. I know you mean well and want what's best for me. But did you listen to what I said the other day? Did you hear anything at all?"

"I heard a daughter being defiant, that's what I heard."

"Not an experienced, intelligent woman capable of making sound business decisions?"

One second passed. Two. Three.

"I don't call you with ultimatums on how to do your job, or suggestions on which detective you should work with and which one you should avoid. I don't do that because I'm not in law enforcement. You're the one with that experience, who's put in the hours to become knowledgeable in how best to do your job. I don't have twenty years in this industry, and yes, right now is a struggle. Eighty percent of restaurants fail within the first five years. I'm working like hell to best those odds by doing what I feel is best for my business."

"Your business or your personal life?"

"Again, and with all due respect, my personal life is also my business."

The silence was deafening. And extended.

"Daddy?"

She looked at the phone. He'd hung up.

"Well, that went to hell in a handbasket," she said to the condo walls, while her emotional ones threatened to crash down around her.

Jamilah came down from the amazing sex high. To his credit,

Rashad had reached out to make sure she was okay. She lied and said she was, that she was busy with work and other avoidant, nonsensical excuses that kept her from having to talk to him while sorting herself out.

Over the next couple days she went from questioning her actions to regretting them, especially because of the wedge it drove between her and her father. She called him to apologize again for her outburst and call a truce. He didn't answer. Not surprised, she left a voice mail. She knew it would be a few days before he came around. James Carver was a stubborn, proud, opinionated man who'd sacrificed a lot to raise her as a single dad. He'd had to fulfill the role of two parents. She understood why he felt it was still his responsibility to protect her, a sense of entitlement when it came to having a say in how she lived her life.

Because she grew up apart from her mother, their relationship was totally different. Except for a phone call here or a birthday card there, Shannon had missed Jamilah's growing-up years and the bond usually formed during that time. Theirs was a casual friendship, two strangers really, who each decided to make room for the other in their life. Jamilah would see her mother next month during the Christmas holiday. If a repeat of last year, they'd have dinner, be cordial, and fill the air with surface conversation, polite inquiries about each other's lives. She'd dutifully ask about her absent half-brother, who was fifteen years younger and who she barely knew. Shannon would politely inquire about James. Maybe this time her brother EJ would be there, and Jamilah could get to know the kid who she shared blood with.

Jamilah held no anger. He wasn't the one who'd been married to her father. Bottom line, though, that motherly advice she needed about men in general and Rashad specifically would definitely not come from Shannon.

Friday arrived. She walked into Side Chic'k exhausted from two back-to-back doubles. Somewhere in the delirium of too much work, too little sleep, and running on energy drinks, the pendulum of emotions finished its erratic swaying and settled in the seat of her soul, where rationale, logic, and who-gives-a-damn had a come-to-Jesus meeting. When it was over, Jamilah decided to not fret over what had happened in the past that couldn't be changed, what took place now that wasn't in her control, or what was in the future that she couldn't yet see. With that mindset, she put on her favorite India Arie, turned up the volume, and had just begun assembling the day's salads when she heard footsteps coming down the hall.

"Rashad?"

He rounded the corner. "The one and only."

After placing his ever-present notebook under the counter, he walked straight over and pulled her into his arms. There was a chance they could be seen from the street, but after a brief hesitation, Jamilah wrapped her arms around his neck and accepted his kiss. When he tried to deepen the exchange, however, she ended the embrace and went to the fridge to cover her conflicting emotions by looking busy.

If Rashad noticed, he said nothing. Jamilah exhaled.

"Would you believe I haven't stopped thinking about you since you bum-rushed my body?"

This elicited a smile. "I did that, didn't I?"

"You did," he replied, taming his locs with his bandanna. "I loved every minute of it."

"Me, too." Jamilah washed her hands and returned to the counter. "Might cost me, though."

Rashad pulled an apron over his sweatshirt. "Let me guess. Your pops?"

Jamilah sighed, not sure how much about her father's continued dislike she wanted to share with a man who disliked him right back. Still, knowing he was exactly who she needed to talk to, she tapped the volume button and lowered India's beautiful voice.

Rashad joined her at the counter. "I don't mind loud music."

"You asked how being with you the other night might cost me."

"Yeah."

Jamilah finished one of the salad offerings, transferred it from the mixing bowl to a display tray. The familiar act was not only comforting but gave her another minute before sharing information that Rashad could not unhear.

Rashad stopped working. "What happened?"

"He called and restated his position. Made sure I knew it hadn't changed. I shared my reasons for keeping you based on sound logic, but he didn't hear a word. He asked me again to find another cook and found out my mind hadn't changed either. I told him I would not be looking for a replacement."

"You said that?"

"For better or worse."

"Impressive."

Jamilah didn't see the admiration in Rashad's eyes as he looked at her. "His anger for not firing me, that's the price?"

"Not just that you still work here. He thinks I like you."

"He'd rather you work around people you don't like?"

"You know what I mean."

"Is he right?"

It was Jamilah's turn for an annoyed tsk. "What do you think?"

"Just because we slept together doesn't mean you're feeling me like that."

"I don't know what I'm feeling. But my dad is pissed. He's used to me following his orders without question. But that's starting to change."

"Change isn't always easy, but often necessary."

"I just have to get comfortable with being uncomfortable. I just don't—" Jamilah swallowed the sob that hopped into her throat and swiped the renegade tear that escaped through her lashes.

"Say it, Jamilah. You just don't what?"

"I don't want to lose my dad!"

Rashad stepped closer and hugged her.

"Love doesn't let go that easy, babe. When he sees you happy and the business successful, he'll come around."

Rashad's words were as soothing as fresh aloe vera. Jamilah hoped they were also the truth.

Twenty-Four

Rashad sat letting his car warm up, on a call with his lead PO.

"Mr. Turner has good things to say about you, Rashad. He hinted at visiting your place of work soon." Rashad heard finger taps on a computer keyboard. "What's it called again?"

"Side Chic'k. With an apostrophe between the *c* and *k*."

"Right. Are you still there only three days a week?"

"Yeah. I know you'd prefer I be somewhere with more hours, but here I'm head chef. I get to use what I learned under my mentor Francisco and get more experience running a restaurant, my ultimate goal. Plus, we're hoping the holidays bring more catering jobs. More customers, too. If so, we can maybe go to being open five days by spring."

"Speaking of the holidays, what are your travel plans?"

"I'm definitely homesick and would love to see my family. Not sure I can swing a ticket, though."

"Because of how well you're meeting your parole obligations, holiday travel for you should be okay. Send me the proposed schedule so that I can take the request through the proper channels, and inform Mr. Turner. It would also be nice if you and I could have a visit while you're here."

Rashad ignored the invisible yet ever-present penal chain around his ankle. "Okay."

"I'm proud of you Rashad. You're staying out of trouble and doing the work."

"Appreciate that."

"Have a good evening, Rashad."

"You, too, Nichole."

Finally, warm air flowed through the vents. Rashad doubted he'd ever get used to the crazy Midwest weather. He'd already checked his watch but looked again and shook his head. It was barely six o'clock but already dark. How did people get used to nighttime coming so quickly?

He left the Side Chic'k parking space without a clear destination. Decided to explore the area, to drive and think. Rashad was restless, antsy. Jamilah was the reason. She'd pulled out several minutes earlier, hoping to catch her father before he went to work to try to patch things up. Rashad wanted to be with her again and had made those wishes known. On Friday night she'd taken a rain check, but he'd stayed at her condo last night. Waking up there felt perfect and weird at the same time. In the middle of the night while Jamilah slept, Rashad had a moment of paranoia. He'd imagined a loud knock at the door followed by officers running in, guns drawn and a smug-looking James leading the charge before hauling him off in handcuffs. Going back to sleep hadn't come easy.

Jamilah had put a lot on the line to be with him. It both impressed and flattered him, yet he still felt a way about it. Her moves applied pressure for him to do the right thing. But what was that, exactly?

Jamilah was everything a man could want in a woman: smart, ambitious, honest, fine. Surprising, too. He would never have thought that the woman who tightened up like Questlove's snare drum at the start of a show would be the passionate lover he experienced. She was classy, in his mind not the type to do casual hookups. They were in the CWWB zone: coworkers with benefits. But what happened if one day she wanted more? There was something about a steady partner that was satisfying, but Rashad didn't see himself in a relationship right now. A personal commitment wasn't on his list of priorities. Until Jamilah had driven over unannounced, it hadn't been on the list at all.

WWJD? Of all his friends, him and Juke were the closet, the voice of reason when Rashad might crash out. He decided to find out what would Juke do. His call went to voice mail.

"Yo, hit me back."

Rashad was acclimating to Kansas City, but he missed his LA friends—Juke, Sky Walka, Eight Track, a politically incorrect nod to this friend's ADHD, Sir Zimbabwe, whose parents were really from there, and PhD, who during his many years in prison had read at least a thousand books. Hands down, Phil Diggs, his government name, was one of the smartest, most knowledgeable men walking upright. His IQ was probably off the charts. Given another set of circumstances, Phil was one of those brothahs who could have helped change the world.

These boys, now men, had known each other since babyhood and, like almost all of their peers and half the melanated teen boys in the world, grew up dreaming to be world-renowned rappers. Sky Walka and PhD came the closest. PhD had a handful of features with famous West Coast rappers and production credits on popular mix tapes. One song with a Sky Walka hook actually reached number two on the hip-hop charts and led to him joining a tour overseas. Eight Track sold a few beats to the TDE camp, where Kendrick honed his skills, and was cast in a couple B movies, basically playing himself, about life in the hood.

There were others, those who'd gone the gang or pharmaceutical route and ended up either buried alive, another term for being in prison, or buried for real. The odds were often stacked against men who looked like Rashad and his homies. Like Tupac, it felt like them against the world. Thus the loyalty.

The camaraderie. The unbreakable bonds. The reason to do three years rather than snitch on a friend. Codes of the culture.

He reached Paseo and the bright neon lights of Side Chic'k's nemesis, Fly the Coop, made a right on to Eighteenth Street, and headed toward Vine. Most of the tourist-attracting venues Charles had told him about were there, plus a jazz venue called the Blue Room and a few restaurants. He was surprised to see that the area made famous during the twenties and thirties was contained in a few blocks. He reached the end of one street, turned onto another and was just about to exit the area when a small sign in a window caught his eye: *Poetry on the Vine*. He put the car in Park, reached for his phone, and quickly typed the name into the browser.

The link led to a Facebook page, Poetryls, with almost two thousand members. Reading the content got him excited. Various artists posted their work or about their events. Written poems, spoken word set to music, video of a podcast. All this happening barely a stone's throw from where he'd been spending his weekends for the past month.

Who woulda thunk it?

He scrolled the page. The next show was Thursday at seven. Unconsciously, he reached over and stroked his ever-present rhyme book. Seeing that sign was like a message from the Universe. It was time to get back on the mic.

Just knowing there was someplace he might spit his rhymes lifted his spirits. He almost called Jamilah but didn't want to take the chance of interrupting a conversation with her dad. He wasn't ready to go home to a quiet house. Charles and Anna were having dinner with Monique and "an old friend," as Anna explained it. He thought about Leon but wasn't in the mood for gaming or sports, Leon's favorite—correction, *only*—pastimes besides listening to hip-hop and Blair. He made his way out of the historic area headed to wherever. He scrolled his phone to a hip-hop playlist. It beeped in his hand.

A seven-two-five area code. Rashad's brow creased. Not a

California area code, for sure, about the only other state be-sides Missouri with people who had his new number acquired after relocating here. Well, he didn't have a warrant and was already on parole. He decided to answer.

"Hello?"

"Ra God!"

Rashad paused, allowed the sound of the voice to reach his brain's Contacts list. "T Bone?"

"I prefer Tyson, the name my mama gave me. T-Bone was the dude I retired when I left the streets. Juke gave me your number. Hope you don't mind."

"It's cool. What's up?"

"Just checking on you. Make sure you're all right. That was a big thing you did for my little brother, and the family. Wanna make sure you're straight."

Rashad nodded. "Appreciate that."

"I hear you're in Kansas now."

"Missouri. Kansas City, Missouri, which is right next door."

"I'm familiar," Tyson replied. "Been to Missouri a couple times checking out properties. KC and St. Louis."

"Juke told me you're in real estate now."

"That's my new hustle. Started flipping houses a few years back. Tripled my money in less than six months. Needless to say, I got hooked."

"That's what's up."

"I hear you're a cook."

"I prefer *head chef.* Has a much better ring to it."

Tyson laughed. "The money enough for you to make ends meet?"

"Hell, no. That's not my main focus. I'm doing it for the practice and the experience. Want to open my own place."

"Ownership goals," he teased.

"Tends to happen when you spend time with grown men telling other grown men what to do."

Tyson's tone became somber. "You sacrificed a lot. Three

years you can't get back. Saved Drew from a potential third strike. Good to hear you're out and striving. When we put that skill and intelligence honed in the street toward a legitimate business, bro, sky's the limit."

"Real talk. Some of the best and brightest minds are in prison. Just needing a chance."

"So…have you thought about ways to make this dream of owning your own business a reality?"

"Several, in fact."

"Talk to me."

For the next hour, Rashad did just that. He mentioned pop-ups, food trucks, and—the biggest risk—a space featuring hip-hop, spoken word and satisfying food. Tyson offered valuable advice and support where he could. Rashad hung up with reinvigorated confidence about his plans, perhaps even a potential partner. For the first time since seeing the red and blue lights flashing that late night on Crenshaw, Rashad saw a future he could believe in.

There was only one question as he pondered the call. Would Jamilah believe in him as much as he believed in himself? Because try as he might to dismiss their connection, he didn't see a tomorrow without her.

Twenty-Five

It had been another busy week. Gusto stayed busy. The holiday season was in full swing. Tips were good, but Jamilah was exhausted. Even so, she checked the Side Chic'k website nightly for catering inquiries. There'd been a few but no deposits yet. Jamilah squashed her disappointment and kept hope alive.

Rashad was having a different experience. The cards he'd passed out at Monique's party were paying off. He'd snagged three catering jobs in one week. They were small, but heck, a win was a win. One for a nonprofit organization, another for a sorority, a third for a church. That Thursday, she called him to hang out. When he failed to pick up, she didn't leave a voice mail.

She woke up to the text he sent after she went to bed.

Just saw your missed call. Phone was off. See you tomorrow

Questions quickly rose unbidden. Where had he been? Who was he with? Why was his phone turned off? And the final, most important one, what was it to her? Rashad didn't owe her an explanation. They hadn't yet put a name on what they were doing, but whatever it was didn't make him accountable to her for his whereabouts.

Why'd she have to go and make things so complicated?

Resisting the urge for more shopping therapy, Jamilah went to the gym instead. Certain muscles screamed and complained from lack of use, but the workout was sorely needed. Helped clear her head. A short time later, she pulled into the lot behind Side Chic'k, next to Rashad's SUV, and just like that, anxiety returned. An unexplainable nervousness hit her gut. Last week's sex romp and the camaraderie that followed suddenly seemed like a long time ago. For all the confidence it had taken to start and run her own business, and the latest brave act to not kowtow to her father, Jamilah still dealt with feelings of abandonment and insecurity. Walter knew about these issues and still stayed with her, even if he did use these same points to maintain a type of control. Time and distance softened the memories of his emotional turmoil and caused her to consider the unthinkable: Had breaking up with him been a mistake?

Locking these thoughts in a vault for safekeeping, she stepped into Side Chic'k, hung up her coat, and entered the kitchen. Nerves turned to squiggles of desire. One thing about it—no one turned her on like Rashad.

"Hey," she said, with as much don't-give-a-shit as she could muster.

"Hey, you. My hands are three inches deep in this flour. Come give me a kiss."

"You want one of those?"

The question came out in a pitch higher than she intended, making what she'd meant to come off as flippant sound desperate instead.

He looked over his shoulder but said nothing, just walked over to where she slipped into an apron and kissed her on the cheek.

"Sorry I missed your call last night."

"No big deal."

"Believe it or not, I was right here in our hood. You ever heard of Poetry on the Vine?"

"Nope."

"Poetryls is the name they use on social media. Anyway, it's an event that happens on Thursday nights at a jazz bar. I noticed a sign last week after deciding to drive around a block or two and check out my surroundings."

"Sounds interesting. How was it?"

"Pretty cool. It had been a while since I hung out with other artists, folk spitting and rapping, doing their thing. You should come with me sometime. I heard some nice work."

Hearing Rashad's explanation made Jamilah feel badly. One missed phone call and she'd thought the worse.

"How'd it go with your father?"

"It didn't."

"Still not talking?"

"He answered my call but had no time to talk. He's working a case. Said he'd call later."

"That's progress, right?"

"I hope so."

Rashad nodded, refocused on the dish being prepared. Jamilah relaxed, a little. She wasn't the most intuitive person, but something felt different about Rashad. He was quieter, more introspective, as though something else besides rap and her father's opinion was on his mind.

"Tell me about your catering gigs."

He became more animated while sharing menu plans. Shasta, Everett, and Caylen arrived. Personal conversation was shelved to handle a surprisingly busy lunch crowd. Dinner traffic was respectable, too.

After closing, as Rashad and Jamilah walked to the back door he asked, "You hang out down here much?"

"Hardly at all. I should probably change that."

"Ever been to that jazz bar I mentioned?"

"The Corner? Yeah, but not lately." Jamilah set the alarm and walked out the door Rashad held for her. "There was an amazing jazz singer named Ida McBeth who used to perform there. She was one of my dad's favorites."

Rashad followed Jamilah to her car. "Maybe your dad and I can go there and, you know, hang out."

Jamilah gave him a look. He chuckled. "Okay, maybe not."

"Unfortunately Ida passed away a few years ago. The thought of you and Dad getting along sounds like a dream. But before that happens, we might see hell freeze over."

She got ready to open her door. Rashad stopped her. "Boss lady, I've got a question. What do you know about the empty space next door?"

"Why, are you getting ready to open up your own jazz and spoken-word bar and knock out your competition down the block?"

"Would you be mad if I did?"

"Not as long as chicken or any of the sides we serve isn't on the menu."

"What? No chicken? Not even wings?"

Jamilah again went for the door. "I'm cold."

"My bad." Rashad opened it. "Does the guy you rent from own both places?"

"I think so."

"Do you have his number?"

"You sound serious." His look confirmed that he wasn't joking.

"Unlock the other side."

She did. He climbed in, rubbing cold palms together.

"So…check this out. I'd have this venue, right. Not just poetry like the place down the street. Mine would feature hip-hop—"

"Of course."

"All sorts of music, really. I'd want a DJ in the mix. It would be a mash up for mostly Gen Xers, Millennials, creatives and geeks, from me hanging with Leon," he conspiratorially added. "A cool spot with positive vibes. No gang stuff. No violence. A place where people our age can socialize and have a good time, and not just on Thursday night."

"You've really thought this out. You're seriously thinking about being my competition?"

"Or your partner. Don't you think we work well together?"

He squiggled his brows, then leaned over and kissed her. What began as an innocent peck quickly deepened. If not for the fact that her newly acquired chef was scheming to set up shop mere feet away, she'd be more open for tongue dancing.

"Wait, Rashad. I want to hear more. How long have you been working on this?"

"All my life, in one way or another. But more recently since I came here for the interview and saw the next door space empty."

"Where would you get the money for renovations?"

"I have connections."

And just like that, the ghost of her father began yapping inside her head.

I thought I taught you better than to hire a criminal... In my twenty-plus years on the force, I've met men like this Rashad character coming and going. You do not want to get involved with the likes of him...

"What kind of connections?" Even though she tried to ask it casually, the question sounded like a plate of suspicion, with a dollop of judgment on the side.

From the change in Rashad's demeanor, he'd eyed her meal.

"Oh, you know. Drug dealers. Burglars who can do a lick or two to cover their part of the investment."

"Rashad, the last thing you want to do is bring criminal activity anywhere near here. Think about your parole!"

"I was just kidding, Jamilah." There was no humor in his voice.

"Oh." She laughed nervously. "A joke. Okay."

He shifted to face her more fully. "I believe I told you during our first conversation that I've committed to changing and am no longer about that life."

Jamilah was too embarrassed to look at him. "You did."

"But you don't believe me."

"I didn't say that."

"Yeah, you did, just not in those words."

She placed a hand on his arm. He yanked it away.

"I didn't mean what I said in the way it came out. I just don't see how someone who only works a few days a week with a catering gig here and there can pull off something like that."

The hole got deeper. Jamilah changed tactics, tried to claw her way out.

"Rashad, I know you're smart, talented, an amazing cook. You can probably do anything you set your mind to."

"You don't really believe that."

"Yes, I do. Old habits die hard, as do stereotypes that have been etched in my head. Forgive me?"

He released a deep sigh. "Okay."

Jamilah lightened her tone, put a smile in her voice. "Where are you headed? Do you want to come over?"

"Not tonight. I've got some planning to do."

With a light kiss on the lips, he opened his door.

"Good night, Jamilah. Drive safe."

Jamilah watched him walk away, knowing she'd messed up. As she backed out and headed for home, she forced away the discomfort. Told herself to stop overreacting. He needed the job at Side Chic'k. Steady employment was a condition of his parole. His plans were plausible, even enticing, but lofty as heck. Even with her high credit score and respectable savings account (which at this moment was quite disrespectful), she'd had to go to three banks and finally her father before securing a loan. Given Rashad's background, borrowing money would be almost impossible. With his limited experience, she also doubted investors would line up. It was a harsh reality, but the world they lived in and one that made her feel more secure about Rashad continuing at Side Chic'k.

He'd learn those hard lessons, and when he found out, she hoped to be the one to make him feel better and love all of the hurt away.

Twenty-Six

For Rashad, the weeks leading up to Thanksgiving were busy ones. He'd stumbled upon a menu that was an all-around hit: smoked then fried turkey wings on slices of stuffing, drizzled with a giblet gravy and topped with love, mac 'n' cheese balls, green bean casserole (inspired by Anna's recipe), a potato dish, and an oatmeal cranberry cookie. After serving it at Anna's workplace, word spread fast. In addition to his work at Side Chic'k, his catering business was booming.

All of the groups he served were complimentary and generous with their tips. But by the time he headed to the airport to spend Thanksgiving with his family, Rashad never wanted to see a turkey wing, cranberry or green bean ever again.

The busy pace was good for him. Helped take his mind off the dagger Jamilah had unknowingly stabbed in his dream of running his own establishment, their businesses side by side. He told himself that her observations were valid, to not be so sensitive. Still, her mindset was disappointing. He was good enough to work *for* her, but not to work *with* her, peer to peer. She didn't believe he could put a plan this big together and execute it. Fortunately, others did. Anna and Charles, Mr. Turner, and Blair and Leon all encouraged him to go for the goal.

Meanwhile, Nichole got the okay for him to fly home. His sister Zara bought the ticket. As soon as the plane wheels touched concrete, he pulled out his phone and called Tyson.

"Hey, man, how you living?"

"Large and in charge!"

"I'm back on the west side."

"Word? In LA?"

"Yeah, you coming home for the holidays?"

"Nah, man. I've got business to handle."

"Cool. That's why I called. Did you get the proposal I sent over?"

"Through Telegram? Yeah, I got it."

"Did you read it?"

"Yes, and liked what I saw, especially the part about hiring people like us, folk with criminal histories who might not pass a drug test. Men and women on parole."

"Good people with bad luck," Rashad said.

"Who's Thomas Turner?"

"My local PO. I want his help in getting the community involved, reaching the locals trying to get back on the right track. He said he had connections to local jails and juvenile detention centers who'd love a way to enhance rehabilitation."

"Man, you've put in a lot of work since we talked."

"Having your freedom snatched and life put on hold for years is a hell of a motivator."

"No doubt."

"I was hoping we'd be able to meet while I'm here. In the meantime, I want to run something past you."

"Go for it."

"How would you like to come on as a silent partner or make an investment? All of these great ideas are nothing without a stack of dead presidents."

Rashad didn't like the silence that followed. But he waited it out.

"Ra God, I'll do anything and everything to help you. But

times are tough right now. The economy is tanking. Y'all's president is acting a fool. People are scared for the future and holding onto their money. The real estate market in Vegas is on a steady decline, and my company's been hit. Trying to stop the bleeding is why I can't come home or make any investments right now."

Rashad tried and failed to not feel deflated. Tyson was his surest bet to the kind of capital for this type of start up. He shook off the hit and started thinking about food trucks.

"Look, don't give up on your spot, man. Give me some time, till after the holidays. Let me see what I can do."

"Appreciate it, Tyson."

"No problem. Give your family my best."

That night, on his way out to see the fellas, his phone pinged.

Hope you have a happy thanksgiving

He started to type a reply, then tapped the number instead.

"Hello."

"Happy Thanksgiving, Boss Lady."

"Thank you, Rashad."

Her subdued response caught him off guard. Normally there'd be push back for the nickname he gave her.

"Are you in Cali?"

"Yep."

"Excited about being home?"

"There's no place like it. These few months away seem a lot longer. I can't wait to see everybody, eat too much, talk a lot of shit, you know how we do it."

He laughed. She didn't.

"Sounds like fun."

"You okay, Jamilah? You sound a little… I don't know… quiet."

"I'm okay."

"Are you having dinner with your pops?"

"Yes, he sent me a text with dinner reservations. We're talking again, but there's still an elephant in the room."

"Whew, glad to hear it's an elephant. If it were about me, there'd be a roaring lion."

"Then, it's definitely a lion, one with an inaudible roar that fills all our silent spaces."

"I'm sorry, Jamilah."

"Not your fault."

"Maybe I can talk to him."

"Not recommended."

Jamilah's mood caused Rashad to drop his shield and speak from the heart. "I'll miss spending the holiday with you."

"Me, too."

"Tell your pops I said Happy Thanksgiving."

"I'll do that. Bye, Rashad."

Thanksgiving arrived, bright, sunny and eighty degrees. Thank you, California. Rashad sat around a table laden with mouthwatering dishes cooked by someone else's hand. All the women, led by Granny Isabel and his mother Katrina, forbade him from helping.

"You do this for a living," they'd scolded, Granny the loudest. "Let somebody cook for you."

Didn't have to tell Rashad twice. He hung out with the men—uncles, cousins, a couple neighborhood buddies, his granny's gentlemen friend—and basked in the good vibes that flowed from the front porch to the back fence. As happy as they were to see him, it didn't come close to how good it felt to be back home. Last night he'd hung out with his boys. Later, him and Juke would go to his mother's side of the family for their traditional dessert-bar finale.

"You look happy, son," his mom said, once the plates had been filled and Zara had finished a long-winded prayer that Rashad thought might last until Christmas.

"The Midwest must be agreeing with you."

Rashad smiled. "It's going all right."

Granny looked at him through narrowed eyes. "Money's good but doesn't bring out that kind of smile. A woman's causing that."

"Back out my business, Granny."

"Baby, when you get to be my age, all business is my business."

Laughter erupted, wrapped itself around him and squeezed tight. He leaned back and soaked it all in. There was no place like home.

On the ride over to Long Beach for dessert, Rashad caught Juke up on his business plans.

"That sounds cool as fuck, man. For real. Wish there was someplace like that around here."

"From what I've seen, there aren't many places for the twenty- and thirtysomethings. Except for the club, and who's going to those? Nobody in my set."

"Mine either," Juke said.

"Everybody's at home by themselves, interacting online. Putting their talent on TikTok or the 'Gram. Nothing against that. I plan to park mine there, too. But I went to a spoken-word night a week or so back. It felt good to be around other people, other artists, vibing off each other. To get the feedback and hear the applause."

"Did you rap?"

"Nah, I wasn't ready for that."

"What do you mean?"

"Juke, I'm rusty!"

"What the hell? Ra, you'd better get back on your game. Stay ready so you don't have to get ready. Feel me?"

"I feel you, cousin. Ain't a word you spoke a lie."

Long Beach was hella crazy, as expected. Rashad left his aunt's house with a stomach full of too much peach cobbler and sweet potato pie and a doggie bag for breakfast.

"You good, Rashad? I'm a little spent, but we can go somewhere else if you want to. I know you'll only be here for a few days."

"No, we can head to the crib. Before I crash, I want to jot down a couple things."

"Lyrics?"

"Yeah, I—"

His vibrating phone interrupted. A text had come in. He tapped the screen and opened the message.

"Ah, hell."

"What's up? Your girl trippin'?"

"Not my girl. A girl, though. I blocked this chick awhile back. She's made a new profile and is trying to ride my dick again."

"Ugh, dude. Leave out the visuals!"

"I didn't mean it like…"

They both dissolved into laughter.

"I needed that laugh, Juke. 'Cause for real, this ain't funny."

"Sounds like some stalker shit, like you went through with Yasmine."

"Don't remind me."

"Got some info on old girl."

"Do I want to hear it?"

"She's pregnant."

"Well, congratu-damn-lations."

The response was said lightly to cover the hurt. Hearing how his ex and former friend had fully moved on sent the dinner and dessert Rashad had enjoyed roiling around in his gut.

"That news upset my stomach."

"We'll stop by Granny's house. She eats antacids for candy."

Once back at Juke's house, where he was staying, Rashad went to the guest room, got comfortable, and pulled out his book. He intended to forget about the news he heard by focusing on his business, to write down potential names for his bar, and run them past Juke tomorrow. But when he opened his notebook, the page he landed on was an unfinished rhyme inspired by a very special side chick.

Started at a party this part that would rock my world
Where an urban man did a scan on a suburban girl
Played no fool. LA cool. Not my type anyway
Let's ride with the lie locked up inside
Mental games that players play
Then…

Flipping to his back, he looked at the ceiling and watched a video of the past few weeks play in his head. Jamilah, in Anna's basement, wearing silk and a smile. Them side by side in the Side Chic'k kitchen, grooving to Kendrick or Valntna or India. In the living room of Jamilah's condo, too hot and ready to make it down the hall. He flipped to the page where he'd written the second verse.

In the kitchen whipped up getting gripped up for last call
Shorty walked into the room with a badaboom that made giants fall
Tried to play it off like a hungry man turning down a meal
Couldn't fake the funk gotta get a chunk of that whip appeal…

"No one does it like me…"

He went to sleep thinking about Jamilah, dreaming about her whip appeal.

Twenty-Seven

Jamilah yawned, stretched, and rolled over, enjoying a rare Friday when she wasn't headed to Side Chic'k. With both Rashad and Everett out of town for Thanksgiving, and Ed's sciatic nerve flaring up, she made the easy decision to close shop for the weekend. Chances were the crowds would be thin anyway, since Thanksgiving saw more travel than any other holiday. Those still in town were probably enjoying leftovers with family. And quite frankly, as hard as she'd been grinding for the past year, Jamilah could use a break. She worked tonight and tomorrow at Gusto, which she didn't mind at all, because tips would likely be great, and then would have Sunday and Monday off. The only thing she knew about one of those days was that it contained a mani–pedi and a full-body massage.

Dinner with Dad was strained but welcome. She made it clear up front that she didn't want to talk about work. Yes, part of that was to not talk about Rashad, which is why she didn't do as requested and pass on a Happy Thanksgiving message to her father. But mainly it was because she wanted to reconnect with the man that was her hero.

"How's your case going?" she'd asked him once orders were placed and wine had been poured.

"Oh, so your job is off-limits but we can talk about mine?"

"Only if you want to. Or we can talk about how pitiful your team looked in that game earlier today."

"My team?" James relaxed, sat back in his seat. "When did you turn traitor?"

"I love the Chiefs, which wasn't enough to keep them from losing."

"Even the best quarterback can have a bad day."

"Think they'll make it to the Super Bowl again?" Jamilah asked.

"If so, I'll be there with bells on. To answer your question, the case is going all right. Got to bust up a little ring trying to form in the city."

"Drugs? Never mind, I know you can't provide details."

"I can tell you it's not drug related but still deals with addiction."

The wine flowed, and so did conversation, easier with each pour of red. Topics discussed went from sports to family and her Christmas plans. Both trod lightly when talking about Shannon. James had forgiven Jamilah's mom for leaving him, but he'd never forgotten. He wasn't exactly sad the new marriage hadn't worked out either. Once outside, he offered Jamilah a ride home.

"Thanks, Dad, but I already ordered an Uber."

"Sometimes it's hard for me to remember that you're grown and independent."

Jamilah heard the catch in his voice. Watched a look of sadness cross his face. Rarely did her dad show emotion, which made it easy to see him as Superman. Beneath that persona, however, was a human being, one who'd undoubtedly grappled with his own demons. It wasn't something they talked about. Jamilah wished they would.

It suddenly occurred to her that she'd never considered how it felt for him to be an empty nester. After leaving home, she'd remained a large part of his life. For the past twenty-plus years, she'd been his sole responsibility and, as such, his main focus. Dating officers, or men like Walter, kept Jamilah in her father's social circle. Perhaps disliking her romantic choices had less to do with controlling her life and more with her father feeling replaced.

"Daddy," she said, hugging him inside his coat. "No matter how grown and independent I become, you'll always be my first love. I'll always be your baby girl."

She felt her father's arms come around her and squeeze tight. "Feels good to hear that, baby girl."

"I mean every word. I love you."

He kissed her cheek and with a smile that reached his eyes replied, "I love you, too."

On Sunday morning, Jamilah took a long, hot shower. Of course she thought about Rashad, wondered how he felt being back home. She'd hoped to hear from him, but when the days went by with only brief responses to her texts, she decided to focus on trying to make the best of her time off.

Anticipating temporary freedom, Jamilah had called up a few of her own friends who in the past year especially she'd basically abandoned. A miracle as huge as Jesus turning water to wine had occurred when she found out Blair also had the day off. Remembering what Rashad had said about her restaurant's neighborhood, because things Rashad had said were never far from her mind, she suggested the group meet up for food and fun at a restaurant near Eighteenth and Vine. She and Blair decided to arrive ahead of the others, for a much-needed catch-up. Upon seeing each other, the two hugged like friends who hadn't hung out in years.

"So good to see you, Blair."

"Same. It's been forever."

"How's work?"

"Hardest job I've ever done. Love every minute. We might get another Michelin star."

"No doubt thanks to you."

"Absolutely."

They ordered drinks, then got comfortable.

Blair looked around. "Would you believe I've never been here before?"

"Me either."

"That's a shame."

"Right? Working right around the corner. Rashad went on a discovery tour of the neighborhood. Made me feel bad about not patronizing these businesses. I used to frequent a couple places, but it's been years."

"I know Rashad went home for Thanksgiving. Glad y'all worked things out."

"I have you to thank for that. Saved my life. I owe you."

"Don't worry, I'll collect. How's it going with you two outside of the workplace?"

"What do you mean?"

"Don't play coy. When you mentioned his name, your eyes twinkled."

Jamilah laughed. "You're lying."

"Sure, but am I wrong? I've seen real shenanigans go on in these kitchens."

Jamilah knew this was true. An image of her and Rashad's shenanigans in and out of Side Chic'k flashed through her mind. Even now, her body reacted to the memory of his tongue down her throat, his hand searching out her good time with his nature steadily rising. What she'd been two seconds away from doing one fine morning with that man in the pantry made her cheeks burn. Only Shasta arriving early had kept her reputation intact.

She trusted Blair, but when it came to Rashad she wasn't ready to go public, even with a best friend.

"Rashad is hot," she offered instead. "There may be a little flirting going on here and there."

"A little? Are you kidding? You need to loosen up, Jamilah. You're acting way too conservative to own a place called Side Chic'k."

If Blair had seen her in Rashad's basement quarters, her big ass in the air and ponytail bouncing, she'd sing a different tune.

"You're probably right," Jamilah responded, impressed that she'd kept a straight face. "Maybe one day I'll take your advice."

Once the other friends arrived, the party was soon in full swing. Jamilah laughed until she snorted, got caught up on both local and national gossip, rocked to good music, and ate decent food. Only now did Jamilah truly get the magnitude of how hard she'd been working and how little time she'd taken to just chill, to be instead of do, to enjoy life and remember there was more to it than trying to build her tiny empire in the restaurant world.

Back home and slightly tipsy, thoughts of Rashad consumed her. When showering, she imagined his fingers following the water droplets down her body and into her heat. She touched herself as she imagined he would. In bed the power of memory surrounding their lovemaking became its own current that flowed through her body like the blood through her veins.

Almost an hour of tossing and turning later, Jamilah was still wide awake. She reached for her phone and scrolled social media. Finally, she gave up the pretense of caring about the World Wide Web of information and brought up Rashad's contact. California was two hours behind KC. Should she give him a call?

No, texting is better. Her fingers hovered over the keys.

Still missing you xoxo

Sappy and desperate. *Ugh*. Delete.

Can't wait to see you. Hope you're having fun

Read like a note from a mother with a kid at camp. Delete.

The temperatures dropped tonight. Wish you were here to warm me up

Closer, but Jamilah felt that text sounded too safe, too nice. Delete.

She plopped back on the pillow, remembering their conversations just before he left. Cordial but lacking the sparks from those earlier days. At times he'd been romantic, a hug here, a kiss there. But nothing had been the same since she'd poured water on his dreams of setting up shop beside her. She'd unintentionally damaged his ego. This text needed to come with repairs. She had to be bold, send something unexpected, something to get his attention. After a couple of ideas that hovered between babbling and begging, she typed a message that was totally unlike her, yet simple and to the point.

I'm lying in bed imaging your big dick inside me. When are you coming home?

Pause. Deep breath. Send.

Seconds later her phone chirped with a one-word answer—Tomorrow—and three smiley faces.

Jamilah was up bright and early Monday morning, thankful to have a whole day to get ready for Rashad. She planned to set the stage for a major seduction and wanted to show up as her best self. She went to her scheduled mani–pedi, then, wanting to give Rashad the night off as well, arranged a delivery from Gusto, for eight that night. Next, she headed for a salon appointment where she'd told her hairstylist beforehand that she wanted extensions. Jamilah envisioned herself as a siren who, while serving Rashad dessert, would only be wearing long hair.

Three hours later, she turned to view herself in the mirror. Her stylist had showed up and showed out on her hair. She looked like a dark-skinned version of Beyoncé as she rode that horse into the football stadium, her curly extensions brown instead of the singer's platinum choice. She smiled, imagining what Rashad would think when she opened the door. The new hairstyle paired with the short sweater dress she planned on wearing with nothing beneath it, would probably leave him speechless.

"How did I do?"

"When it comes to this hair business, you're the truth!"

They walked to the cash register. Jamilah put in her card, her pin numbers, and added a big tip.

"Ooh, wow, sis. Thank you," the stylist said.

"I love it. Wish I could give you more."

Jamilah waited for the transaction to go through. She watched the stylist push a few buttons.

"Everything okay?"

A moot question, Jamilah knew. In a rare act of using business for personal reasons, she'd used the Side Chic'k account specifically because her personal account was running on fumes.

"It's declined." The stylist's voice was apologetic. "I tried three times."

"That's strange. No problem. It might be some type of fraud alert. My bank is good about that. Hold on."

She rifled through her high-interest highway-robbery credit card choice selections and selected one she prayed wasn't maxed out.

The stylist beamed. "There we go."

Jamilah took the receipt. "Thanks again. Happy holidays."

"You're welcome. Same to you."

Jamilah couldn't wait until getting home for answers. As soon as she reached her car, she tapped her bank app and pulled up the business account.

Her jaw dropped.

The balance that only a few days ago showed a healthy five figures now showed $102.18. There had to be a mistake. She called her personal banker. Ten minutes into the conversation she sat stunned. There'd been no mistake. The Side Chic'k business account had been garnisheed by a relative...good old Uncle Sam.

Still numbed to the point of a zombie state, Jamilah drove toward her father's house on autopilot. Doing so wasn't a conscious thought but rather a knee-jerk reaction. Dad's was where she always went when there was trouble. He opened the door with a frown on his face.

"Jamilah?"

She remembered her hair transformation and managed a weak laugh. "It's me, Daddy."

He backed away to allow her entrance, shaking his head.

Glad for the disaster distraction, Jamilah reached the living room and hid growing anxiety behind a model turn. "Like it?"

"What was wrong with your own hair?"

"Nothing. Just thought I'd switch it up for the holidays."

His look was skeptical. "That the only reason?"

He sat in his favorite recliner. She sat on the couch. "Don't act like me changing hairstyles is different. Remember when I turned thirteen and you let me get my ears pierced and hair braided with those waist-long extensions?"

"I took you out for steak and lobster, your first date. Will never forget it."

"Me either. The picture of us from that night is one of my favorites."

They both sat silent, cherishing the memory.

"We've been through braids, crochets, weaves… I think everything but a full-blown afro."

"Don't tell me that's next."

"Can't promise, Dad. I hear they're making a comeback!"

This got a laugh from him. For the briefest of moments her problem faded, and the friction-causing lion they had yet to discuss loped out of the room.

"What brings you by? Don't get me wrong. You're welcome anytime. But we just had dinner the other night."

Jamilah took a fortifying breath and then jumped off the cliff.

"The restaurant is why I came over, Daddy. Remember that problem I had with the IRS two years ago?"

"Yeah, you set up payments to handle what the accountant missed."

"Well, I'd fallen behind in those payments, and unfortunately the government didn't want to wait for its money. They garnisheed my bank account." She paused, gathered her frayed emotions. "The business is broke. I need your help. It's only temporary," she quickly insisted. "Like I said, business is up. We were already thinking about adding Thursday back to the schedule. I'm cautiously optimistic about being back to full schedule by summer. I also had the website revamped to pull in more catering clients like the ones during Thanksgiving. So...this would be a temporary loan."

"How much are we talking?"

"Five thousand would keep us from having to close the doors, though ten or fifteen would provide a cushion for anything unexpected. I feel safe in saying we could start paying it back in ninety days and return whatever we didn't use."

"You keep saying *we*, as in you and the *chef*, as you call him?"

"As in the team—Rashad, Ed, Shasta, Everett."

"What about a bank loan?"

"I tried that a few months ago."

"Before the account got garnisheed."

"And before business picked up. Now that it has, and with these plans in place, we're all excited about getting back to a full-time business. We all want Side Chic'k to win."

"So do I, baby girl. And I might be able to help you." Her father's demeanor changed. "But not as long as you're working with a felon. I get why you might not understand or agree, but I still don't trust that joker." His voice softened. "If you want me to lend you my money, then you have to be ready to take my advice. I have to have a say about where I'm investing. And you have to accept my terms."

"What are the terms?"

"You're not going to like it, but it's time for you to make a tough decision, baby girl. That smart cook you've got over there or a loan to make sure you have a business to cook for. Because I have to follow my conscience. My mind is telling me that you can't have both."

Jamilah sat stuck between a rock and a hard place. Her daddy had silenced the lion's roar.

Twenty-Eight

The red-eye flight Rashad took from LA back to Kansas City arrived Monday morning. At first, he'd been upset with Zara for that schedule, an ungrateful attitude since the trip was her gift. But the red-eye was nonstop and the lowest fare. His sister figured by eleven o'clock on Sunday night, his visit was basically over anyway. She was right, and the flight wasn't bad at all. Because of the full, tight schedule, however, Rashad hadn't met with Nichole.

After getting his luggage, he took a bus to his car, texted Mr. Turner, and went directly to his office. He liked Nichole but related better with Mr. Turner, who reminded Rashad of a grandfather. Looked a little bit like the actor Morgan Freeman and possessed that same affable personality exhibited in many of the characters Morgan played. From their first meeting, Mr. Turner made it clear that he believed in him. Said he saw something in his eyes that looked like success. Similar words used to come from Rashad's father. The older man had filled a space Rashad hadn't known was empty.

He walked in to a big smile, dap, and shoulder bump as always, then took a seat.

"How's it going, man?"

"No complaints, Mr. Turner."

"Good. Good. How was your Thanksgiving?"

"It was good." Rashad shared highlights from his trip LA. "Reconnected with family, friends."

His local PO gave him a look.

Rashad grinned. "Not like that. I towed the line, Mr. Turner."

"That's what I like to hear. Any updates on the plans to one day open your own business? I really like what you sent so far. Ambitious, but I can see its potential success."

"Like you, everyone likes the idea. All I need is a millionaire looking for somewhere to invest his money."

"Don't we all."

"I thought a friend of mine might become an investor. He's in real estate and has done pretty good."

While hanging out with family, Rashad had considered what Jamilah had used, a cosigner. He had someone in mind, just had to get up enough nerve to ask her. If it happened and she said yes, he'd tell Mr. Turner. Until then, he'd stay quiet. To get turned down would leave him all out of options. No need to jinx this last attempt.

"Yeah, that market is tricky right now. Bad decisions by folk who shouldn't be in power has this country going to hell in a handbasket and no way to jump out. I assume you'll return to Side Chic'k this week?"

"Yeah, on Friday."

"I'm still planning on making it by there. I hear the food is good."

"The food is exceptional."

"Ha! That's the spirit, son. Keep doing your best, and don't let go of your dreams. Believe in yourself. Believe you can make it. Everything's possible when you believe."

Rashad left Mr. Turner's office feeling like he'd attended a holy ghost revival. He reached his car and immediately called Jamilah. The text she'd sent the previous night had both surprised and aroused him. It felt good to know he'd been on her mind. She'd stayed on his, more than he cared to admit. He'd think about her at the oddest times, like when driving to Long Beach, or cruising Slauson, or hanging out with family in LA. How it would be for Jamilah to meet his sister, mama, and especially granny.

Money's good but doesn't bring out that kind of smile. A woman's causing that.

Granny was right. Even though things between them had gotten shaky lately, Jamilah did make him smile. So much so that their meeting time, seven o'clock, now seemed forever away. It was early and he should probably go home, but since she was off on Mondays maybe they could hang out all day together.

He tapped her name on his screen and got voice mail. He ended the call and sent a text instead of leaving a message.

Back in town. Not far from you. Want to meet up?

With his plans for Jamilah to light up his life on hold, and no desire to spend the day at home alone, he called Leon, who welcomed him to stop by. He'd mentioned his plans but wanted to go into detail about the gaming room he envisioned and make Leon part of the team.

As soon as Rashad bounded up the steps, Leon stood at the door.

"Glad you hurried up, brothah," he said, as a chill caused his teeth to rattle.

"With all that good weather in LA, I'm surprised you came back here."

"Wasn't easy."

Even as he said those words, Rashad knew they weren't true. Jamilah's text had him so fired up he could have flown back without a plane, just on that feel-good energy.

Three hours after arriving at Leon's house, Rashad had a hard time leaving. An ecstatic Leon, pumped from the possibility of focusing on what he loved and getting paid for it, had peppered him nonstop with questions, comments, suggestions, and ideas. In between, they'd played a couple games, listened to hip-hop, and eaten Blair's delicious leftovers.

"I gotta go, man," Rashad said, this time not only standing up but heading purposefully toward the door. "Don't worry. You don't have to present your plans tomorrow. Right now these plans are just that. There's a long road between dream and reality."

"That's okay. I'm still going to start working on it. My ideas are already crystalizing. I need to get in that building ASAP and take a look at whatever room we'll be using."

"Slow your roll, QNA. And keep what we discussed between you and me."

"Rashad, seriously, I can't thank you enough for including me. Don't worry. Nobody's going to steal this genius idea."

He took Rashad's hand and began to pump it. If Rashad didn't know better, he'd swear Leon got misty-eyed.

"I've been looking for work. It's shit for jobs right now, man. I've either got too much experience, too little, or not the right kind. It was starting to get to me, I'm not going to lie. So even for this light at the end of a tunnel…man, just thank you."

Rashad wasn't prepared for Leon's next move, long, gangly arms wrapped around him.

"Bro! Chill out with the emotions. I asked you to be my business partner, not my girlfriend. Damn!"

Rashad shoved the Quiet Nerd Assassin away with a smile, then held out his fist for a more manly fist, shoulder bump and slap on the back, the unspoken trifecta of gestures between men like him.

"Nah, man, seriously, I understand. Keep working on your plans. Keep believing it will happen. Everything's possible when we believe."

On that Thomas Turner–inspired note, Rashad practically ran to his car, actually laughing out loud. He headed home for a shower, maybe a quick nap. There was no proof he'd pull off having his own place, but he believed it could happen. He tried to remember the last time he'd felt this pumped, this motivated, this full of possibility.

He couldn't think of one.

He'd checked his phone a couple times. Jamilah hadn't called or texted back. It was almost three o'clock. Before leaving Leon's driveway, he tried again. Still no answer.

It was unusual to not be able to reach her. Had she changed her mind about the plans for tonight? He sent a text.

Hey boss lady, you okay? Want to talk about tonight real quick. Am I cooking? Going out? Hit me back.

He'd almost made it home when his phone rang.

Finally.

"I was about to send law enforcement out to look for you," Rashad joked. "You know it would have to be a serious situation, because I don't rock with them like that."

Silence. And something else…a sniffle? No.

"I was joking, Boss Lady." He looked at the phone. Still connected. "Jamilah. What's wrong?"

"Dinner's canceled."

"What? I didn't hear you."

Jamilah cleared her throat. "There's no need to come over for dinner. And don't bother showing up for work this week either."

WTH? A bad feeling passed over Rashad's body like somebody had died.

"Why wouldn't I come to work?"

"Something happened. I lost a lot of money. I'm probably gonna have to shut down."

"Sit right there. Don't move. I'm coming over."

Twenty-Nine

Jamilah thought she'd run out of tears, but the sight of Rashad as she opened the door reopened the fountain.

"Hey, come on, now," he said, taking her into his arms and running his hands over the Rapunzel-like hair that, after lounging on the couch and the bed, made her look less like Beyoncé and more like someone whose finger had met an electrical outlet.

"Shh. Come on. Let's sit down."

They did. Rashad walked into her kitchen and found a bottle of water in the fridge. He went to the bathroom, ran cold water over a washcloth, and brought both back to her.

"Here, wash your face."

Jamilah took the facecloth and breathed slowly as she held it over her eyes.

"That's it. Now drink this water."

She dutifully obeyed.

He reached over, gently lifted her chin with his fingers, and used his other hand to swipe away an errant tear.

Jamilah walked over to a box of tissues on the bar counter. She walked into the bathroom. Rashad heard the nose-blow, a flush, and a door opening. All the while he had one question.

What happened?

She sat down, reopened the bottle, and took a long swig. Rashad remained quiet, giving her time to collect herself.

When she began speaking, her voice was soft. She looked away from him, toward the large-paned windows, unconsciously wringing her hands as she spoke.

"I had an ongoing issue with the IRS. Worked out a payment arrangement. Fell behind when business slowed. They garnished the business account. Left Side Chic'k with a whopping one hundred bucks."

"Without any notice?"

"They sent them. I just hadn't seen them. I'd signed up to go paperless, and somehow they didn't make it to my main inbox. They went to another file."

"Damn, babe. I'm sorry that happened to you."

"Me, too." She took another swallow of water.

"As bad as having all my money stolen is, that isn't the worst thing that happened today."

"What could be worse than that?"

"My father's ultimatum. The business or you."

"You told him about us?"

"I was distraught, Rashad, but not crazy." She described the visit with her father. "I think he was secretly okay with what happened. Almost as if getting his way was the most important thing. He doesn't know you but never liked you. Always wanted you gone. All he saw was your paperwork, never Rashad the person. Getting garnished swung the ball of power back in his court. To keep my business I have to play by his rules."

Rashad took her hand. "You know there's no love lost on this end regarding your father. But still, cut him some slack."

"Like he cut you some?"

"You're his daughter. He's trying to protect you. He's not used to being questioned. As law enforcement, he's used to his commands being followed. I'm a threat because you went against him and took my side. You've bruised his ego. Men have big egos."

Jamilah gave him a look and offered her first real smile of the afternoon. To Rashad, it was like sunshine on a cloudy day.

"We can be stubborn. We don't like being wrong. But guess what? The man he wanted to run out of your life might just be the one who can help you save your business."

"How?"

"I don't know. But I believe I can, so it has to happen."

"Rashad, to keep my business, you have to get fired. Why would you help me when you need a job?"

"Because I care about you, Jamilah." He reached up and tenderly tucked an errant tendril behind her ear. "And I'm ride-or-die with those I care about."

The room became silent. Rashad jumped off the couch. "Have you eaten?"

"No. Not hungry."

"I'm starved, baby. I saved my appetite for tonight, so now there's a hole in my stomach."

When Jamilah remained silent, Rashad got up and did what cooks do. Went scrounging around in a seldom-used kitchen and made magic with eggs, cheese, and a can of mixed veggies.

Jamilah sat wondering what had just happened. His declaration of caring had left her breathless. The quick mood shift left her speechless and confused.

He brought Jamilah's plate to where she sat. Watching her scarf down his food gave him immense pleasure. "Changing your mind about food in a can?"

"I never said I was against all canned goods. We've got them in the pantry. I just said I prefer fresh, organic, and locally grown."

Jamilah finished her plate, set it on the coffee table, and drank the second water he'd brought her. "I wasn't hungry until the smell of your food made my mouth water. I hadn't eaten all day.

I appreciate you coming over, Rashad. I was in a dark place.
You cheered me up. Fed me. How can I thank you?"

"I can show you better than I can tell you. Come here."

She scooted over to close the distance between them. He ran
his hands through her tresses and began kissing her all over her
face. The soft, measured foreplay, like banked embers, quickly
roared into a flame. Rashad pulled off his T-shirt, then stood to
remove his jeans. Jamilah followed suit, throwing her sweater
and yoga pants on top of his pile.

He laid her on the couch, kissed her with passion, his hips
matching the swirling motion of his tongue. Jamilah spread
her legs to accommodate him, ran her hands up and down his
back. She grabbed his hard ass and squeezed. It was as though
a muscle there was connected to his manhood. His penis grew
faster than a lying Pinocchio's nose.

Feeling his girth, her lips quivered and became slick with
dew. He shifted for better access to her pussy. Jamilah had a
different idea. She grabbed his dick, kissed his thick, sensitive
sac. He hissed, then sighed, giving in to the pleasure. She slid to
her knees and employed the same techniques he'd used on her
that first night. Kissed his chest. Tugged his nipples. Outlined
his six-pack with her tongue. Teased the hair outlining his sex,
while massaging his penis into a masterpiece resembling steel.

"Hmm."

She kissed the tip, then sucked him into her mouth. His hips
created a rhythm of their own, bringing him in and out of her
wetness. Her mouth became a vacuum, her lips delicious friction. He grabbed fistfuls of hair and directed her actions. Only
sheer will and honed discipline kept him from exploding.

"My turn." His voice was raspy, a near growl as he pulled
her from the couch, picked her up, and carried her to a wall.
Using it as an anchor, he raised her high, then slid her wet
flower down on his thick stem. Like salt and pepper. Eggs and
bacon. Shrimp and grits. A perfect pairing.

Jamilah's world shattered while pinned against the wall. He

continued the welcome assault, pounding and thrusting, until there were no more juices. He led them to the bathroom. They took a shower together, then went to her bed where, after just toweling off, he made her wet again. He eagerly lapped her up. Tickled her ass, his lips and tongue doing things that Jamilah had never experienced.

"Rashad! Oh my God, please!"

He lay down and directed her to climb on top. "Ride me, baby."

Jamilah did as commanded. She twerked on his pole, bounced up and down, with no idea the vision of loveliness she made. Breasts jiggled. Hips did a slow grind on his heat. Long, curly tresses tickled him everywhere.

After several minutes of a slow sensual dance performed on his pole, Rashad heard Jamilah's breath catch in her throat. Her gyrations increased. The bouncing intensified. Her mouth went slack. Soft *oh*s kept emitting from her throat until her muscles clenched, her body almost in suspended animation before a powerful orgasm sent her spiraling. She collapsed beside him, her position perfect to perform his finale. He lifted her leg, entered one final time and within minutes claimed his own release.

They lay spent, breathing heavily, sweaty, satisfied. When she opened her eyes, they met his, already staring at her.

"What?" she asked, running a hand through his locs.

"We have a problem, Boss Lady."

"The money. I know."

"Not that. I think I'm catching feelings for you. That wasn't supposed to happen."

"That's what you meant earlier by *ride-or-die*?"

He nodded. Kissed the tip of her nose.

"I think Daddy suspects what I haven't acknowledged. I'm catching something, too."

Their laughter turned into a sensuous kiss. The atmosphere shifted. Something between them did, too. Whatever this was they were doing was forming into something, beginning to take on a name. *Relationship? Partnership? Friendship? Soul mates?*

Jamilah didn't know which name to give it, but one thing was for sure. Whatever this was that was being created between them was something her father couldn't control.

"Thanks again for coming over," she whispered.

"Thank you for the invitation and such an enthusiastic welcome home." He cuddled her against him and added, "I like your hair."

Thirty

Rashad barely slept that night. The next morning after leaving Jamilah's house he jumped on the phone.

A groggy voice answered. "Rashad?"

"Sorry for calling so early, Zara. I waited as long as I could."

"Did something happen? What's going on?"

"I'm dealing with a situation over here and need your help."

"What kind of help?"

"A loan."

A beat of silence and then, "How much?"

"Five bands."

"Five thousand dollars?" Zara shouted. His sister was wide awake now.

"What kind of trouble have you gotten into?"

"No trouble, sis. Seriously, everything's good. It's where I work, Side Chic'k. The business I told you and Mama about."

"You want me to lend you money to lend to the person that's supposed to pay you? I know it's early, brother, but make it make sense."

Rashad gave Zara the rundown on what had happened. He also shared his idea for a start-up next door.

"This time next year, Zee, both spots will be jumping! We just need a little help getting over the hump."

"I can give you something, Rashad, but I don't have five thousand just lying around."

"What about taking out a loan, or cosigning for me?"

"No can do. Jason and I are saving up to buy a house. This is Cali, where homes cost more than some countries' GNP. I can't upset my debt-to-income ratio. I've got to maintain my credit score."

Rashad was discouraged, but he hid it from Zara. "That's cool. I get it. How much can you spare?"

"Five hundred, maybe a thousand. Let me check and call you back."

Zara called back before Rashad could step in the shower. It wasn't good news. Her fiancé had put a quick ix-nay to the oan-lay. Said they had no money to spare.

"All that belief bullshit," he mumbled, feeling dejected. Everyone said hard work paid off, but how long did it take? Twenty, thirty years? In his old life, he could clear twenty thousand in a week, ten days tops. That was no longer an option. Neither was failure. He needed a job. Jamilah needed a break. Leon was waiting on the green light to design a hit game room. Young men in the system needed a chance. Mr. Turner believed Rashad could provide it.

"This has got to work," he insisted to whatever entity listened. "I believe in myself. I believe in this dream. It's got to happen. Something's got to give!"

Rashad took a long, hot shower. His mind never shut off. He stood there, water streaming, imagining his dream realized. Saw the black walls, gold lighting, rugged interior. A long bar, small stage, enough space for dancing. Closed-off game room with high-speed internet and plenty of outlets. Rashad remembered Leon's excited face and broke into a smile. Reaching for the shampoo, he imagined the menu. Stuff the patrons could eat with their hands. Reasonably priced but pulling a profit. There wasn't a place quite like what he envisioned anywhere that he knew of.

Just a chance, he prayed to whatever God might hear him, while toweling off and heading back into the bedroom. He heard vibration mode and reached for the phone.

Another notification from the dating site. He'd meant to block his fling's new profile, but with all that was going on he hadn't had time. He clicked on the site, blocked the new profile, deleted his profile all together, then angrily tossed the phone on his bed.

Pacing, he racked his brain for an answer to Jamilah's dilemma. He'd left another message with Tyson, and even hit up his uncle Melvin whom he'd rarely spoken with since getting released. No responses yet. Frustrated, he went upstairs to grab what for him was a rare beer from the fridge. He returned to a missed call from Tyson, and remembered the bad taste their last conversation left in his mouth.

"Yo, Tyson. Sorry I missed your call."

"No problem. Got a question, though."

"What's that?"

"Do you believe in miracles?"

"Hell, yeah."

"Good. 'Cause I got one that just might be headed your way."

Jamilah reached for the brush to tame her long curls. She was meeting her father at the bank and wanted to look like a business owner. He was transferring money out of his IRA, something that he could have done over the phone without her present. But for some reason, he wanted to handle the transaction in person and wanted her there.

After securing her hair in a high ponytail, she reached for a rarely worn navy pantsuit. It had been a splurge purchase when business was high, a light Merino wool that breathed and stayed cool, paired with a white, sleeveless top and gold jewelry. She returned to the bathroom to apply a light powder, a touch of mascara, and gloss on her lips.

"Be happy," she told her sad face. "Side Chic'k is still standing."

Rashad would land on his feet. He hadn't left her. He cared about her beyond the restaurant. The thought brought tears that she quickly blinked away. He was her ride-or-die for real!

Jamilah walked into the living room and gathered her purse and keys. Her eye caught on a trinket she'd held on to from the Thanksgiving dinner with her father. Was it just a few weeks ago when they'd enjoyed fine dining, seemed to bury the hatchet, and told each other how much love was still there? Hadn't she told him that, no matter what, she'd always be his daughter? Was that declaration not enough to restore his trust in her, to know that she was smart enough to not do something dumb?

Evidently not. Time to get what felt like blackmail over and done. She reached for the tote carrying a change of clothes. If the transaction went smoothly, she could make sure her personnel were all set for Friday and still work her server shift.

The bank wasn't far, ten minutes away. She lucked upon a nearby place to park, got out, and fed the meter. She didn't see her father's car and assumed he'd parked in the garage. Taking a breath, she mounted the stairs, reached the door, and pulled the gold handle.

Her phone rang. She stepped inside, quickly pulled it out of her purse, and read the screen.

"Hey, Rashad."

"Jamilah, where are you?"

"I can't talk now. I'm at the bank. My dad—"

"Has he completed the transaction?"

"Rashad, what are you asking me—"

"The money. Has he given you the loan?"

"No. I just got here. I'm going in now."

"Don't do it, Jamilah. I've got you."

"Got me? What do you mean?"

"Is five thousand enough to keep Side Chic'k going for, like, a month or so? There's an opportunity for how you might get more funding. All legit, Jamilah. Nothing illegal. I'll explain later, Boss Lady. Just please, if you want to stay out of your pop's prison, don't take that check!"

Jamilah stared at her now-blank screen. She looked up to see her dad walking toward her.

"We're waiting on you," he said, in greeting. "Let's go."

She didn't move. Couldn't. Rashad's message had frozen her on the spot.

"Come on, now, baby girl. My friend managed to squeeze me in, but he has another meeting."

"I'm sorry, Daddy. I can't."

His brow creased. "Can't what?"

"Um, something's come up. An emergency. I've got to go now and figure it out."

"Figure what out? Who was on the phone?"

Jamilah heard the questions but didn't have time to answer. She was off and running, already halfway down the steps.

When she arrived at the restaurant, Rashad stood in her parking space. She jumped out. He rushed over, pulled her into a bear hug, and held on tight.

"Rashad, I can't breathe."

"Oh, sorry, baby."

"What's going on?"

"It's crazy, Jamilah. Come on. I'll explain everything."

Rashad sat her down and did just that. Told her about a friend named Tyson with business ties in Las Vegas. About a partner who'd met two young Asian guys with more money than they knew how to spend. How'd they got talking about music and hip-hop, and gaming and tech. One thing led to another, and Tyson broached the subject about becoming investors. Which led to Rashad spending over two hours on a conference call, and getting five thousand dollars wired in good faith toward their future plans.

"This is overwhelming," Jamilah said when he finished. "If

they're interested in helping start up your business, how can you use that money for mine?"

"That's the crazy part, Jamilah. It's not so much about what business I'm pushing. These guys believe in me! First off, Tyson can sell life insurance to a dead man. He obviously talked me up before the call. Told them about my life as a chef. My music and connections. I'm still reeling myself from everything that happened. They're all flying up next week to help me figure it out."

Jamilah stilled, even as her heart began an erratic thump in her chest.

"A week?" she asked softly, her nerves stretched to the limit and feeling like they'd break if she yelled. "I don't have a week, Rashad. That money is needed now."

"It's already been wired to Anna's bank. I made sure that she got it before I called you."

"How did this happen?" she asked him.

Rashad shrugged. "Tyson called it a miracle the way all this went down. And you know what, Boss Lady? I believe him."

Thirty-One

"I've got to go, Rashad. I've got to try to reach Daddy."

"I understand." He got up and helped her into her coat. "Stay in touch so I know you're okay. Call me if you need me."

"Thanks for everything."

"You're welcome."

Hours had passed since Jamilah had run away as her father hurled questions at her back. The dust of anxiety had settled. Her adrenaline flow had returned to normal. Now, with the catastrophe of potential bounced payments averted, and Side Chic'k on solid ground for at least thirty days, the gravity of the decision she'd made weighed as heavily as a cement shawl, her jewelry an albatross around her neck. In the light of temporary solvency, the magnitude of her decision and its possible consequences loomed. She'd given the wrong impression for all the right reasons. Once again, in the battle of Daddy versus Rashad, Rashad was the victor.

She hadn't left her dad hanging completely. Once they'd driven to Anna's house, picked up a cashier's check, and deposited it in a new account Jamilah created (just in case the IRS decided to spin the block), she'd sent him a carefully worded text. The message wasn't entirely true but not a whole lie ei-

ther, rather filled with creative license, the veil of open interpretation, and a generous amount of plain old CYA.

OMG, Daddy. First of all I'm okay. Please don't worry. So sorry
for all the confusion, having to cancel the meeting and my
abrupt departure. That call I was on in the bank doorway was
from an investor who wants to act as a silent partner and adviser to Side Chic'k. I had to move quickly to secure the arrangement, one of ongoing financial support as needed, for
the next few months. You have done so much for me and this
business. I'm forever in your debt and didn't want to add to
what I already owe you.

Please send me the name of the bank manager so that I can
offer a personal apology for having to cancel. I would also like
to meet with you for lunch or dinner (my treat!) to give you a
more detailed explanation of what's going on. Love you so
much, Daddy. Always your baby girl.

Technically, Side Chic'k did have new investors. Jamilah
hadn't met them yet, but a couple of young Asian men with
money had sent a good faith installment to Rashad for business expansion. He'd generously decided to expand the business already in operation, upgrading his status from head chef
to partner. Silent, because this change in status would not be
shared with her father. For the next few months, or until Side
Chic'k's financial picture stabilized, Rashad had also offered
ongoing financial support by funneling any extra money made
from his growing catering business into the Side Chic'k cof-
fers. A detailed record would be kept and paid back with no
interest at whatever time the business could afford it. His real
estate friend, Tyson, would be their adviser, along with another friend of his who also happened to be a CPA. Jamilah
loved her dad immensely, and remembering that vulnerable
moment she'd witnessed on Thanksgiving outside the swanky

steak house, she felt uncomfortable with being less than truthful. But given his immovable stance regarding Rashad, and her growing love for the man he despised, it was the best comprise Jamilah could offer.

So far, she'd received no response.

She pulled up to her father's well-manicured community. It wasn't the home she'd grown up in. Five years ago, her father had downsized and moved into a newly built grouping of single-level duplexes, all laminated wood, stainless steel, vaulted ceilings, and low HOA fees. His truck wasn't in the driveway. He rarely parked in the garage. Still, Jamilah exited her car and knocked on his door.

No answer.

She returned to her car, retrieved a Post-it note and quickly scribbled a simple message.

Stopped by. Please call. Jamilah.

For the next two days, Rashad practically lived at her house. When she wasn't serving at Gusto and he wasn't on a catering gig, they were at her dining room table mapping out strategies for growing Side Chic'k's business. She also took the time to really listen to Rashad's plans about how he wanted to expand their enterprise—his words—by opening up a place next door. One night, after releasing stress through a round of lovemaking, she felt especially honored when he asked her to help with a possible name for the venue.

"I want it to be something that reflects my experience," he told her, as they cuddled under a supersoft throw. "That will resonate with brothahs who've been in the system and sound cool to our friends who haven't."

"What about the music and gaming, do you want that in there somewhere, too?"

"Would love to give a shout-out to hip-hop, a lifeline to so many in the culture. When we rap, it's called *spitting*. When we write, they're called *bars*. I've been playing around with those ideas a little bit."

"Let's hear what you've got."

He turned to a page in his book. "Bars is the first name I came up with. It's catchy, with a double entendre, which is a quality ingredient of a good rap lyric."

"I like that too," Jamilah agreed. "But it's rather general."

"And people might think it's just a drinking establishment. Plus, there are so many bars that if I'm just called Bars, then potential customers could end up anywhere."

Jamilah leaned over to look at his list. "Prison Poets, Rashad? Um, no."

"Ha! Heard. What about Felon Foodies?"

"Ugh! Sounds like a place only for criminals. I couldn't cop a meal.

"Music and Mayhem? Now, that's a possibility."

Rashad squeezed her shoulder. "I thought so, too. In fact, it's my favorite so far."

Jamilah sat up. "Hey! I've got the perfect choice—Main Man!"

From Rashad? Blank stare.

"My place is Side Chic'k. Yours is Main Man. Get it?"

"Unfortunately," he deadpanned.

She laughed. "Heard."

As she entered the kitchen on December's first Friday, Rashad's greeting was full of optimism, his overall attitude these days.

"What's up, Boss Lady?" Rashad pulled a couple chicken packs from the fridge.

Heading over to grab an apron, she stopped midstride. "What the heck is that?"

"These," he said holding a large pack of drumsticks, "are what the chicken runs with. These," he said of the huge pack of wings, "are how they fly."

"We prefer to buy and break down the whole bird. Blair says it—"

"Who said?" Rashad placed a hand to his ear. "Who?"

"It keeps the meat fresher. And I believe it's cheaper, too."

"Negative on both counts. What keeps the meat fresh is buying less more often, which means shopping more, and knowing where to shop to get the best buys. Now, I thought we'd resolved this whole thing about the kitchen when I tossed out Blair's bible."

Jamilah's eyes went wide. "You did what?"

"Tossed it out." He waited for impact. "Out of the kitchen and into the storage closet."

"I can't stand you," Jamilah jokingly admitted, even as she allowed herself to be pulled into his arms. "You get on my nerves."

"You love me on your nerves, and a few other places."

"Ha-ha."

He kissed her forehead. "Whose kitchen is this?"

Jamilah knew where this was going. He'd found ways to get her to use his rap name since opening up about that part of his life and giving her a peek into some of the contents of his precious rhyme book. She didn't have time to stroke his big ego—his definition, not hers.

"Okay, come on. Let's cook."

He refused to let her go. "Whose kitchen?"

"Ra God's kitchen," she mumbled.

"I can't hear you. Whose kitchen?"

"Ra God's kitchen! Now, let me go."

They fell into the comfortable camaraderie they enjoyed when working side by side. With about thirty minutes until the rest of the crew arrived, Rashad spoke again.

"You heard from your pops yet?"

"No, unfortunately." Said with a sigh.

"Give him time. He'll come around."

"I don't know, Rashad. What I did was pretty awful."

"You really feel that way?"

"No, but he does. I'd bet the biz on that."

For a few moments, the sounds of smooth jazz and neo-soul filled the room as they prepped and pondered individually.

"Boss Lady, I've been thinking."

"That's always dangerous."

Rashad laughed. "I've gone over everything about your business. Inventory. Operations. I think I've figured out your problem."

"What problem?"

He made a sound, a cross between a tsk and a breath. "All of them."

Jamilah walked to the pantry and gathered the condiments that would turn regular chili beans into barbecued bliss. She tamped down the anger rising from his audacity. The guy hadn't been at her business three months, and now he was the expert on running it?

Okay, there was that little thing about mistakes and accounting and the IRS. And being garnisheed and the falling-out with her father and Rashad's five thousand acts of largess that had kept the lights on and the doors open.

But still.

"You want to hear my suggestions?" he asked when she returned.

"Do I have to?"

"You need to listen to somebody."

"Excuse me?"

"I didn't stutter. You've got a good thing going here. Clever name, clear marketing concept, and me cooking some of the best food in the city, maybe anywhere."

"If you must say so yourself."

"Damn straight. If I'm not for me, how can I expect anyone else to be?"

He had a point.

"You just need to tweak a few things here and there. I have a plan."

"You have a plan?"

"Yeah."

"*You* have a plan for improving *my* business?"

"If you haven't noticed already, I'm pretty good at making plans and getting shit done. I put together something, kinda like a business plan."

"A plan for my business, the one I created, kept running through blood, sweat, and tears, and worked myself into exhaustion over."

"Yeah, that one." He washed and dried his hands, walked over to a leather backpack and pulled out his phone. "It's brief, just a couple pages. I'll text it to you."

Jamilah crossed her arms, incredulity replacing anger. "You're serious. You want to text me your new-and-improved business idea for how to pull my restaurant out of the two-days-a-week toilet and restore my business to a level that you don't even know."

"I just sent it to you," Rashad spoke to her back. "You're welcome!"

Jamilah exited the kitchen carrying a tray of condiments for the tables, her chagrin at his boldness quickly replaced by the humor of the situation.

Rashad was a certified trip. She'd never met anyone like him. Cocky, all alpha, a natural born leader. But if one could back up their self-aggrandizing comments, was it boasting or pride? Rashad was right. She did need to make changes. He had followed through on a dream that could very well become reality. Jamilah didn't want to consider his suggestions. She hated the feeling of him being right. It was a petty and childish position. But she didn't want to budge.

The crew arrived. They opened for business. The room filled up quickly. As she walked an order to the kitchen, the tinkling doorbell announced another set of customers. She clipped the order to the order wheel, then returned to the front where a group women stood waiting. While reaching for the one-page, laminated menus to give them, she was struck with a discomforting revelation.

She was acting exactly like her dad.

"Good afternoon, ladies. Three for lunch?"

"Is this where that cook Rashad works?" one of them asked.

"Yes," Jamilah offered, after a slight hesitation that didn't make sense. It was common to tout the chef of a restaurant known for good food. His pic added to the website had helped to boost business. So why was she feeling some kind of way about their obvious interest? They might drool over him at lunchtime. But most nights, he was in her bed.

The second lady in the trio, wearing loud colors, lots of makeup, and flaming red hair said, "Can you have him come out? He, um, catered a lunch for my mother's work. She said he's cute and single and from California. And that I need to meet him."

The third woman said nothing. Just flipped back blond-tinted tresses and kept looking toward the kitchen.

Jamilah scanned the dining room, offering no response to their overt thirstiness. There were few seats left.

"Would y'all like to sit at the stools along the wall? I don't think we have a table available right now. As you can see, we're really busy, but I'll let Rashad know you're here."

The woman who'd inquired about him peered toward the kitchen, then questioned her friends. "I guess that's all right. Why'd you choose such a small place for your business?"

Jamilah swallowed a mouth full of sarcastic responses, smiled, and answered, "Because it's chic."

After taking the women's orders, Jamilah entered the kitchen. "A group of admirers await your presence, great king," she teased, before placing the order on the wheel.

"Why? They just got here. Haven't tasted my food."

"You catered a workplace lunch and were highly recommended."

Rashad broke out into a wide smile. "That's what's up."

Shasta delivered their drinks. Jamilah helped with their meals. "I passed on your request to the chef," she told them. "He'll be out shortly."

A short time later, Rashad passed her on the way to the table. She watched as the one who'd been the most silent sat up straighter in her chair. She was pretty, Jamilah admitted. A manufactured beauty, but it worked. Jamilah discreetly eyed their interaction as she moved around the room. All of them flirted, but when the quiet one spoke Rashad looked visibly uncomfortable.

After he returned to the kitchen, the women left in a whirlwind, the kind that could pick up a house and bring it down on a wicked witch. Jamilah followed Rashad into the kitchen.

"What the heck was that about?"

"Nothing."

"Didn't look like nothing."

"A misunderstanding, that's all."

"At one point, the conversation looked pretty serious."

"She was mad because I'm not into her."

"Were you ever?"

No comment.

"Is there something going on there? Wait, don't answer. It's none of my business. But I do have to give you this heads-up, Rashad. Having side chicks wreak havoc at Side Chic'k is the last thing we need."

Thirty-Two

Remembering how it felt when Brigit betrayed him, Rashad didn't wait to come clean. That night, as he and Jamilah prepared for bed, he told her the whole story, about swiping right on a girl whose name he still couldn't remember.

"I was frustrated, angry," he finished. "Your dad's words still in my ear. Fresh out of a job. No plans to see you again. It was before we got together, Jamilah. Casual sex, nothing more."

"Did you use a condom?"

"Of course."

"How'd she know you worked at Side Chic'k?"

"My cards are all over this city. Word gets around." Rashad rubbed a hand through his locs. "She's mad because I blocked her on the app before eventually completely deleting my account. Hopefully today she got the message. I don't want her. Period."

There was a long pause before Jamilah answered. "I have no right to be angry about what happened that night. Emotions were charged for all of us, and we hadn't been intimate. But I guess it's time to have"—she made air quotes—"the conversation. To define exactly what this is.

"So…what is it?"

Rashad thought for a moment. His eyes bore into hers. "Complicated."

An hour and some change later, they'd reached an understanding. Because theirs was a multifaceted situation, with both personal and professional ties, they agreed to a friendship-with-monogamous-benefits label. If either had an outside itch that needed scratching by a side chick or rooster, they'd let the other know beforehand and give them the choice to fly the romantic coop.

They would make their business partnership more official. When Rashad spoke to Tyson about next week's visit, he also mentioned wanting to discuss with the investors the five-thousand-dollar investment he'd made into Jamilah's already-established venue. A full-blown explanation had already been mapped out on why the businesses working in tandem would benefit all involved.

"Are you ready?" Jamilah asked Rashad when Thursday arrived and he prepared to drive to KC's Country Club Plaza.

"Born that way," Rashad replied, with more verve than he felt. "You heading to Side Chic'k to start preparations?"

"With a stop at the Young Family Farm on Wayne and the farmers market. I want everything to be perfect."

Rashad leaned in, squeezed Jamilah's booty. "I'd say you've got that covered."

She tucked down the collar of the casual black linen button-down that Rashad paired with his signature black jeans. His locs were freshly twisted, his face clean-shaven but for a small goatee.

"You look amazing."

"Wish me luck."

Jamilah offered Rashad a sweet kiss on the cheek. "Give 'em hell, baby. You got this."

Rashad bumped Kendrick all the way to the meeting. By the time he arrived, he was cool, calm, and collected. Life had prepared him for this moment. He believed it would happen.

He deserved it all. And at the end of the day, everything would be all right.

He reached the lobby, checked the signage, then headed down the hall to the designated meeting location. He tapped on the door, then opened it. His eyes landed on Tyson, who stood immediately and offered a welcoming smile.

"There's the man!" he said, coming forward to offer a soul brother's handshake. "Good to see you again, Ra God—my bad, Rashad."

"Likewise, Tyson. Good to be here."

"Let me introduce you around the table. This is my real estate partner, Jimmy. Our accountant, Steve. And our Asian brothers here to make unique yet sound investments and big money, Yuchen and Bo."

Rashad rounded the table shaking hands, looking each man in the eye.

"It's a pleasure, gentlemen," he said, after taking the seat Tyson offered. "I look forward to creating a lot of currency with you brothahs. Thanks for taking time out of your busy schedules to meet with me."

"It is our pleasure," Yuchen replied. "We like your idea. Hip-hop, gaming, and food. Good combination."

Rashad nodded at a slender young man with expressive eyes who looked nineteen but who Tyson had told him was actually thirty-four. Bo, the shorter, rounder, more serious looking of the two was twenty-six but looked older than Yuchen.

"Tell us more about what was in your proposal," Bo said.

Rashad was meticulous as he laid it all out. First, he touted the unique concept of Side Chic'k, and how his corner connected business would help boost the whole block. After sharing a bit of Eighteenth and Vine's rich history, he presented the plans for his baby. He excitedly shared how hip-hop, gaming, and food could intersect, how one could enhance the other, and how now was the perfect time to strike with a concept that no one else had.

"Our generation has gotten away from social gathering," Rashad finished. "I don't want to separate gamers from their pleasure but give them a trendy, interactive, social environment to have a good time."

The men were clearly interested and asked several questions. About PR and marketing, budgets, and competition. Profit margins and equipment. Renovations and time frames. Tyson's partner Jimmy, who'd flown in with Tyson to scout commercial properties to flip, chimed in as well. For the next few hours, the men strategized and organized and finally came up with a plan that was both workable and agreeable to all involved.

"Starting slow and then ramping up makes sense. Conservative budget. Minimum reno. Heavy concentration on targeted marketing. And brothah," Tyson finished, "I love the whole community involvement and rehabilitation idea about employing felons and others who find it hard to get a job."

"That's my favorite part, too," Steve admitted, a fact that might have surprised those who judged by appearance. "And honestly, that's the part of your story that brought me on board."

Steve could have been stamped *Made in the USA*, just like baseball, hot dogs, apple pie, and beer. He wore a CPA's uniform: plaid button-down shirt, khaki pants, and sports jacket. Reddish-brown hair, sparkling green eyes, skin bronzed from an afternoon with eighteen holes. House in the suburbs. White picket fence. Two kids and a dog. The American dream. But his life hadn't always looked like that. His dad had been a heroin addict. Overdosed when Steve was a teen. Mother made ends meet as a dancer on the Strip. Steve had pulled himself out of the gutter with willpower and grit. Used a knack for numbers and near photographic memory to become top-tier in his field. Instead of forgetting where he came from, he remembered to reach back with a hand to help other souls climb out of hell's grip.

"Is your PO still offering assistance?" Tyson asked.

Bo interrupted. "What's a PO?"

"Parole officer," Rashad said. "A person one reports to after being given an early release from prison.

"Mr. Turner is very enthusiastic about these plans," he continued, answering Tyson's question. "He's already speaking with members of the judicial system and city hall on ways I might be able to partner with some of their programs."

Steve leaned forward. "That's fantastic. And economical. We can structure a part of your business as a nonprofit arm, to be eligible for grants and other governmental assistance."

Tyson looked at his watch. "If there are no more questions, I say we wrap up here and head over to the building, find out if there's any way we can contact the owner, and get access inside."

"I have a question," Bo asked, with a sheepish expression. "You from LA, right? Do you know Kendrick Lamar?"

"They not like us!" Yuchen surprised Rashad by chanting, the first time Mr. Super Rich acted his age.

"No, I don't know him," Rashad answered, good-naturedly. "But I have friends who do."

"I hear you have good barbecue," Bo said, as the men gathered belongings and headed toward the lobby.

"The best," Rashad glibly replied. "But today, you'll be dining at Side Chic'k. We're opening up just for you."

As soon as he was out of earshot, Rashad called Jamilah. "We did it, baby! Everything's a go!"

"Oh my gosh, Rashad. That's amazing. I'm so proud of you."

"I'm proud of us, Boss Lady, and on my way over. The guys will meet us in an hour."

"I can't wait until my dad sees what we're doing together. Prove to him there's real skill, intelligence, and value in some of the men behind bars."

Rashad narrowly missed being rear-ended. He almost slammed on the brakes midblock. "Wait, what did you say?"

"I know, it took me a minute to come around. But I finally see everything you tried to show me. That so many men like you have so much to offer."

"No, the last part. Where they're doing their time."

"Behind bars?"

"Baby, you're a genius. I can't believe I didn't think of it myself. Ooh, I'm going to make you come so hard tonight."

"What are you talking about?" she replied laughing, and Rashad pictured her body's reaction.

"Boss Lady, you have just captured the essence of my venue with words that convey what I write, the music I want to high-light, and the people I want to help and inspire. You've just named my establishment—Behind Bars."

Thirty-Three

The month of December passed in a blur. Other than a text from Anna inviting them to a holiday bash at Monique's house, Rashad and Jamilah barely noticed. Jamilah quit working at Gusto and joined Rashad to better manage the increased foot traffic at Side Chic'k and Rashad's catering gigs. Thursdays were added back to the restaurant schedule. Ed was hired part-time.

When not cooking his sexy ass off, Rashad was consumed with the expansion and ways for Side Chic'k and Behind Bars to mutually survive and thrive. There were regular conference calls with his partners in Vegas and visits with Mr. Turner outside of those regarding parole. With Rashad's diligence and marketing prowess, business continued to grow. Most companies now relied solely on the internet to advertise. Rashad pulled on his street marketing prowess and created colorful cards that were placed everywhere. With the help of Mr. Turner, an army of teens blanketed the area, touting what he and Jamilah called their Holiday Hookup, an expanded menu that ran throughout the month of December. Thanks to Steve, Side Chic'k's books had been completely overhauled and automated. Both businesses would run through an app that he managed, which he guaranteed would prevent any future tax trouble.

The overall atmosphere was festive, but not everyone sang "Jingle Bells." Jamilah and her father were still fighting. For two weeks after the infamous bank meeting, he ignored all calls and texts. Jamilah returned to his house and saw lights on inside, yet no one answered the door. Then finally, as Rashad and Jamilah dressed for the holiday brunch, Jamilah's phone flashed a familiar number.

"Hey, Daddy."

She heard a heavy sigh before he responded. "Jamilah."

Clearly, James wasn't going to make this easy. "I'm glad you finally got back with me. So much is happening. I wanted to share."

"We've both been busy." A pause and then, "How are you?"

"Fine." *Horrible.* "I hate us not talking, and fighting like this. You're the only parent truly in my life."

"Yet even that didn't stop the betrayal."

"How did I betray you, Dad? I made a business decision, based on knowledge and belief. Why does a decision I make in what I believe to be my best interest have to be a strike against you?"

Rashad walked into the suite from the bathroom. The last thing she wanted was those two to fight.

"Listen, Daddy. I'm on way to an engagement, but I'd love for us to clear the air, see if there's some way to reach a resolution before I head to Denver for Christmas."

"I'm not sure what good it will do, Jamilah. We're on different sides of the street, and I don't see any middle ground."

"You might, after hearing what's happening. Maybe breakfast one day next week?"

"Sure. I'll call you."

On the way to Monique's, conversation was muted. She didn't expound on what her father had said, and thankfully,

Rashad didn't pry. At one point, he reached over and squeezed her hand. For Jamilah, that simple move was the best way he could have responded.

They arrived at a home loudly broadcasting the holidays. Elaborately hung lights twinkled from the roof and nearby trees. Solid white lights lined the walkways. Jamilah reached for the holiday bag containing a bottle of creamy peppermint liqueur and a crystal mug set and looked at Rashad.

"Ready for the interrogation?"

"Not at all, babe. I should have prepared. So tell me. Are we coworkers, business partners, or two grown folks fucking and minding our business?"

Jamilah's mouth dropped as she punched him. "Rashad!"

They were still laughing as Rashad rang the bell.

"Did I tell you that you look good enough to eat?" he whispered, nuzzling her neck and slipping hands where they didn't belong in public. "I think I'll skip dessert and have you instead."

"Ooh, baby, stop that! But later, bon appétit!"

Just as Rashad removed his hand from under Jamilah's coat, the door swung open and Monique announced, "Happy holidays!"

"Hello, again," Jamilah said, with a hug and air kisses. "Thanks for inviting me to another one of your parties. I had such fun last time."

Monique looked beyond her to Rashad. "So I hear."

Before Jamilah could react, Monique winked, took the gifts Jamilah offered, and led them inside. Jamilah was about to join Charles and Anna across the room when she caught the blur of a bright red 'fro in the kitchen.

She hurried toward her friend. "Blair!"

Blair turned, laughed, then gave Jamilah a big hug.

"Oh my goodness! It's so good to see you. I had no idea." They hugged again.

"I know. I told Leon not to say anything in case my day off turned into another day called in to work."

Jamilah looked around. "So you're cooking today, on your day off?"

"No, thank goodness. It's from my work, but catered. This spread is compliments of the head chef himself."

"How swanky!" Jamilah set down her purse on a chair and pulled up her sleeves. "Here, let me help you."

"I see you and Rashad arrived together," Blair said.

"Yes."

"I don't know why you're trying to keep what is an open se-cret. The fact that his pickle has filled your pita pocket is writ-ten all over your face."

The old friends caught up on each other's lives while ar-ranging the ritzy fare from Blair's place of employment. Soon a group that included two women from Anna's ladies' organi-zation sat down to a table laden with goodness.

At first, conversation centered around the food. Blair had chosen exquisitely. Juicy lobster. Perfectly cooked scallops. Spicy crab legs. Porterhouse steaks. And sides that, while delicious, Jamilah felt were not better than Side Chic'k. Of course, she might be biased based by a certain affinity for the cook.

The conversation changed to the upcoming fundraiser that Anna and the members of their social group were organizing.

"Mom, tell me more about this contest or whatever you're planning," Blair asked her mother-in-love. "Leon says it's a Soul Train line."

"Not just any line." Monique wiped her mouth and set down her napkin. "But one of the most exciting things to happen in our city since our guys won the Super Bowl. One long enough to break the *Guinness World Records* book."

"There's actually a record for that?" Rashad asked.

"Absolutely," a woman named Latonia said. "It happened in 2021, through a BET-sponsored event in New York City."

"Harlem," Latonia's friend Roslyn added. "Marcus Garvey Park. It was BET's fiftieth anniversary, I believe, and the awards show was being hosted in Harlem. They won with an official number of five hundred and thirty-six, with a Guinness person there to document it and everything."

"An adjudicator," Latonia clarified.

Jamilah noticed Rashad being especially intrigued. "Where is this happening?"

"We're still working on that," Anna answered. "The committee has floated a few ideas. The Plaza, of course. Union Station. Downtown."

Rashad made a show of being pseudo-annoyed.

"I can't believe y'all aren't stating the obvious answer. This needs to happen near our businesses, Boss Lady." He looked from her to the others. "An area known for soul music. Black musicians. Black music. This party has to go down at Eighteenth and Vine."

Thirty-Four

Rashad and Jamilah enjoyed the city's New Year fireworks from her plate glass windows. Unfortunately, the explosions didn't end after the countdown from ten to one. For the next two months, Rashad learned more about real estate, leasing, renovation, and equipment than he thought he'd ever want to know. Turned out getting the investors was the easy part. When the owner heard about Rashad's plans of ex-criminals being rehabilitated through employment, he balked at giving him a lease, even one that came with a clause to pay one year in advance. This was to get around Rashad not having a credit history or established bank account. Even after Tyson agreed to cosign, the owner hesitated.

In the end it was Yuchen Wang and Bo Peng who settled matters. They bought the building.

The morning Rashad met with the real estate agent and got the keys to the space, everything became surreal. Jamilah asked if he wanted her to come with him, but he said no. The journey from prison to adjunct property owner hadn't happened in a vacuum, but those initial dreams had happened when he was alone. That's how he wanted to enjoy this moment. By himself.

Anyone entering that corner space on a block in its infancy

of gentrification would have seen a discarded old building with little to offer. Rashad saw the opposite. He saw the wooden floors, now covered in dust, dirt, and all kinds of trash, clean and polished. Same with the long bar with the broken mirror behind it. Rashad saw a refurbished anchor of the room, a granite top, a brightly tagged backsplash. He envisioned ragtag furniture and seating arrangements. Benches mixed with chairs. Tables in different shapes and designs. A hodgepodge of furniture mirroring the diverse crowd and experiences he hoped to draw in. Everywhere he looked, Rashad saw potential.

Thanks to Mr. Turner's connections, renovations got underway rather quickly. He'd worked in KC for decades and knew some of everybody. Permits, licenses, and other administrative paperwork bypassed the usual channels. It didn't mean life was a cakewalk. The worlds of real estate, construction, and retail spaces were not for the faint of heart. For men like Rashad, who'd survived the streets and prison, too, there was no mountain that could not be climbed...or moved.

When he brought Jamilah over the following Thursday morning, it was harder for her to see his vision.

"I could never start from scratch like this," she all but whispered, clearly overwhelmed. "The place next door had already been renovated. My contribution was light fixtures and paint.

"If anyone can pull this off, Ra God, it's you. Your tenacity, intelligence, and self-determination will be more than enough to see it through."

Her words, especially using his rap name, were wind beneath his wings. Rashad's confidence soared, as did his growing and deepening feelings for Jamilah. So much so, that he invited her to his next meeting with Mr. Turner.

"I wanted you to meet my business partner," he said proudly, leading Jamilah into Mr. Turner's office, a space made small by the amount of books, newspapers, magazines, and papers that covered every surface except the chairs. There were even stacks on the floor.

"Jamilah Carver. Nice to meet you," Jamilah said, hand outstretched.

"Likewise." Mr. Turner's look, while respectable, was also admiring. "Are you the brains behind all this brawn?"

"At least a good ninety percent," Jamilah quickly responded with so much authority Rashad laughed out loud.

"I'm just kidding. Rashad has an eye for aesthetics and a head for marketing and business. My restaurant, Side Chic'k, is better with him as head chef."

"How is everything progressing?" Mr. Turner asked, once they sat down.

"Feels like two steps forward and three back sometimes. Having the paperwork handled helps out a lot. But there are shipping delays, supply shortages. We've had to continually tweak the drawings based on what materials we can get. At the end of the month, Tyson is going to relocate here temporarily until we get past the main obstacles."

"After this week, I should have some good news to help the bad go down better. I have a meeting scheduled with a buddy of mine over at the Department of Corrections to go over your proposal. No doubt he'll bring in a few others from city government, maybe the county.

"I'm glad you two are working together," he continued, his eyes now on Jamilah. "We have a growing number of women in these detention centers and jails. They need to see a path as well. Business owners like you are perfect for lighting the way. I'm sure you already know that, though. James must be proud of you."

Jamilah did not try to hide her surprise. "You know my father?"

"I do."

"Mr. Turner knows everybody," Rashad proudly announced.

"How do you know my dad?"

"You might say we grew up together. I'm a few years older.

But we came from the same small Kansas town. Knew his family. His daddy."

He turned to Rashad. "How do the two of you get along? Considering that you work with his daughter, I'm assuming you've met."

"Unfortunately."

Jamilah was quick to defend her dad. "His view isn't personal. It's based on what he's seen on paper. He doesn't really know Rashad."

"He considers anyone whose been to prison a bad influence that she shouldn't hang around," Rashad added.

Mr. Turner steepled his fingers, looked over his glasses, and eyed Jamilah closely. "You ever meet your granddaddy?"

"I think once, when I was really young. But he died a long time ago. Daddy never mentions him or any of the family really, other than those I know here."

"He never told you why he became a policeman?"

She slowly shook her head. "He's never told me and, Mr. Turner, for all my life that's a question that I've never thought to ask."

"You should ask him," Mr. Turner suggested. "And about your granddaddy. It'll give you a better understanding of his reaction toward this young man and others like him.

"Meanwhile, I have a boring meeting to attend that'll put me to sleep." Mr. Turner shuffled papers as he prepared to leave. "I'll let you know how next week's meeting turns out."

"Thanks for all your help, Mr. Turner."

Rashad and Jamilah watched the mentor turn and walk toward his car before heading to theirs parked across the street.

The ride was quiet as they headed toward Side Chic'k. "Are you going to ask your father about his father?"

Jamilah looked out the window. "I don't know."

"You don't? Sounds to me like it's some important information, some history about your family that you don't know about."

"Maybe I don't want to know," Jamilah testily replied. "Maybe it's better not knowing, which is why Daddy never told me."

Rashad snuck a glance at Jamilah, watched as the family narrative James had probably concocted now threatened to unravel. It hurt to think that Jamilah would rather live a lie than know the truth because the truth might expose a hypocritical father.

"Would it be so bad to find out your family isn't perfect? To learn there may be a hardhead or two swinging off one of those tree branches?"

Jamilah turned even more toward the window. Rashad let it go, but the conversation was far from over. If Jamilah didn't ask her dad about what Mr. Turner said, Rashad most definitely would.

Thirty-Five

Jamilah was glad for prep as an outlet. Instead of using the food processor, she chopped veggies by hand. Took her frustration out on carrots, onions, and potatoes. She was nervous about what Mr. Turner had said, terrified to know what her dad might be hiding about his father. He'd kept whatever it was to himself for thirty years. Surely it couldn't be good.

It took the whole of lunch service for Jamilah to come around and admit that Rashad was right. Whatever had happened with her grandfather was a part of her lineage. Good or bad, she needed to know. Once the dining room slowed down and they'd gotten through most of the prep for the dinner crowd, Jamilah texted James.

Met Mr. Thomas Turner today. He says he grew up with you and to ask about my grandfather. Has me curious. When you get a minute, please call. Xoxo

For the rest of the day and most of Friday, conversation was cool between Rashad and Jamilah. She didn't invite him over, and he didn't invite himself. At work, each spoke when spoken to, but mostly only when necessary. It didn't help that her dad hadn't responded to her text nor to the phone call she'd placed last evening. Fortunately, Ed kept up a senseless banter, but by Friday afternoon even he noticed something amiss.

"Lover's quarrel?" he asked Jamilah when it was just the two of them in the kitchen together. "Don't worry, I'm not going to tell your Daddy. But even Stevie Wonder can see the two of y'all are a pair."

Ed's words prompted Jamilah to change her perspective and think about the potential development in her family from Rashad's point of view. What if he were right and her father was hiding something nefarious that had happened in their family? And whatever that was had influenced his decision to enter law enforcement? How would that affect how Jamilah viewed her father, and even more, how would it potentially explain his disdain for Rashad?

Friday night after closing, she took baby steps over the bridge of reconciliation. "I took Mr. Turner's advice and asked about my grandfather."

"Oh, yeah?"

Jamilah nodded. "He hasn't answered yet."

"Interesting."

"He's been very busy," she countered. "I know at least one case he's very involved in, and there are probably others."

Rashad made small talk with Caylen who'd finished cleanup, then reached for his notebook. "See you tomorrow, Jamilah," he said, also on his way out.

"You want to come over?"

"Yeah, but Tyson is going to be here before we know it. I've got work to do."

Jamilah and Rashad left in separate cars. She was tired but didn't feel like going straight to her empty condo. After driving around the block, her eyes fell on the Blue Room, where she'd occasionally gone to listen to jazz with her dad. She'd never gone there solo, but sitting at the bar for one drink didn't sound so bad. Maybe she'd run into a friend or—who knew?—maybe even her father.

After getting a glass of cabernet, she turned her attention to the jam session happening on stage. The musicians were respectable but felt nothing like the music of Ida McBeth's era or even further back to this intersection's heyday. She could only imagine how it would have been to see Charlie Parker blowing his sax in Jay McShan's band. Or witness a lesson in jazz by Bennie Moten, who her dad said taught Count Basie. Or get an earful of the blues shouting Big Joe Turner. Or hear Duke Ellington telling the audience to take the A train.

Still, she enjoyed being out more than she realized and made small talk with the people nearby. She'd almost finished her wine and was considering another when she felt a tap on her shoulder.

She turned around with a smile, half expecting to see her father. It wasn't him. The smile dimmed.

"Walter. Hi."

"Fancy seeing you here," he said good-naturedly, as though they were old buddies. He looked around. "You with James?"

"Nope, just me."

"What's a pretty lady like you doing alone on a Friday night?"

Even though the comment made her feel a tad uncomfortable, Jamilah managed a smile. "I just got off work and decided to unwind with a glass of wine. Actually," she said and drained the glass, "I was just leaving."

"Jamilah, wait."

Jamilah looked pointedly at the hand he'd placed on her arm. He removed it slowly.

"It's good to see you."

"Where's your fiancée?"

"Out of town. One of her sorority sisters is getting married."

"And you're not with her?"

"Heavy workload. Couldn't be helped. In fact, something came across my desk involving Side Chic'k possibly working with young women in the system. Some type of rehabilitation program?"

"The idea is in its infancy, but yes, we want to offer young people coming out of jail a safe place to make an income."

"We?"

Jamilah realized too late the door she had opened. Didn't mean she couldn't keep the chain latched.

"There are a few businesses with similar goals."

Walter eyed her intently. "I never knew you to be interested in social change."

"I wasn't, until I was." She slipped off the barstool and adjusted her purse strap. "Take care of yourself. Congratulations on your engagement."

"I thought you could do better than selling food for a living. But the law is demanding, and being a civil servant can be taxing. Sometimes I miss the easy life of kicking back with a good piece of chicken."

"Good-bye, Walter."

"Tell James I said hello. And if you ever need anything, call me."

Driving home, Jamilah played the comparison card. Couldn't help it. Walter and Rashad couldn't be more different. Being reminded of the type of man she'd left behind made her uber aware of the one that she had.

The next morning, she arrived at work and walked straight over to Rashad. "I'm sorry."

"For what?"

"My attitude after meeting with Mr. Turner. Getting angry at you for your accurate assessment of me not wanting to face what sounds like a sketchy family past. Forgive me?"

"I'll think about it."

Jamilah almost missed his lip's slight upturn, starting the journey on the way to a smile. Unfortunately, it wouldn't last long. The second customer who came through the door that Saturday was the woman from the dating website. The last person either of them wanted to see.

Thirty-Six

Rashad looked up as Jamilah approached him.

"She's back."

One look at her expression, and he knew who'd come into their place, and probably not for the chicken or sides.

"What should we do?" Jamilah asked.

"Take her order. Then ignore her. That's what I'm going to do."

Jamilah didn't trust herself to not go off, so she sent Shasta to wait the table. When the order came through, it included the name he couldn't remember: DeeDee. She asked to see the chef. He wouldn't be interacting with her now or in the future, and he instructed Shasta to pass on the message. He hated involving the young woman, but Rashad had to draw a line. He had to convince DeeDee that he meant business. The last person you wanted to mess with was the one who fixed your food.

He spent the night with Jamilah. Having her beneath him again, and then on top and sideways, felt like home. DeeDee returned on Sunday just before closing. Jamilah informed her it was too late to order. When the protests started, she simply pointed to a sign near the window.

We Reserve the Right to Refuse Service to Anyone.

"I hope she doesn't become a problem," Jamilah said, after locking the door and turning around the Open sign.

"She's already a problem," Rashad replied. "I just hope one that doesn't last long."

After work, he returned to Anna's house and called Juke to implement the plan he'd mentioned when back home for Thanksgiving.

"You ready to move to KC?" Rashad asked, after small talk.

"Leave LA?" Juke said, as though Rashad had relocated to Mars.

"We talked about this back in November!"

"No, you talked," Juke clarified. "I listened."

"I know, it's a big ask. Big risk, big reward. I need someone I can trust to help manage the business."

"I've never run a venue like that."

"Neither have I."

Juke told Rashad he'd think about the offer. Over the next few days and in between the catering jobs he accepted to keep his bottom line tight, Rashad reached out to a couple more of his homeboys he wanted on the team. He couldn't handle the cooking for two spaces but knew exactly who'd do the job right. Other key positions included scheduling and security. Leon was over all things gaming. He hadn't stopped planning and creating since the first mention in October. Mr. Turner agreed to oversee the staff that would work with those from the system. Tyson agreed to temporarily act as a floater and handle everything else.

In between cooking, constructing, and constant coordinating, Rashad and Jamilah tried to have a life. After almost a month went by where they barely saw each other outside of the kitchen or the construction site next door, when neither could remember how long it had been since they'd had a real conversation that didn't somehow involve food, they scheduled a date night. They couldn't completely escape talking about work, but the couple's package purchased at a spa in the suburbs helped them work out all kinds of kinks.

"Is it supposed to be this hot?" Rashad had been ready to enter the highly touted Himalayan salt sauna, but the blast of heat changed his mind.

"All right, Mr. California. I thought you liked hot?"

"Yes, but not hell. It's hell-hot in there."

"Are you gonna let a woman experience something you can't handle?" Jamilah brushed past him and took his hand. "You'll get used to it. And you'll love it."

"Or I'll come out like my chicken. Fried to a crisp."

Once Rashad acclimated to the temperature and quit complaining, he relaxed against a pillow.

"I thought the massage was going to be the best part of this. I haven't sweated this much since working out at Venice Beach."

"What about last night?" Jamilah teased.

"Just a warm-up." He tied his locs with a leather band. "I can almost feel the toxins running out of my pores."

Jamilah poured water on the salt rocks, then leaned forward for the steam bath on her face. "I got a call from Anna."

"About the line, no doubt."

"She's so excited. Monique, too. She said she felt bad for asking but wanted me to know that if I had any spare time as July approaches, they'll need all hands on deck."

"How hard can it be to line people up in teams of two and get them to dance down the street?"

"I have a feeling I'm about to find out."

Jamilah lay back on the cedar bench and allowed her body to fully relax. She could have cursed when the face that floated into her conscious was surrounded by a halo of blond-tinted hair.

Instead of running away from the troubling thought, she said, "Haven't seen the Stalker in a while. When was the last time?"

"I thought we were supposed to be relaxing. And here you go rattling my nerves."

"Sorry. She just popped up in my mind."

The Right to Refuse sign hadn't deterred DeeDee from her mission. She came back several times. After trying and failing to get Rashad to come out, she'd post up at the table with the most direct line of sight to the kitchen and try to get noticed. Wintertime didn't prevent her from dressing inappropriately in catsuits that left nothing to the imagination or tops that barely held in her breasts. One day Jamilah realized she hadn't seen DeeDee at all, now labeled the Stalker. A day turned into a week. And then two. And now almost a month.

"I told you that eventually she'd get tired of coming around. A woman like that needs attention. She wasn't going to get it from me."

"Speaking of women, I'm kinda nervous about the meeting coming up at the detention center."

"Baby, that was one helluva segue."

"Ha! Guess thinking about how crazy she acted made me wonder what choices all those young women made that landed them in the system.

"I don't mean to sound bougie, but I don't know what that life is like, can't imagine participating in an action to land me behind bars. What can I share that will make their lives better?"

"You can tell them your story. Everyone dreams. Share yours. How it started with watching the Food Network when you were a kid and you imagining being on TV. Talk about your ups and downs, the struggles you went through in opening up a business. Think of something that all women have in common. Like your obsession with men. You can tell them how I came into your life, swept you off your feet, and made you the happiest woman on the planet."

Instead of balking, Jamilah slid over and gave Rashad a kiss. "Now it's time for the cold treatment. Let's go jump in the pool."

Rashad and Jamilah left the spa with two new bodies.

"We've got to do that once a month," she said.

"At least," he agreed and sealed the promise with a fist pound.

In the car, Jamilah's phone rang. "Hey, Daddy." She looked at Rashad. "No, I'm not at home right now. Is everything okay? Ah, you saw the construction. That's going to be Rashad's music and gaming venue. I've wanted to speak with you about it, but you haven't had time."

Shaking her head she said, "There will be food served, but it won't be competition. Different hours, menus, customer base. It's not just him. There's a team working with us to ensure the success of both businesses."

Jamilah rolled her eyes. "Yes, Daddy, I said *us*. Rashad and I are partners. In business," she hurriedly added as Rashad slid a hand between her thighs.

Jamilah swatted his hand. "It's been forever since you've patronized my establishment. I'm starting to take it personal..." She nodded. "Okay, this Sunday. See you then."

"Still not ready to tell Daddy that I'm banging his daughter?" Rashad teased.

"He already knows. I'm sure Ed told him."

"Ed knows?"

"I never told you what he said?"

"No."

She repeated Ed's Stevie Wonder line.

"Are you ever going to confront your pops about his daddy?"

"I've asked him. Vocally and in writing. Maybe one day he'll tell me. For now it's enough that we're talking again and he's ready to eat food that you cooked."

Thirty-Seven

Anna's call for all hands on deck came sooner than Jamilah expected. St. Patrick had not yet had his day when she was asked to join their meetings. By then, Jamilah considered Anna a friend and was the first one Rashad and Jamilah admitted to being a couple to. Somehow, it was easier to tell her than someone in Jamilah's circle. Most days, the thought of being Rashad's woman sent her over the moon. At other times, her pesky issues reared their ugly heads and sent her second-guessing.

Side Chic'k, for instance. When around Rashad, Jamilah put on a brave face, all excited about the Behind Bars venue. Privately, though, she worried about him opening up next door. Would the result be as they hoped, with both businesses solvent? The preparations to open had them barely seeing each other. What would happen once the doors opened and the customers came? When attractive women inevitably patronized his establishment, female artists or musicians who shared his creativity, or like Shelby, dreamed of making him the main character in their personal story? Rashad was handsome, sexy, and now a business owner. Any one of those traits could give him his pick of women, and now he had a trifecta. Throw in that he was an expert in the kitchen and the bedroom? They'd become like

DeeDee the Stalker and camp out at his venue. Jamilah shuddered at the thought.

And the biggest concern? What happened if what Jamilah and Rashad had didn't work out and they were forced to dissolve the partnership? Hers was the established business, yet in that scenario, depending on the time frame, Jamilah couldn't help but believe she had the most to lose.

Thank God for Anna and the SOS—the Society of Sisters— the group organizing the *Soul Train* event. Talking and laughing with Anna or listening to the ladies throw shade and gossip was the perfect balance to Rashad and his testosterone-driven team. What started out as a fundraiser centered around besting a record had morphed into an all-day event. Jamilah never knew so much went into what had been submitted to City Hall as a parade. The festivities would take place in and around the intersection of Eighteenth and Vine. There would be vendors and food trucks. Singers and steppers and other creative acts. High schools had signed up marching bands, who would also be counted as participants.

While she was focusing on *Soul Train* and Side Chic'k, Rashad juggled everything else. Overseeing the Behind Bars renovation. Working with Mr. Turner on the detention/parolee program. A grant had been submitted that, if approved, would cover training and hiring for Behind Bars, Side Chic'k, and other businesses where a trade could be taught or a skill learned. Unfortunately, in getting BB off the ground, Rashad's catering business became a casualty. However, the former hustler and natural entrepreneur had gathered contact information everywhere he fed people. Once his website was up, this information would be entered into a database. Rashad would have a customer base from day one.

Jamilah's phone rang, bringing her back to the present. She rose from the couch, stretched, then hurried to grab her cell phone off the counter.

"Hello?"

"Jamilah, it's Anna."

"Hey, Anna. How are you?"

"The truth? Overwhelmed."

Jamilah walked into the kitchen. "What's going on?"

"We've handled most of the details for the line and set up an application process for businesses that want to participate. Now comes the hard part, working out all the logistics. There are so many moving parts. Because of how many people we're anticipating, our permit may take longer to process. I've learned there may need to be a preapplication meeting and a neighborhood meeting with all of the businesses along the route. We have to work with the City Planning and Zoning Committee. The mayor's office."

Jamilah heard Anna getting more frustrated. "Trying to break a world record. What the heck was I thinking?"

"It does sound like a lot. But, Anna, we can do this. Over the past several months I've watched your godson do the impossible, over and over again. Don't tell him I said this, but he's taught me a lot. Including how to eat an elephant."

Anna laughed. "One bite at a time. That's his granny talking. It sounds simple enough, but I can't figure out what to bite first."

"Me either, but I might know someone who does."

Jamilah hung up from Anna and scrolled her Contacts for a number she hadn't used in almost a year. Her hesitation was brief before she tapped the number.

The call was answered on the second ring. "Jamilah?"

"Hi, Walter."

"This is a surprise."

Jamilah chuckled. "For me, too. When I saw you at the Blue Room, you said to call if there was ever something I needed."

"I said that. And I meant it. We were friends before we started dating. I took that friendship, and you, for granted. I owe you an apology."

Jamilah was caught off guard. This was a completely unexpected direction from where she'd planned to lead the conversation.

"An apology for what?"

"In short, for being an asshole. Through my current engagement I've learned that much of what happened that led to our breakup, well, it wasn't you, it was me."

"Wow, apology accepted."

"Good. What can I do for you?"

Jamilah was reeling from Walter's revelation. She almost forgot why she'd called.

"It's, um, yeah. It's about a fundraising event happening in July involving a *Soul Train* line…"

Jamilah believed she'd fully gotten over Walter. For the most part, she had. But something about his apology, acknowledging his role in the demise of their relationship, gave Jamilah a validation she didn't know she'd needed. She'd been right all along. She wasn't crazy. Justification replaced insecurity. Confidence replaced trepidation. Even though she'd ended the relationship, a part of Jamilah had still felt abandoned. She'd been underappreciated and undervalued. Leaving Walter had been the right thing to do.

Nowhere was that fact more evident than when she was with Rashad. Tonight they entertained Leon in Jamilah's condo, happily stuffed from one of Rashad's dishes labeled Cellblock Cuisine, made with Ramen noodles, canned tuna, and crushed tortilla chips. The ingredients sounded simple enough, but it wasn't a run-of-the-mill tuna casserole. Rashad always had secret ingredients that he refused to reveal. Jamilah was still waiting for the magic contained in that long-ago wonton dish.

"Is Blair going to be able to get off for the Fourth?" Rashad asked.

"She's already put in the request, so we're hoping."

Jamilah stood and began gathering dishes. "It's so cool that the Fourth actually falls on a Saturday. A round of fireworks is the perfect way to celebrate breaking a record."

Leon drained his glass and handed it to Jamilah. "How many dancers do you need to break the record?"

"A lot," Rashad said.

"Around five-, six-hundred," Jamilah added.

"Are y'all ready for the crowd that's going to be on your block? You're gonna need hella chicken in that joint."

Jamilah sighed dramatically. "I've dreamed of the day that I'd need hella chicken."

Rashad followed Jamilah into the kitchen, grabbed a water, then pulled Jamilah back against him.

"That is the official opening weekend for Behind Bars," he announced, fondling Jamilah like they didn't have company. "I'll be ready for anything."

As usual, Leon's eyes were glued to his phone. Knowing he'd be enthralled in whatever game he played for hours, Rashad quietly led Jamilah into the bedroom and softly closed the door.

Thirty-Eight

"Is this blindfold really necessary?"

Jamilah tugged at the bandanna Rashad had secured before leading her to the new door that now created an inner pathway for the adjoining businesses. Renovating the building, inside and out, had been happening since February. Now, in May, it was near completion. For the past three weeks, except for the construction crew, Behind Bars had been off-limits. Today Rashad couldn't wait to give Jamilah the big reveal.

"Keep walking," he instructed, while holding her hand. "Now turn. Over here. A few more steps. Okay, stop."

He stepped behind her and untied the bandanna. Jamilah opened her eyes. One hand covered a mouth now wide with amazement. Rashad stood silent, beaming as she did a three-sixty turn.

She threw her arms around Rashad. "This is incredible!"

"No, baby," he said, returning her hug. "This is hip-hop."

"When you said the walls would be black I didn't get it, but…"

"That graffiti is popping, isn't it? And wait until dark, when the black lights hit that fluorescent paint. Patrons will be transported to Compton, or Inglewood, or Queens, or the Bronx."

"I don't feel like I'm in Kansas City, that's for sure. And what's that say?" Jamilah read the oversize painted banner. *"Higher Infinite Power Healing Our People.* Very creative. Did you make that up?"

"I can't take credit. That belongs to Professor Griff, back when he was with Public Enemy. Most who enjoy the genre now don't know about its uplifting, conscious beginnings. Back then, there was a message in the music, one that inspired and empowered. That's why I rock with Kendrick, and creatives like him. His is the highest profile of any artist bringing that original spirit back."

Jamilah admired the rest of the decor, a blend of modern, rugged, and street. Exposed brick complemented the original wood found beneath layers of dirt and grime, and years of neglect. Different style tables hosted mismatched chairs. A long bench occupied one wall. An equally long bar filled the other. At various intervals, the walls held blank spaces.

"What goes there?" Jamilah asked.

"Masterpieces from local artists that I don't know yet."

Rashad checked his watch. "We've got to hurry this up. The fellas land in just over an hour."

Jamilah appreciated the plain but superclean bathroom. She was jealous of his kitchen. Leon's game room looked like something out of NASA. She imagined gamers going in there and staying for days.

They walked back through the adjoining door and into Side Chic'k. "We should be back around six-ish depending on traffic. Are you sure you don't mind us taking over your spot?"

"Not at all. Your gas isn't on yet, and we're closed today. Plus, I can't wait to meet these friends you've talked so much about. They're like characters in a movie."

With a kiss good-bye, Rashad hit the road. Heading to the airport felt surreal. He couldn't count the times he'd imagined hanging out in this new city with his old crew. He was equal parts nervous and excited. On his word, these friends had agreed to pull up their lives and move to Kansas City. He'd told them it would be more than worth it, that in this smaller, less competitive market, they all could get paid. Rashad hoped his crystal ball was accurate and that he hadn't lied.

Rashad parked the roomy Kia Telluride he'd rented in the cell phone lot. His fingers tapped out a melody on the steering wheel as he waited for the text from Juke that they'd landed. Moments later, just after Tupac told women to keep their head up and right before Biggie realized it was all a dream, two words flashed across his cell phone screen.

We here.

Rashad smiled. Got your luggage?

Just landed.

Hit me up when you get your bags.

Ur supposed to already be at the carousel holding a sign with our names. Wearing a limo hat and shit. ☺

STFU!

Ten minutes later, Rashad pulled up to the curb where five knuckleheads had everyone's attention just by being themselves. His heart swelled, and if he allowed himself to be an emotional kind of guy he might have even gotten misty-eyed. Except for Antonio, who he'd met in prison, these men had known him since he rode a Big Wheel and had left their lives and comfort zones to help him realize a dream. He thought back to the thousands of hours spent doing just that, dreaming, envisioning how their lives would look one day. In the early days, most of those fantasies ended up with them somewhere on stage. Wearing big chains and rocking the mic in front of thousands. A bunch of scantily clad ladies clamoring to claim even a few seconds of their time. The next N.W.A., taking over the world. For Rashad that dream had contracted and expanded, shifted and morphed into various versions of itself. It had been redefined to what would happen next month with a soft opening. Still built around a mic. Still rocking a stage. Same…but different.

"Damn, man. You got us out in the middle of nowhere!"

"Bro, you went country when country wasn't cool."

"Nah, Eight Track, Shaboozey made that shit cool again."

Shouts and hugs. Disses and laughter. Six grown men, one who shopped in the big-and-tall store, piling into the SUV. The space was tight. He could have arranged a rideshare with two cars. But these were friends who at one time had split hamburgers and tacos and four hot dogs five ways. Moving separately would have changed the dynamic and made the experience less rich and memorable.

"We're hungry, dog," Antonio said. "Take us to your restaurant so we can cook something."

"Great idea. Consider it an unofficial audition for a job in my kitchen. You probably need to sharpen your skills."

"Man, my skills are sharper than a blade that just kissed a whetstone."

"Speaking of lips," Sky Walka segued, "how's the female population around these parts?"

"How would Ra know?" PhD asked. "He's too ugly to catch one."

"He's got a shorty," Juke said. "Hasn't said that much about her, but I peeped that puppy dog look when you were back in Cali and got a text."

Rashad blew him off. "Don't believe what's been created in Juke's imagination. A puppy dog look has never graced this face."

The chatter continued nonstop until Rashad pulled up to Side Chic'k when suddenly, all at once, the car went quiet.

"Rashad, you shouldn't have," Antonio murmured. "You didn't have to bring me a welcome gift."

"Man, what are you…"

The sentence died on his lips as the reason for the sudden silence walked toward his car. Blonde-tinted hair. Pretty face. Enticing breasts threatening to spill over. And a smile that sent Rashad's spidey senses straight to the moon.

"Fuck."

"Who is that?" Juke asked, with obvious interest.

"Bad news. Come on, y'all."

Four car doors opened. Rashad walked with purpose toward the restaurant's entrance. Various comments sounded behind him. A hand pulled his arm.

"Rashad!"

He took a breath, determined to stay calm and shake DeeDee the Stalker. "We're closed."

Her voice turned flirty. "Doesn't look like it."

"I'll open for you, mami," Antonio drawled.

"Rashad, can we talk? I've been trying for months, and you keep ignoring me."

"That should tell you something."

He watched as Jamilah came down the hallway, stopping short when she took in the scene. He shook off her arm.

"I think one of my friends is trying to get your attention."

The Stalker followed his line of sight and saw Jamilah.

"Why are you acting like you don't know me, like we haven't been together? I knew you were special, going places, and that I was supposed to be your girl."

Rashad turned then, looked her straight in the eye. "Is that why the last words out of your mouth were about money?"

"Why not?" DeeDee pouted. "Men like you always have it like that."

"Whatever you're looking for, I don't have it. You're *not* my girl. Go. Away." He entered the shop. DeeDee tried to follow. "I told you we're closed. Now, back up."

"You're not going to be able to forget me this easily," she yelled through the glass.

Livid, Rashad opened the door up just enough to tell his homeboys, "Follow that pathway and meet me around back."

"Should we call the police?" Jamilah asked, clearly vexed. "She was trespassing."

"Technically, she was on the sidewalk. Public property."

"How did she even know we'd be here?"

Rashad shook his head. "Bad karma is all I can think. In another lifetime, I must have really fucked up."

Rashad listened as his friends joked about her in the dining room. Wasn't a damn thing funny, but they didn't know that. He decided to ignore their ignorance and shift their attention.

"Fellas," he said, pulling Jamilah out of the kitchen and wrapping an arm around her waist, "this is my lady, Jamilah. Jamilah, this is family."

Very quickly, the incident with DeeDee the Stalker was forgotten as chicken fried, music blared, and everyone caught up on each other's lives. Rashad basked in watching Jamilah with these friends who were like brothers. More than once, he saw her and Juke talking and laughing. God only knew what lies that boy told. They plied Jamilah with stories about Rashad's boyhood and life in the Jungle. They were appropriately impressed when he walked them next door.

"Let's test the sound system," Juke suggested.

"It's not hooked up yet," Rashad said.

"Damn, cuz. That's the first thing that should have happened. Even before you opened a can of paint!"

Rashad hadn't intended to entertain his friends at Side Chic'k, but before they knew it, three hours had gone by. He was tired and they opened tomorrow. With a yawn, he suggested they get the place cleaned up so he could drop them off at the hotel. He was in the kitchen when Juke came around the corner, no joke in his expression.

"Police are headed this way," he said, his voice low and trepidatious.

"Probably not," Rashad answered. "They patrol the area. It's all good."

"They're at your door," he explained.

Rashad grabbed a towel to dry his hands and followed Juke into the dining area. Sure enough, two officers stood just beyond the entrance looking their way.

He quelled the familiar angst that arose from being allergic to law enforcement. Gathering himself, he opened the door and calmly asked, "Officers, may I help you?"

"We're looking for Rashad White," the taller of the two said, as the shorter one looked beyond him to the other men inside.

Rashad's heartbeat quickened, though his voice remained casual. "That's me."

"Rashad White," the officer began, pulling out cuffs, "you're under arrest."

Commotion broke out behind him. Jamilah rushed to the door. "What is this about?" she demanded.

"Ma'am, stand back or you'll be arrested for obstruction."

She stood her ground, eyed his badge. "Officer Henley, is it? This is a mistake."

"What's the charge?" Juke yelled out.

"Assault. Let's go."

"Don't worry, baby," Rashad told Jamilah. "Call Tyson," he yelled to Juke. As they led him to the police car, he looked across the street and saw DeeDee, disheveled and with a tear-stained face, smirking in the shadows.

Thirty-Nine

Once the cops left, all hell broke loose, all at once.

"This is ridiculous!"

"Can't go nowhere without running into those clowns."

"*Assault?* That's crazy. He's been too busy working to have time to fight."

Jamilah broke away from the hubbub and ran for her phone.

"Please pick up," she murmured, as she tapped the Speaker button. "Come on, Daddy. Please!"

The call went to voice mail.

"Daddy, it's me. Rashad got arrested! It's a mistake, Daddy. Please call me back ASAP, as soon as you can."

She joined Rashad's friends in the dining room, listened as Juke called Tyson and relayed the news.

After listening, Tyson said three words. "On my way."

"It was her." Jamilah rushed to the door and yanked it open. She scoured the block from one side to the other, walked to the corner, down the alley and back. Adrenaline pumped so hard her feet barely touched the ground. Jamilah knew the person behind this, as sure as she knew her name.

When she returned to the shop, the men gathered around her. PhD turned spokesman. "What do you need us to do?"

"I don't know," Jamilah said, sinking into the nearest chair. "I need to reach my father. I've got to get to Rashad."

She almost broke then. Juke hurried over and squeezed her shoulder. "Stay strong," he all but demanded. "This isn't Rashad's first rodeo with some bullshit. We'll find out what happened and whoever did this and do whatever it takes to get him out."

"You think it's that girl?" Antonio asked Jamilah.

"I know it is."

She told his friends the whole story, from that first swipe right until tonight.

Sky Walka turned a chair around and sat in it backward. "Something about her seemed off to me. She's gorgeous, but something about those eyes…"

"I wasn't looking at her eyes," Antonio mumbled.

Except for Jamilah, the levity was appreciated. As for her, she sat angry and plotting, suddenly very aware of how unsuspecting people ended up in jail.

Tyson arrived, phone pressed to his ear, wearing authority like a tailored suit. "I've got one of my contacts reaching out to a local attorney. We won't be able to do anything until we know what this is about."

"A woman scorned," Juke said, and told Tyson about the earlier encounter.

"Look, guys, I appreciate you wanting to help. But I need to handle this. My father is in law enforcement and—"

"Your daddy's a cop?"

"Former cop, current detective…and a damned good one."

The tone in how she answered Juke dared anyone in the room to speak against James Carver.

"Just hang on until I hear from my dad. He'll know what to do. In the meantime, I can drive y'all to the hotel."

"I'll handle that," Tyson answered.

He walked over and offered a light hug. "You go take care of your man."

After the guys left, Jamilah became frantic. Rashad getting arrested replayed in her head. She called her father a dozen times. Texted him, too. Unable to sit still, she drove down to the police station in her father's former precinct. There, she saw familiar faces but no one who could help her.

"If he just got arrested, that information might not yet be in the database," one officer said. "And even if it was, we couldn't release it."

"But you know my father!"

"Sorry, Jamilah. It's police procedure. As a detective, James might be able to move a little differently."

"Can you at least tell me where they took him?"

An older man Jamilah remembered from years ago said, "Jackson County Detention Center, most likely. He can probably get bonded out in the morning. Till then, my advice is to go home and try to get some rest. James has been tied up with an ongoing investigation. I'll personally try to contact him and have him call you."

Jamilah drove home on autopilot, too shocked to cry. She wanted to wake up from this nightmare—Rashad housed in the same facility as the men he hoped to hire.

Once home, the tears came. A flurry of thoughts assailed her. Unbidden, old recordings of her father began to play in her head, about thugs and criminals not to be trusted. She shook her head against the onslaught. Rashad had changed. He wasn't the same man who had spent years in prison.

But what if by some random chance her father was right? What if she'd misjudged Rashad's character, allowed attraction and desire to cloud her view? Eyes narrowed, she peered into the soul of an average female. Most women she knew wouldn't act like the Stalker, become obsessed with a man after only one night.

"No!"

She refused to believe that Rashad was anyone other than the man he'd been since she first laid eyes on him at Monique's party. Seeing one of his bandannas on the table, she walked over and grabbed it, returned to the sofa with his scent close to her heart. She vowed not to fall asleep until she heard from her dad.

Several hours later, however, she was being gently shaken awake.

"Jamilah."

The voice sounded far away, as though speaking through water. Clearly, she was dreaming. That reality drew a fresh set of tears.

"Jamilah, it's me. Wake up."

Her eyes fluttered open.

"Rashad?" She sat up, rubbing her eyes in disbelief. "Rashad!"

She jumped up and into his arms. "Oh my God! I can't believe it. How'd you get out of jail? How'd you get here?"

"I brought him here, baby girl."

A gasp, as Jamilah whipped around to see her father standing near the door.

"I know I'm dreaming now," she said, again rubbing her eyes.

"No, Boss Lady, this is real," Rashad assured her.

Overcome with emotional exhaustion, Jamilah sank to the couch. "I don't understand."

"Why don't we all sit down?" her dad suggested, taking a seat in a nearby chair. "It's time the three of us had a conversation that's long overdue. First of all, Rashad, I owe you an apology. I misjudged you horribly and made life for you tough when it didn't have to be."

Jamilah sat as still as a statue, afraid that if she moved, then like a mirage, her father would disappear.

Her dad ran weary hands over his face. Only then did Jamilah really notice the bags beneath his eyes. He looked tired—no, weary. As though he'd aged since their war of wills began.

He looked at Rashad, sitting by Jamilah. "Recently, your PO, Thomas, paid me a visit. Told me we needed to talk. That I'd gotten you all wrong. He knows how stubborn I can be and

wasn't surprised when I didn't want to hear a thing he was saying. Fortunately, Thomas is just as bullheaded as me and one of
only a handful of folk who can call me on my bullshit and get
me to listen. That's what I did, Rashad. I sat there and heard
what he had to say.

"He told me about your place next door and the program
for prior offenders the two of you have put together. Told me it
was your idea and how impressed he was that you'd brought it
to him. He shared a few more things, using the type of colorful
language that doesn't bear repeating. He forced me to consider
you and this situation with Jamilah from a different perspective
than the one I'd held. For making you out to be the one I read
on paper and not the one here helping my daughter, I apologize and hope that one day you can forgive me."

Jamilah felt Rashad place an arm around her. "After what
you shared on the ride over, I forgive you right now."

"What did he tell you?" Jamilah asked.

"It's a long story and still an active case, so I'll only say so
much. For the past two years we've been working to crack a ring
of…*thieves* for lack of a better word. Women who target men
with either high profile or questionable backgrounds, threaten
to cry wolf, or rape, or assault…and then blackmail them into
giving them money to drop the charges."

Jamilah jumped to her feet. "I knew it was her! She set you
up." And then back to her father, "Rashad was set up, wasn't
he?"

"The accuser has established a pattern that would make such
a conclusion likely. But it's been hard to get the kind of evidence that will stick. Without clear-cut video surveillance or a
credible witness, instances like this are he said, she said. That's
why it's such a hard case to crack.

"She's not working alone. We believe it could even be some
type of ring, with a leader at the top giving them advice, helping them plot and using his or her know-how of the law to keep
the scheme going. They've had a level of success. Some men

who don't want to or can't afford that type of accusation, or to fall into public scrutiny, would rather pay up than seek justice."

"Isn't there something we can do?" Jamilah returned to the couch as a thought occurred. "We've got her on video! Her and Rashad argued right at the front door!"

"Rashad told me about her restaurant visits, and what happened earlier. A good attorney could explain all of that away as lovers fighting."

Jamilah's shoulders sagged in defeat. "If she keeps getting away with the crime, it'll keep happening. One of Rashad's friends believes there may be mental issues. What if she comes after him again?"

"A warrant has been issued. For now, that's all I can say."

"Daddy," Jamilah began after long moments had passed, "what do I need to know about my grandfather?"

"Everything," James finally answered. "And one day I'll tell you. For now, suffice it to say that he was an abuser who mistreated my mama, your grandmother. I was too young to defend her and vowed to one day become a police officer and lock his ass up. He died before I could make good on that promise. Locking up everyone else who breaks the law was the next best thing."

You know that moment in the classic *The Wizard of Oz* when the picture changes from black-and-white into Technicolor? The come-to-Jesus meeting in her condo brought that type of change. While all her life Jamilah had known her daddy, in the days and weeks following his unburdening, she finally got to know James. Science fiction movies often spoke of jumping timelines and multiple dimensions. Jamilah came as close to something like that as one could experience in a human lifetime. As flowers bloomed, rain fell, and spring eased into summer, Jamilah found herself in a whole new world that looked nothing like her old life.

Side Chic'k now bustled with color and life. Antonio, trained by Rashad, now ran the kitchen alongside him. Shasta had been joined by Daniela, Berniece, and Kim, young women who'd avoided jail time by enrolling in the program inspired by Rashad, designed by Mr. Turner, and facilitated by the Department of Corrections. Professional photos of the food Side Chic'k offered lent splashes of color to the decor, and were perfectly showcased against the stark white walls. Jamilah adjusted her business hours to close at eight thirty, before Behind Bars's entertainment started at nine.

Rashad's official opening coincided with the *Soul Train* event, but in the weeks leading up to the big day, he conducted a series of soft openings to work through the kinks. The energy was as he'd envisioned, with a diverse group of twenty- and thirtysomethings enjoying gaming, music, and food.

By far, the biggest change Jamilah witnessed was with her father. It was as though her dad had carried the sins of his father. In telling the truth to Jamilah, a weight was lifted off his neck. He was still swamped with work but texted more often, made quick stops at Side Chic'k, and actually complimented Rashad on the Behind Bars concept.

Jamilah had once said that to see those two get along, hell would have to freeze over. A part of her still left the house looking for ice.

Forty

The first Saturday in July arrived bright, hot, and humid. Inside Jamilah's air-conditioned life, all was well with her world. She snuggled up next to Rashad, still marveling how much her life had changed. None of what happened had been expected: Blair leaving, meeting Rashad, him coming to work at Side Chic'k, them becoming lovers, and now them being in business together. No one, not a prophet, seer, or tarot card reader, could have convinced her that any part of the life she now experienced would happen. Ever. Yet here she lay, satiated and satisfied from last night's lovemaking, with a man who her father not only accepted but respected, proving to someone as nonreligious as Jamilah that indeed there was a God.

Smiling at how good she felt and how fortunate she was to be lying beside this awesome man, she looked up into the eyes that had mesmerized her from the beginning.

"Hi," she said shyly because he'd caught her sneaking a peek.

He kissed the top of her head. "Sup."

She chuckled. "Sup."

He kissed her lips this time.

"Spam and bologna."

Jamilah frowned, turned to her side to see him more clearly. "That's what's up? Spam and bologna?"

"Those are the mystery ingredients in the wonton soup that got me hired at Side Chic'k."

"Wow." Jamilah felt like she'd touched the holy grail. "Finally laying bare your secrets. I really am special."

"Told you."

"Thank you." She shifted until she straddled him. "If it weren't time to get moving and we didn't have such a long day ahead, I'd ask you to make me happy again like you did last night."

"Baby, if you don't want to engage in a duel, I suggest you hop off my sword."

The two took a shower together, making quick work of washing off last night's sexual shenanigans. Knowing she'd be wearing a wig later on, Jamilah pulled her shoulder-length flat-iron into a ponytail, and in preparation for the scorching heat donned a simple, oversize white T-shirt over a pair of cotton shorts that hit just above the knee. A silver chain with the words *Side Chic'k* in cursive, a gift from her father on the restaurant's one-year anniversary, hoop earrings, and a grouping of thin silver bangles were her only accessories.

When Rashad reached for his standard black denim jeans, Jamilah said, "You might want to wear those linen slacks I bought you. It's going to be crazy hot today."

"I'll be all right."

"Said like someone who hasn't experienced Midwestern humidity."

Sure enough, even though it was barely seven o'clock, they stepped outside into nature's version of an oven.

Rashad threw an arm up as though he could shield himself from air. "Man! This heat is crazy."

"Told you."

"Wow!"

"Want to go back?"

"Nah, but I might be pulling out that dashiki long before it's time to go down the *Soul Train* line."

Soul Train. Who knew that a TV show that went off the air when Jamilah was ten would now have such an impact on her life. Even though to break the record the Society of Sisters only technically needed five-hundred and thirty-seven dancers, they had set a loftier goal, one thousand people, to ensure a long reign in the record books. They had faith that fun-loving citizens from the Show Me State would show up and show out.

Word of their intentions, and the knowledge that the monies raised from the event would go into developing after-school music and arts programs in the city helped boost not only the interest throughout the metropolitan area but also media coverage. Educational venues from middle school through college responded with participants wanting to dance the line, as had marching bands, sororities, fraternities, dance schools, and personnel from professional sports organizations. Cities and towns from as far away as St. Louis had inquired about attending and participating. All of the major news outlets and newspapers had run articles on the upcoming event.

Anna, Monique, and Latonia had been interviewed, along with other members of the committee. Because they were serving as one of the sponsors and the coordinators for the food truck festival coinciding with the dance line, Side Chic'k and Behind Bars got tons of free publicity. As busy as it had been leading up to this big day, Jamilah's jaw still dropped when they exited Paseo toward Vine. Cars and people were everywhere. Food trucks lined their designated street. The atmosphere was clearly festive, with many of the attendees already wearing the attire popular in the seventies, eighties, nineties, and early aughts, when the classic television show created by Don Cornelius appeared on televisions across the country every Saturday morning. Approaching the security-manned barricade, she was thankful for the placard Anna had insisted they take to allow direct access to the alley behind their businesses.

"We'll get there early," Jamilah had informed her.

"Not early enough," had been Anna's correct answer.

They parked behind their businesses and entered through the back door. In a short time Rashad had expertly assembled a stellar crew, led by an ex-Cholo gang leader, Tomás Rodriguez. With tats covering almost every visible part of his body except his face, and an intimidating scar running across his chin, most people would see this young man coming and clutch their purse. For sure, he'd been a respected figure in the streets of New Mexico where he was born and raised. Having turned the page in his life and started a new chapter, the man Mr. Turner had introduced to Rashad and Jamilah was funny, smart and a natural leader. Anyone watching the team work together under his supervision would have sworn they'd done so for years, not weeks.

Tomás looked up and smiled when he saw Rashad and Jamilah. She waved at him but continued through the adjoining door to check on the Side Chic'k crew. Unlike Rashad with Blair, Antonio had had no problem following Rashad's "bible." He fit right in with her other employees.

A couple hours later, satisfied that everything was in place and running smoothly, the two changed into their outfits. Along with matching dashikis, Jamilah donned a large bright auburn afro, ridiculously big hoop earrings and extra-wide mustard-colored bell-bottoms. Rashad cocked an oversize black-striped denim apple cap to the side, paired with that same pattern in a pair of bell-bottoms, and he stuck an afro pick sporting a clenched fist in the leather band holding his locs. The two were ready for their closeup. *Right on!*

Less than a minute of walking down the street and around the corner, Jamilah's jaw dropped. Rashad stopped in his tracks. Both were expecting a large crowd, but neither was prepared for the sea of people stretching down two blocks and spilling into the side streets. Red and blue lights signaled a police presence.

"What happened?" Rashad asked.

"I don't know." Jamilah pulled out her phone. "Maybe crowd control?" she added, shooting off a quick text to her dad.

Red and blue lights down here. Anything going on?

She placed a hand on Rashad's arm. "Let's check it out."

Moving closer, they heard the buzz and felt the excitement. Rashad moved calmly yet cautiously, placing a protective arm around her, his eyes fully alert and scanning the crowd.

She pulled out her phone to text Anna, but it buzzed in her hand.

Crowd control. Many more than everyone expected.

Jamilah replied with a smiling emoji. Are you here yet?

Later

You dancing?

No

Daddy! It's the world record!

LOL We'll see

Anna and Charles were at the sign-up booth, representing the eighties like two who'd actually lived through the era.

"What's up, LL Cool J!" Rashad and Charles bumped fists, Rashad laughing as he took in the man who'd become a mentor of sorts sporting a fire-engine-red B-boy tracksuit, red Kangol bucket hat, and ginormous faux-gold double-roped chains.

"Hey, Anna." Jamilah offered a quick hug before stepping back for a head-to-toe. "Who are you?"

Anna feigned having a heart attack. "How dare you not recognize the queen!" She turned to show Jamilah the words emblazoned in gold across the back of a black military-style shirt that she paired with shiny gold pants like MC Hammer wore in his "U Can't Touch This" video, a classic.

"Ladies first," Jamilah said, still clueless.

"Hey, bae," Anna said to Charles. "Jamilah doesn't know Queen Latifah."

"You're Queen Latifah? I know her. She plays on *The Equalizer*. But she doesn't dress like that."

Anna and Rashad shared a knowing look. "Youngins."

Jamilah looked between the two of them. "What?"

"I'll tell you later, baby." Rashad placed his arm around Jamilah's shoulder and drew her close.

Leon walked up, wearing his standard attire, khakis and a faded T-shirt boasting a picture of a bandanna-wearing Tupac Shakur.

"That's your outfit?" Jamilah asked skeptically.

"Given I'm one helping to tally the number of line participants, Tupac helping me rep the nineties is the best I can do."

Considering the importance of his assignment, showing up sans outlandish costume was immediately excused.

"Where's Blair? And Monique?"

"Blair's working. She's hoping to get off early, though, so she can be a part of history. Mom is on her way," he said as he looked around, "if she isn't here already."

The crowd continued to grow. At one point, an excited Juke came up, passing out flyers as he neared them.

"Check this out. Tonight's official grand opening is going to be fire! A few pro ballers, the KC Chiefs cheerleaders, and the honorary *Soul Train* dancers all said they'd stop by Behind Bars tonight."

"I hope you're keeping our capacity in mind," Rashad warned. "We can squeeze in a hundred and fifty tops, and that's both buildings. I don't want any problems with the fire department."

"It's cool. Everybody knows that tonight's affair is semi-private, but I, um, kinda threw in a special."

Rashad's eyes narrowed.

"For the rest of this month, I told the ladies they could get in free between eight-thirty and nine, with a two-drink minimum."

Rashad groaned. "Who's going to keep track of that?"

"A cute little shorty you'll meet later on tonight." Juke winked, kissed Jamilah's cheek, and was soon lost in the crowd.

Temperatures continued to swelter. The organizers decided to start the *Soul Train* line early, before the crowd diminished. A popular DJ from a local radio station took to the stage and got everyone's attention. There was a brief program where the mayor spoke and gave keys to the city to the three original *Soul Train* dancers who'd graciously accepted invitations to attend. He also proclaimed it Soul Train Line Day in Kansas City. Jamilah wasn't surprised to see Walter on the podium with other officials. He wore a suit. His fiancée was dressed like the attorney she was.

Party poopers!

A small army worked together to coordinate the dancers, who'd start fifty feet up the block and dance down to the iconic intersection of Eighteenth and Vine. A popular former DJ from KPRS, the legendary first Black-owned radio station west of the Mississippi, and longest-running on the radio to date, one that had played much of the music highlighted on *Soul Train* throughout its thirty-five-year run, joined the younger man on the turntable. Together they compiled and began playing a multidecade soundtrack of the seventies, eighties, nineties, and aughts. "Rapper's Delight," the first national hip-hop hit. "Walk This Way," the first crossover. R and B. Funk. Disco. New Jack Swing. Couples, groups, and troupes bumped, pop-locked, slid, shuffled, and danced their way down fifty feet of concrete, cheered on by an enthusiastic crowd that spanned the ages from five to eighty.

Roughly two hours later, Leon, along with his team of counters and the professional staff that had been sent from Guinness, huddled on a corner of the intersection, comparing iPads and iPhones.

A petite woman sporting a cute gray bob and a pair of bifocals perched on the tip of her nose slowly mounted the stairs and pulled down the mic to address the crowd.

"Good afternoon, everyone. What a fun time we've had watching these participants break the record for the largest, longest *Soul Train* line! The official count for those involved stands at nine hundred and seventy-two. With that being said…"

A murmur went up from those who'd remained, mostly the dancers who'd participated. Clearly, they weren't happy being so close to but not quite reaching their goal of one thousand.

"One K. One K," someone began to chant, a mantra quickly picked up by the crowd, and growing in both volume and intensity.

The representative from Guinness was clearly not used to this type of pushback. She turned to those still huddled near the stage. Soon, the legendary DJ from KPRS bounded up the steps. Using his arms, he motioned for quiet.

"To reach our goal of one thousand, we need twenty-eight people," he said, looking out at the crowd. "We're sooo close. Is there anyone, anywhere in the crowd who has not gone down the line. Don't try to cheat," he admonished. "We'd hate all of this hard work to get disqualified."

Soon, Juke and his boys were scouring the neighborhood, pulling out shop owners, customers, even the police officers milling around to have a turn down the line. Comic relief came in the form of Ed's friend, Russell, at least two if not three sheets to the wind, agreeing to boogie down the line only if they played his favorite artist, James Brown.

He shimmied and shook in a loud lime-green, yellow, and

orange plaid suit with lapels wide enough to fly in a tornado. Everyone surrounding him sang and clapped along as he strutted while shouting, "I feel good!"

"Nine ninety-eight," the DJ said, after Russell reached the area in front of the stage. Y'all, we can't stop now. We've got to reach our goal."

By now all of the organizers had joined the group near the stage—Jamilah and Rashad, Anna and Charles, Leon and Blair, who'd arrived in time to be participant number eight hundred and ninety-two.

"Look!" a little girl squealed, while pointing toward the other end of the block.

Someone with a megaphone said, "Hang on, guys. I think we have our last two!"

Jamilah squinted. A garishly dressed couple walked toward the middle of the street. The DJ put on "Cool Like That," a Digable Planet smash.

"No way," Jamilah murmured, unconsciously moving forward to peer at the couple coolly strutting down the street.

"That's Monique!" Blair exclaimed, punching Leon in the side.

"That's my mom," he agreed. "Who's the guy, though?"

"I'm not sure…" Blair squinted, then reared back as recognition dawned. "Jamilah! Girl, no! Isn't that—"

"My daddy," Jamilah responded, incredulously. "Wearing faux leather and a braid wig with beads like Rick James on his worst day? I can't believe that's him."

Rashad sidled up beside her. "Um, I'm pretty sure that's your father. Or, as Dave Chappelle would say in tribute to 'Super Freak,' 'That's Rick James, bitch!'"

Several hours had passed since the official count had been tallied for the biggest *Soul Train* line—one thousand and one—the final person arriving at the last minute, popping wheelies with his wheelchair as he rolled down the street to a seventies beat.

Rashad passed the dining room on his way to the Behind Bars stage. Jamilah was talking and laughing with David, a nineteen-year-old KC native recently released from doing eighteen months in lockup. He smiled at how comfortable she was around the young man, knowing that a year ago, given his background, she probably wouldn't have given him the time of day. She caught him looking and waved him over. He cocked his head toward the other side and pointed, letting her know he had work to do. He thought the rap he'd planned to perform was finished. But a few bars kept swirling in his head, begging to be added. He had to put them down.

On the way to the stage where tonight's participants were signing up and milling around, he passed James and Monique sitting at the bar. James had removed the beaded braids and traded the faux-leather jumpsuit for a pair of jeans. A casual, black shirt brought him more into alignment with the reserved figure Rashad had met on most occasions.

Didn't matter. Rashad wasn't going to let that *Soul Train* image of James go any time soon.

"What's up, Rick?"

James eyed Rashad over a sip of scotch. "Rick retired."

"Maybe. That doesn't change the fact that the cat is out of the bag. Beneath all of that conservative machismo is a super freak. Right, Monique?"

"Watch it, son."

Rashad raised his hands. "You're right. My bad." He held out his fist.

James remained motionless, his look somber. Rashad lowered his arm.

"Come on, James," Monique gently chided. "You know how kids play around."

James's expression was stern as he slowly offered up a fist bump. "Okay, but don't make it a habit."

Backstage, it was like old times, his homies standing around laughing, likely talking shit, or as his granny would say, *tell-*

ing lies and swatting flies. For a brief moment, a second even, the scene felt like déjà vu. He stopped, took in the tableau of his boys—Juke, Sky Walka, Eight Track, and PhD, standing in his establishment, happy, doing what they loved. If he wasn't such a hard-ass, he would have shed a tear or two. But he had a bad-boy reputation to uphold. Tears didn't fit in with that. Instead of joining them, he walked to the area behind the DJ and picked up the notebook he'd left there. Except for the last page, it was all filled up. Fitting, he thought, as he found his song "Whipped" and, after repeating the verses a few times in his head, wrote down the addition. He read it back, then went outside and with only the trees, stars, and a stray dog for an audience, did the whole song. The last bars he'd added felt like it had always been there. He turned around and headed back into the building. He was psyched. He was ready.

Showtime.

Jamilah saw him as soon as he entered and made a beeline in his direction. "Hey, baby, I was looking for you. What were you doing out there?"

Rashad hadn't told Jamilah he was going to perform. "Getting some air," he lied.

Her eyes narrowed. She took a step toward him and tried a surreptitious sniff.

"Back up off me, woman, I was not out there smoking." Laughing, he pulled her into an embrace. "Why would I need marijuana when I can get high on you?"

Jamilah looked up, kissed him. "Baby, if you can make a lie sound that good, don't ever tell me the truth."

"It's all true."

"I love you, Rashad."

Her words flowed over Rashad's skin like water, then seeped into him like hot, fragrant oil.

It wasn't like he hadn't been told those words before. But here, now, in this place, with this woman, the phrase hit different. It sounded real, heartfelt, like how it did when his granny said it. Like she'd cross hot coals barefoot, fight a bear, take on any and everybody if they came against him. Just like he would for her.

"Thank you, baby. I love you, too."

Rashad saw Eight Track motioning him over toward the stage. "Be right back," he told her.

Jamilah saw Blair and joined her on the dance floor.

Juke finished a rap he'd penned called "My Block," a respectable representation of the positive side of growing up where they were from. Close-knit families. Loyal neighbors. Backyard barbecues. Street racing. Lowriding. Block parties. Even the way a life was celebrated when somebody died.

"Thank you for the love, Kansas City," Juke said, taking a humble bow. He threw up a sign and added, "Westside!"

The crowd was appreciative, especially the Gen Xers, Millennials and Zoomers in the building. Juke walked from the stage into the crowd and was immediately surrounded by congratulators and well-wishers. Rashad's attention quickly shifted from his friend to the stage, a familiar set of butterflies coming to hang out in his stomach. Tonight it was as if they'd invited a cousin or two. Rashad berated himself, wondering why was he so nervous? He knew what he was about to do was the right thing, the only way his life could go right now. He'd never been surer about anything in his life.

"All right, people," the DJ said, once again commanding the crowd's attention. "We're about to wrap up tonight's performances, but right now I'm especially happy to welcome this next act to the stage. See, this brothah had a dream, and while a lot of people told him *no* when it came to making it a reality, he kept saying *yes*. To himself. But hey, he can tell his story better than I can."

Rashad looked out in the crowd, saw Jamilah straining to find him behind the stage. He stepped back a little farther into the shadows of the curtain and a large speaker dominating that side of the room.

"Ladies and gentlemen, please put your hands together and help me welcome an amazing chef, a talented rap artist, and part owner of the newest and best spot for rhymes, late-night grub and gaming in the city, Rashad 'Ra God' White!"

The audience cheered. Some whistled. His homies hollered. The air was electric. He could feel Jamilah's surprised eyes on him and purposely didn't look in her direction. Not yet.

He reached DJ David. They shared a fist tap and shoulder bump before he took the mic.

"So like you heard, my name is Rashad, the Ra God. Most of you know me as the head chef at Side Chic'k and now here at Behind Bars, but a few people also know me as somebody who rhymes. I want to give a special shout-out to Poetry on the Vine. I see y'all in the building. Everyone, give it up for all the artists in the house!"

The noise swelled to a crescendo before quieting back down.

"They're the first group I shared my art with after moving here from Los Angeles. They were welcoming, supportive, and encouraging when I shared what I planned to do here. In fact, we have something exciting in the works that we'll be announcing soon, so stay tuned.

"This piece I'm going to perform tonight was inspired by a few people. One of them is Kendrick Lamar, one of my favorite rappers. He did a song called 'Luther,' sampling Luther Vandross. It reminded me of my aunties, friends' mamas, and grandmothers who I knew used to groove to that old R and B music. I liked that vibe, you know, and have created something that I hope you'll like, too. It was inspired by my favorite woman in the world, my grandmother Isabel Porter, who is probably the only reason I'm not dead or still in prison, and also—" he finally looked over "—by a goddess, a queen, Jamilah, who's one of the reasons I decided to never go back there. Thank you for helping me be a better me."

He quieted, his shoulders rising and falling from a deep,

calming breath. He looked at DJ David and nodded. The instrumental music began.

"For those of you too young to know or too old to remember, I'm rapping over a Babyface classic from the late eighties, 'Whip Appeal'. My song is called 'Whipped.'"

The instrumental began. Rashad closed his eyes, his head bobbing to the music.

Started at a party this part that would rock my world
Where an urban man did a scan on a suburban girl
Played no fool. LA cool. Not my type anyway
Let's ride with the lie locked up inside
Mental games that players play
Then…

Rashad looked directly at Jamilah, who'd moved to the front of the stage.

In the kitchen whipped up getting gripped up for last call
Shorty walked into the room with a badaboom that made giants fall
Tried to play it off like a hungry man turning down a meal
Couldn't fake the funk gotta get a chunk of that whip appeal…

"No one does it like me…"

The singer's melodic sampled hook perfectly complemented the brash staccato of Rashad's heartfelt delivery. He stood with his head slightly bowed, and continued rapping. It was as if those watching had entered his private domain and accidentally stumbled across an audio diary. There was something both powerful and vulnerable about him, something that pulled in the listener and made them hang on to every word. Rashad lifted his head and was pleasantly surprised when a few of the older couples eased into already-tight aisles, wrapped their arms around each other, and began to slow dance. His eyes scanned the appreciative expressions on those present until finally, just before filling the chorus of sorts with his own hook, he focused on Jamilah again.

"Whipped—don't deny that part.
Stripped—of the armor that hid my heart.

Ripped—from a vibe not right for me.
Dipped—into a love that's destiny."

As he rapped the last two lines, a miracle happened. Any other time he would not have welcomed what had Jamilah distracted and missing his public declaration of love, but considering the circumstances, he completely understood. She'd turned and watched as James and Monique joined the other couples on the dance floor. Her father nodded, and smiled.

Rashad would always remember her face as she returned her gaze to him. An expression painted with joy and mixed with wonder. She blew him a kiss and stood totally enraptured as he serenaded her with the final verse.

"Sometimes to stay alive brothah gotta leave his neighborhood
Thriving and striving. For the journey for the greater good
Write my own scripture, be my own myth, serendipity
Time to leave behind that which is no longer serving me

He had Jamilah's full attention now. He walked over and delivered the bars he'd just written directly to her.

Heart Whipped. Mind Stripped. Life Ripped. I'm like wow.
No Fear. False Evidence. It's not Real. I know that now.
What's on my mind is a sign what I'm thinkin 'bout
Your forever man, time to meet the fam, let's plan a trip to Granny's house."

"No one…"

Jamilah stood transfixed at the edge of the stage. He watched as a single tear trickled from her right eye, down her cheek, and off her chin, followed by one that took that same journey from her left eye. He imagined she'd absorbed the enormity of the message he'd delivered. Hearing the words out loud, with her, in front of an audience, affected him, too. Once something was heard, it couldn't be unheard. Was he really ready to go on this journey with Jamilah? To have a true, committed relationship?

The answer was definitely *yes.*

His eyes softened as he looked at her. "Come here, baby."

The gratitude and admiration that shone in Jamilah's eyes

made Rashad's heart almost burst out of his chest. He leaned over as she reached him and pursed her lips for a kiss. They shared a quick smooch before he introduced her.

"Anybody who's patronized our establishment knows Jamilah already. She owns Side Chic'k, which she created and built from the ground up. I want to publicly thank her for taking a chance and going into business with a knucklehead like me, and while I'm at it, a shout-out to my godmother, the goddess Anna and her husband, Charles. To my mother Katrina White who I'm sure would have loved to be here. To Monique, Anna's friend, who was the first to take a chance on my culinary skills after I arrived in Kansas City, and to the first man Jamilah looked up to and loved, her dad, James Carver. Big up to you for raising a beautiful daughter."

Someone handed him a flute of champagne. "Thanks to everybody for helping me change the narrative, for making hip-hop positive again, for having a safe space to hang out together, for showing it's possible to change your life. Thanks for helping me spread the message that great things can happen from those who were once... Behind Bars!"

Rashad left the stage with Jamilah and after wading through a sea of well-wishers, pulled her into a tight embrace. The sound of Kendrick's "Luther" swirled around them. He took a sip of bubbly, then held the flute up to Jamilah's lips.

"Did you order this as part of your stock?" she asked?

"Just for tonight."

"Need I remind you that your business just opened and will take several months, maybe years, to break even?"

Rashad pulled her closer, grinding against her. "Enjoy the music, Boss Lady."

"You're sipping champagne on a beer budget. Just sayin'."

"No," Rashad said, as he again shared the drink. "You're sipping champagne on this bad boy's budget."

Jamilah slid her hands across Rashad's toned back and laid her head on his shoulder. "In that case," she murmured as the song ended, "let's grab another bottle to pop at a more…private celebration."

"Watch it, girl. I'm ready to shoot off a few fireworks right now."

"The party's in full swing. No one will miss us." Eyes sparkling, Jamilah grabbed his hand. "Let's go!"

★ ★ ★ ★ ★

LET'S TALK

Romance

For exclusive extracts, competitions and special offers, find us online:

- **f** MillsandBoon
- **X** @MillsandBoon
- **O** @MillsandBoonUK
- **♪** @MillsandBoonUK

Get in touch on 01413 063 232

For all the latest titles coming soon, visit
millsandboon.co.uk/nextmonth

FOUR BRAND NEW BOOKS FROM
MILLS & BOON MODERN

Indulge in desire, drama, and breathtaking romance – where passion knows no bounds!

2 BOOKS IN ONE

STOLEN BY A SICILIAN
Jackie Ashenden   Caitlin Crews

Babies to Bind
2 BOOKS IN ONE
Tara Pammi   Rosie Maxwell

2 BOOKS IN ONE
TO HIRE AND TO HATE
Michelle Smart   Annie West

2 BOOKS IN ONE
KEEPING THE Enemy Close
KIM LAWRENCE   BELLA MASON

OUT NOW

Eight Modern stories published every month, find them all at:

millsandboon.co.uk

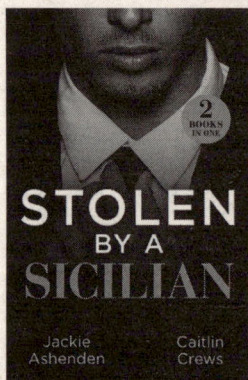

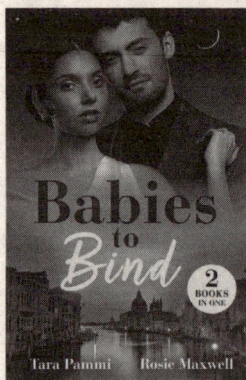

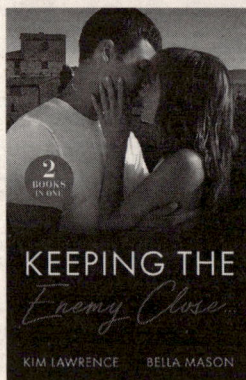

TWO BRAND NEW BOOKS FROM

Love Always

Once Upon
a Second
Chance

2
BOOKS
IN ONE

Kate Hardy · Michele Renae

Juliette Hyland · Clare Miles

Matches
in a
Million

2
BOOKS
IN ONE

Be prepared to be swept away to incredible
worldwide destinations along with our strong,
relatable heroines and intensely desirable heroes.

OUT NOW

Four Love Always stories published
every month, find them all at:

millsandboon.co.uk

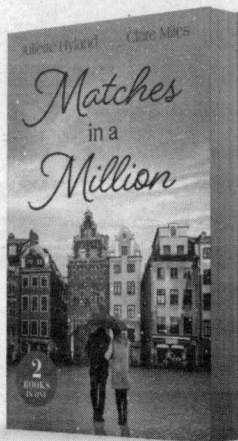

MILLS & BOON

THE HEART OF ROMANCE

A ROMANCE FOR EVERY READER

MODERN

Prepare to be swept off your feet by sophisticated, sexy and seductive heroes, in some of the world's most glamourous and romantic locations, where power and passion collide.

HISTORICAL

Escape with historical heroes from time gone by. Whether your passion is for wicked Regency Rakes, muscled Vikings or rugged Highlanders, awaken the romance of the past.

MEDICAL

Set your pulse racing with dedicated, delectable doctors in the high-pressure world of medicine, where emotions run high and passion, comfort and love are the best medicine.

Love Always

Celebrate true love with tender stories of heartfelt romance, from the rush of falling in love to the joy a new baby can bring, and a focus on the emotional heart of a relationship.

HEROES

The excitement of a gripping thriller, with intense romance at its heart. Resourceful, true-to-life women and strong, fearless men face danger and desire - a killer combination!

afterglow BOOKS

From showing up to glowing up, these characters are on the path to leading their best lives and finding romance along the way – with plenty of sizzling spice!

To see which titles are coming soon, please visit

millsandboon.co.uk/nextmonth

OUT NOW!

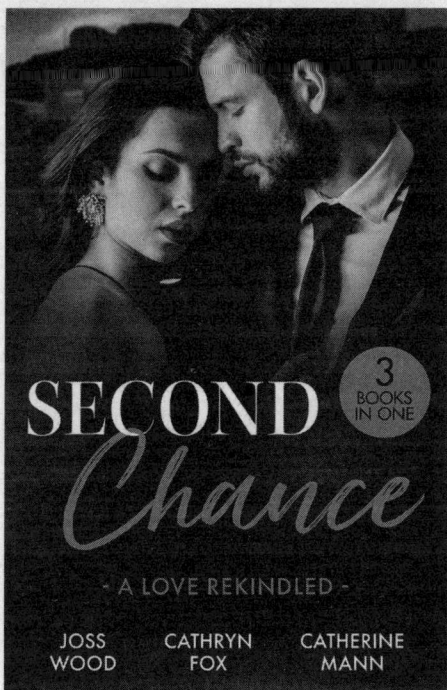

SECOND
Chance

3 BOOKS IN ONE

- A LOVE REKINDLED -

JOSS
WOOD

CATHRYN
FOX

CATHERINE
MANN

Available at
millsandboon.co.uk

MILLS & BOON

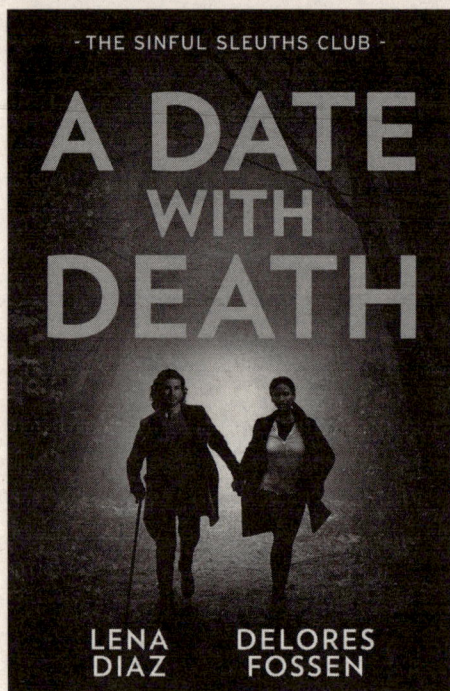

OUT NOW!

- THE SINFUL SLEUTHS CLUB -

A DATE
WITH
DEATH

**LENA
DIAZ**

**DELORES
FOSSEN**

Available at
millsandboon.co.uk

MILLS & BOON